Blood in Grandpont

Blood in Grandpont

Peter Tickler

ROBERT HALE · LONDON

© Peter Tickler 2010
First published in Great Britain 2010

ISBN 978-0-7090-9096-0

Robert Hale Limited
Clerkenwell House
Clerkenwell Green
London EC1R 0HT

www.halebooks.com

The right of Peter Tickler to be identified as
author of this work has been asserted by him
in accordance with the Copyright, Designs and
Patents Act 1988

2 4 6 8 10 9 7 5 3

Typeset in 10½/14½pt Palatino
by Derek Doyle & Associates, Shaw Heath
Printed in Great Britain by the MPG Books Group, Bodmin and King's Lynn

CHAPTER 1

'Damn it!' Jack Smith's shout echoed around the empty stairwell of number 19 Brook Street, one of a row of once very ordinary, but now very desirable Victorian terraced houses in that area of Oxford – just to the south of the river – known as Grandpont. Grand Pont means the Great Bridge – even Jack Smith's schoolboy French stretched that far. But as far as he was concerned, what Grandpont really spelt was money, or so he hoped – an area in which to expand his business. However, at this precise moment in time none of this was on his mind, because the fact was that his thumb ruddy well hurt. He looked at the blood running down the side of his forefinger, and swore again, though this time less loudly, for what was the point when there was no one to hear and no one to commiserate with his pain. Finally, he wiped it on his overalls, and turned his attention back to the floorboards.

For the next five minutes, he worked silently and with increased care as he eased up boards one by one. Most of them resisted him stubbornly, but as he approached the corner, he encountered two shorter pieces which popped up with only the slightest pressure. He sat back on his haunches, and then looked at his watch. Time for a fag break. But the looseness of those last boards had registered somewhere inside his brain as being odd, and even as he felt inside his top pocket for his Silk Cut, he leant forward to take another look. He frowned at what he saw, removed his hand from the cigarette packet, and slipped it instead into the floor-space. When it re-emerged some ten seconds later, its fingers were wrapped firmly round a dusty, hessian-wrapped object some 60 centimetres square. He paused, as if uncertain what to do with it, but then put it down on the floor and carefully began to untie the string which was holding the hessian in place. He did so with a sense of anticipation, for whatever it was, he was pretty sure it must have been put there deliberately, hidden in fact, by the previous owner presumably – not that he knew who that was. Jack Smith was a central heating engineer and South Oxford wasn't his normal stamping ground. He lived off Headley Way, which links Marston to Headington, and it was around there that he had established a solid reputation for reliability and a willingness to turn out at all hours. Of course, he worked further afield, and had in the last few years found himself working more and more for clients in the Summertown area of North Oxford. And it was one of these – Geraldine Payne, a dentist with a surgery in Beaumont Street and a flat towards the northern end of the Banbury Road – who had brought him south of the river Isis to rip out and replace the archaic plumbing and heating system of a house she had purchased in Brook Street. All he knew of the previous owner was what he had been told by Mrs Thompson from next door, that she was a tight-fisted old git with a reputation for scraping a coin along the paintwork of any car left outside her house in 'her' parking space.

The string around the hessian had been tied with a double bow, and it took the fingers of Jack Smith some little time to worry it open. The radio had been on all morning, and what with him being so focused on what he was doing – and then on the painting that he discovered inside the hessian wrapping – he failed to hear the noise of the front door being opened, and then shortly afterwards clicking shut. It was only when Coldplay's 'Fix You' began to fade that he heard the noise of leather soles on the uncarpeted boards and realized that someone was climbing up the stairs. He started guiltily, and quickly tossed the hessian over the painting.

'God, I thought you were Geraldine,' he said as a woman appeared.

'She said I would find you here. Why is your mobile turned off, Jack?' she demanded. 'The shower you installed is leaking, and I'm not happy.'

Jack lifted his hand defensively. 'I left it at home. Sorry. But I'll come and take a look at the shower on my way home. I promise.'

'You'd better do more that take a look,' she said. He was still on one knee on the floor, and she now bent down so her face was close and intrusive. She glared and he flinched. If looks could kill, his brains would have been splattered all over the wall. 'You'd better bloody fix it, Jack Smith.'

'Sure, of course,' he gulped. Despite his bulk, he was easily intimidated.

'What's that?' she said. Her eyes had moved to the piece of hessian, which was partially, but not wholly, covering the painting.

'Nothing,' he said, unconvincingly.

'In that case, you won't mind me taking a look,' she said, and she leant across, her hand out.

Reluctantly, he pulled the hessian to the side, picked the painting up, and passed it over to her. 'I found it,' he said. 'Under the floorboards.'

She took it from him, and studied it for some time, appraising it. 'I guess you'll be giving this to Geraldine, then?' she said eventually, her eyes still on the painting.

'Finders keepers, I reckon,' he said.

Her eyes looked across at him, and fixed themselves firmly on his face. 'Fancy making a bit on the side, do you, Jack? Bit of an art expert, are you, in your spare time?' Her voice was mocking and sarcastic. 'You've been watching too much *Cash in the Attic* if you ask me.'

'It looks quite old, I reckon,' he said. 'I was thinking I might take it to that auction house in Hythe Bridge Street and ask them what it was worth, and—'

'And the first thing they are going to ask,' she cut in sharply, 'is where you got it from.'

'Oh!' he said uncertainly.

'It's nice, though, in a quaint sort of way,' she continued, her tone softening. 'I wouldn't mind buying it off you.'

His eyes narrowed. 'I wouldn't mind buying it off you!' he mimicked, and then laughed, pleased with himself. 'You've as good as told me it's worth some money.'

She put the painting down on the floor, and then opened the bag that hung by a long strap from her shoulder. 'I took a hundred pounds out of the cash point earlier this morning, so why don't I give you that and in return—'

'Fifty-fifty,' he said firmly. 'You find a buyer and we split it fifty-fifty.'

She stared at him hard, and then down at the painting, which he had picked up and was holding on to protectively, as if afraid that she might try to grab it and do a runner. A smile broke suddenly across her face, and she clipped her handbag firmly shut. 'OK, you've got a deal.'

'And don't even think of trying to cheat me,' he said threateningly, 'because if you do—'

'Jackie boy!' She spoke softly, her voice a mixture of cajoling and caressing, as if he was a big dog that needed gentle, yet firm handling. She was kneeling on the floor immediately opposite him. 'In my book,' she murmured, 'a deal is a deal.' Her face had drifted imperceptibly closer to his, and he was suddenly conscious of her perfume, so intense that it was unnerving. 'So why don't we shake on it . . . or something.'

He said nothing, taken off his guard by the turn of events. Her smile became a grin, and she moved even closer until her lips brushed against his cheek. 'What do you say, Jackie boy?' she whispered into his ear.

He grunted, still uncertain. He was way out of his comfort zone. 'Suppose . . .' he began, but he got no further, because her forefinger was on his lips and her face was opposite his, and just inches away. He flinched backwards and gulped.

She nodded towards the door beyond him, which was standing open. 'It looks like there's an old bed in there, Jackie boy. What do you say? Shall we take a look?'

Ten minutes later she extricated herself from his sweaty grasp and began to dress. He lay stretched out across the bed, watching her through half-closed eyes. 'Hey, what's the rush?' he said reproachfully. 'Don't go yet.'

The woman smiled bleakly back at him, but said nothing as she buttoned up her blouse, and then bent down to pull her black ankle boots on. Her bag was lying on the floor where she had dropped it, and from this she now retrieved her mobile phone.

'Hey!' he said, his eyes now fully open, 'you're not ringing up your friends to brag are you?' And he laughed. But only very briefly. And then the expression on his face changed. 'What the hell are you doing?'

What she was not doing was making a phone call. Rather, she was holding her mobile out in front of her and taking a photograph – of him, naked. 'Just taking out insurance, Jackie boy.'

'Insurance?' he shouted, sitting up now. 'What the fuck do you mean?'

'Insurance against you causing trouble, Jackie.' She clicked her mobile shut, put it back in her bag, and then took out a purse. 'Because if you think I'm going to settle for a fifty-fifty split, when you can do nothing on your own, then you're a bigger fool than you look. I've got the cards now, and this is the deal.' She had removed some notes from her purse. 'Five £20 notes. Hot from the cash point. That's for you. And whatever I make, I keep. And if you so much as whisper "It's not fair" then I'll go round and pay your lovely wife a visit. Got it?'

With that she turned, went out of the open door, and clipped briskly down the stairs. Jack stared after her, his mouth open, until he heard the front door open and slam shut. Then he shivered, swore, and reached down for his pants.

' 'Bye, Mrs Russell!' Lucy Tull called out cheerily. But if Sarah Russell heard the farewell of the dentist's receptionist, she gave no apparent sign of having done so. Through the half-open door, Lucy watched

Monday's final patient begin to descend the stairs, and then pulled a face after her. 'Miserable cow!' she said, not entirely silently.

'Is there a problem, Lucy?' Lucy turned in embarrassment at the sound of Geraldine Payne's astringent question. Her employer was standing in the other doorway, the one which led into the inner sanctum of her dental surgery, and her face was a picture of disapproval.

'No,' she said hastily. 'No problem at all.'

But there was no chance of her being let off easily. 'We are a people business,' her employer continued, 'and a key part of your job is to be nice and polite to all our customers, and to be totally professional at all times. So, if you are finding that difficult to achieve, then despite your protestations I believe that we do indeed have a problem. A very serious problem. Do I make myself clear?'

'Absolutely clear,' Lucy replied.

'Hm!' Geraldine continued to glare at her assistant, even as she unbuttoned and pulled off her white work coat. She dropped it in the middle of the floor and picked up her handbag from the nearby chair. 'That requires a wash,' she said dismissively, before walking across the room, out of the far door, and off down the stairs. Lucy said nothing.

Downstairs, Geraldine Payne emerged from the front door which she shared with two other dentists, an osteopath, and a homeopath, and turned left. She walked a dozen paces, and then turned left again into St John's Street. She walked north along its western pavement until she reached a side-street where she stopped and fell into conversation with – remarkably – the self-same Sarah Russell who had exited her dental surgery only two minutes prior to her. A casual observer would have seen them engage in an intense, and at times animated conversation, though quite what they were talking about would have been hard to divine as they spoke in low tones, conscious of the fact that other persons beside themselves used this highly priced street to pass from the city centre of Oxford to the environs of Wellington Square and Little Clarendon Street with its university offices and trendy shops and eating and drinking establishments. However, while most of the passing pedestrians walked obliviously on, one slowed and then stopped. This not so casual observer did so because he knew them both.

Joseph Tull was an eighteen-year-old for whom the expression disconsolate youth might have been especially coined. His hair hung diagonally across his face as if it couldn't be bothered to do anything else, his one mode of movement was a slow slouch, and even now he was running ten minutes late for his five o'clock tutorial at Cornforth College. Cornforth was not, as its name might have implied, a part of the university. Rather, it was one of a number of private educational establishments which had taken root in the city, trading on the kudos that an Oxford address gave them. Joseph Tull knew Sarah Russell via his parents, though he also knew her as an officious and unsympathetic administrator of Cornforth, and he knew Geraldine because she was his dentist too. And right now his dentist was hugging his college's administrator. It might have been merely a hug of friendship or comfort, though Joseph's suspicious nature doubted it. And then he smiled. For even from a distance he could see that Geraldine Payne's hand, which had started high on Sarah Russell's shoulder blade, was slipping gradually downwards, towards her waist, and then even further until it came to rest, albeit briefly, on her right buttock.

'Glad to see you're working hard!' Joseph didn't need to turn round. He knew Lucy Tull's voice only too well.

'Hi, Sis!' he said, apparently unconcerned by her sarcastic greeting. 'People watching is more fun,' he continued, 'especially when you know both parties.'

He nodded towards the two figures further up St John's Street, who had now disengaged from their close encounter. Sarah Russell was resuming her walk north, towards Wellington Square, while Geraldine was retreating into the side alley, her mobile phone in her hand.

'Don't call me Sis,' she snapped. 'You know I hate it!'

'I do,' he agreed, as he moved off himself up St John's Street. 'See you, Sis!'

Dr Alan Tull left his surgery at 3.45 p.m. This was earlier than usual on a Wednesday, because although he never had an afternoon surgery on that day, he liked to use the time to catch up with his administrative tasks. And normally, as he cycled home, he did so with a sense of pleasure at another day over, for he was not a man for whom work was the only thing that mattered. He liked his job, even loved it at times, but he liked not being at work too. Today, however, he would have given anything to be working late rather than going home early to the meeting that he knew awaited him.

It took him approximately seven minutes to cycle home, home being a spacious and comfortable house in the very desirable Bainton Road, overlooking to the front the sports grounds of St John's College, and to the rear the canal. Negotiating entry to the house took very nearly another five minutes: entry through the front door; unlocking and unbolting of the back door; unbolting the side gate and wheeling the bike through it; bolting the gate again; and then locking the bike to the immovable object of a metal bar that he had had fixed on to the back wall of the house. Alan Tull had no intention of making the life of either bike thieves or house breakers easy.

He had barely re-entered the house when he heard the doorbell ring violently. He started, despite the fact that he was expecting a visitor, and then walked reluctantly through the kitchen, along the short corridor, and across the hall.

'Good afternoon, Graham,' he said as he opened the door, trying to pretend that it was just a social visit.

The man who stood framed in the entrance was, in contrast to the angular Alan Tull, short and stocky. The doctor knew that he could be little over 30, yet he had already conceded much ground in the battle against baldness, not to mention the battle of the bulge. What remained of his hair was still defiantly black, but despite the circumstances Alan Tull was sufficiently vain to feel smugly pleased that his own grey hair was more abundant even at his age.

'Do come in,' he said with a welcoming gesture.

Graham Drabble gave a curt grunt and thrust himself past his host into the hall. 'Is anyone else here?' he demanded.

Alan Tull shut the door, and shook his head. 'Just me.'

'In that case, let's get it said here, and then I'll go. I've no wish to stay longer than I must.'

'It's good of you—' Alan began, but he never completed his ingratiating response, because Drabble had launched forcefully into the attack.

'I want you to resign, Doctor, and if you don't, I will make it my job to run you out of the medical profession.'

Alan Tull gulped. He had been expecting a rocky ride, but the bluntness of Drabble's approach caught him unawares, and he felt a surge of nausea rise from his stomach. 'Please, Graham,' he said feebly. 'Let's talk about it calmly, reasonably.'

'I'm perfectly calm, Tull,' Drabble replied loudly, 'and I have thought things through with all of my reason. Just answer this one question. Are you going to resign?'

'Of course not!' came the reply, less feeble this time. 'Everyone makes mistakes from time to time.'

'From time to time!' There was incredulity in his voice. 'The fact is, Tull, that for six months you misdiagnosed my mother. It took you half a year to refer her for a scan, and because of your incompetence she's going to die long before she should have done. And none too pleasantly, either!' His voice, at first a noisy bluster, had become strident with distress. 'Either you resign, or I'll hound you until you're struck off the medical register.'

Tull felt his heart pounding. It was fear, and he knew it, though part of him – the rational part – told him that he had no reason to be afraid because he couldn't possibly be struck off for what had happened. But he knew he could have done better, should have spotted it sooner. He felt guilty about that. 'Graham,' he said, summoning up all the shreds of assertiveness that were scattered around his body, 'the BMA is not going to find against me for this. You know they won't. I'm sorry, really sorry, but no good will come of this. I've known your mother for years. She's been a patient at the practice for almost as long as I've been a GP. What we should be doing is concentrating on providing her with the best possible care. It's amazing what can be done, nowadays.'

Drabble laughed, a single high-pitched explosion that ricocheted around the room with such force that Tull almost ducked to avoid it. 'Next thing is you'll be telling me that she was your favourite patient!' And Drabble laughed again.

'I don't have favourites.' Alan Tull prided himself on his professionalism, and even in the midst of stress this controlled his reaction. 'Of course, I care a lot about my long-standing patients. I get fond of them. That's only natural.'

'You get fond of them!' The tone of Drabble's statement made Tull look at him sharply. He might be a bit bumbling, but Tull was no fool, and instinctively he realized that their conversation was leading into deeper, more dangerous waters.

'Would you rather I hated them?' he retorted, but he was floundering. He was paddling in the sea, the water was up to his knees, the sand was sucking at his feet and the tide was coming in.

'Fondness is a dangerous thing,' Drabble was saying. 'Especially when the object of your fondness is a vulnerable, trusting woman, and you are unable to keep your feelings under control, Doctor. I was looking on the web only the other day. It's amazing how many GPs get struck off for sexually abusing their patients.'

Tull gulped, and his mouth gaped, but at first no sound came out, as the sickening reality of where this was all leading dawned on him. His right hand pulled distractedly at his thinning hair, until finally some words came. 'What are you accusing me of,' he said breathlessly. 'Because I can assure you I have never—'

'Who are they going to believe, Doctor? You, or the testimony of a dying or – by the time it comes to a head – dead woman? And does it matter, anyway, when rumour and gossip is so much more effective than the laboured progress of justice? If you don't resign, and soon, your reputation will be ruined. The choice is yours, Doctor!'

'Marjorie would never say I abused her,' Tull insisted, his face now the colour of the palest parchment. 'Never!'

'First you abused her medically, and then you abused her sexually. That's what her testimony will confirm.'

'But she can't say that. It's not true,' he said desperately.

'Oh, but she will,' Drabble said harshly, before he turned towards the door and wrenched it open. 'I'll give you a couple of days to think it over, Doctor,' he snarled. 'Then I'll take action.'

At the same time as Graham Drabble was uttering his final threat, Sarah Russell was sitting – another world and half a continent away – in the café of the Peggy Guggenheim Collection in Venice. One of the perks she had established for herself as administrator of Cornforth was to be one of the staff who, each October, supervised a select group of students on a visit to Venice. Sometimes she wondered about the educational benefits of these trips, but they were valued by the parents and even more so by their offspring. No doubt both parties were glad of some time off from the other. Right now, she herself was off duty, while one of the museum staff took the students round some of the key paintings and sculptures in the collection. Opposite her sat Maria Tull, née Scarpa, whose fluency in Italian, family connections in Venice, and knowledge of art were three compelling reasons why she – despite not being a member of the college staff – was the other regular adult presence on these Venetian trips.

They had been sitting there, each with a cappuccino, in an uncompanionable silence for some ten minutes. Sarah was studying the menu, although they had already agreed to eat at a café they had identified as they walked to the museum from the Academia Vaporetto stop. Maria was leafing through a copy of *Vogue* magazine, and was enjoying reading the Italian language again as much as she was scouting out the upcoming styles. When she reached the end, she looked up and pushed it across the table.

'You ought to take a look,' she said.

Sarah abandoned her feigned interest in the menu and looked

across at her companion.

'Ought I?' There was sharpness in her voice. 'Why?'

'Well, look at you!' Maria said, waving her arm expansively. 'You could still be an attractive woman if you tried. Of course, ideally you ought to lose some weight, but even so.' She paused, allowing the jibe to sink in. 'Have you not looked at the women of Venice, and the way they dress? They have style, they think a lot about their appearance, and the men appreciate it.'

'I'll dress the way I want,' Sarah said firmly, conscious that they were in a public place, and conscious too that she could never compete with Maria in the style or figure stakes.

'You need to try a bit harder, dear,' she said leaning forward conspiratorially. 'Take it from me.'

'When I want your advice,' Sarah hissed, 'I'll ask for it.'

Maria looked back, her smile and gaze unwavering. 'Did Dominic ring you this morning?'

Sarah stiffened, and leant back, as if to put more space between the two of them. 'Why do you ask?'

'Because, my dear, he rang me. He wanted to know if I'd had any luck with finding a new source for him. He's probably told you he's fallen out with Carlo?'

Sarah winced. Dominic never told her anything about his business. So of course he hadn't told her about Carlo. He had decided early on in their marriage that she wasn't the asset he needed in the world of antiques, and so he had looked around for someone else to assist him. First it had been James, until he'd done a runner with his brother's wife, leaving his own wife with three children under five, and then it had been Maria. The fashionable, antique loving, half-Italian bitch who sat opposite her now and dared to lecture her on how she should bloody well dress to keep that bastard of a husband interested. She knew only too well how to keep him interested, and it didn't involve the latest Italian fashions.

'Just remember,' Sarah said icily, fighting back the fury inside, 'Cornforth employs you to look after the students, not to go antique hunting round Venice.'

Maria smiled, conscious that she had got under Sarah's skin, but conscious too that she needed her cooperation. 'I'm here, aren't I? But I would like some time off tonight or tomorrow. No doubt you do too?' The smile got even broader. 'Why don't you choose? And I'll fit in round you.'

Sarah nodded. 'I'll think about it.' They were the words of surrender, reluctantly given.

Maria stood up, her mission accomplished. *'Perfetto, mia cara!'* she gushed loudly. 'I'll go and find our students. You enjoy the magazine!'

Sarah watched her move across the floor. She moved smoothly. Despite her high heels, she seemed always to move smoothly, even up and down and across the many bridges and steps of Venice. Not for the first time, Sarah wondered about Maria and her own husband. Not that they were conducting an affair: she was pretty sure of that. If anyone was at risk from Dominic in that department, it was most likely Minette, that pretty little nineteen-year-old back in Oxford. But Maria and Dominic were up to something. She was damned sure of that.

Lucy Tull arrived home just before 5.30 p.m. Unlike her father, she locked and left her bike in the front garden before entering the house. Her mother was in Venice, and Joseph was rarely back at this hour, so when she heard noises from the study, she divined quite correctly that her father must be home.

'Hello Daddy,' she called cheerily, pushing the door open.

'Hello, dear.' The slurred reply and the half-empty bottle of whisky on the desk told its own story.

'Daddy!' she exclaimed. 'What on earth are you doing?'

The alarm in her voice failed to register with him. He smiled goofily at her and raised his glass. 'Just having a snifter,' he burbled.

Lucy was used to dealing with challenging behaviour at the dental surgery. Patients who panicked just as they were about to be injected, and patients who turned up late and then got stroppy because they were told to come back another day. In such circumstances, she believed in decisive action. She moved swiftly forward, detaching the glass from her father with one hand, and picking up the bottle with the other. 'That's quite enough,' she said, as if she was his mother and he was a naughty boy.

He looked at her, squinting slightly, his head at an angle.

'So, are you going to tell me why you're drinking at this time of day?' she asked firmly.

He whimpered plaintively. 'All right.' Then, slowly and not very steadily, he proceeded to tell her all about Graham Drabble's visit and the background to it. 'I'm ruined,' he said at the end, and began to sob. 'What am I going to do?'

Lucy, who had remained standing throughout, looked down at him in disgust. She wanted a father who would stand up and fight for himself, not a quitter. She loved him dearly, but right now that feeling was buried deep beneath others.

'Have you told Maria?' she asked, for she refused to refer to her stepmother in any other terms.

'She's in Venice,' he mumbled, as if mobile phones had never been invented.

'I know she's in Venice,' she snapped irritably. 'For God's sake,' she continued after a pause, 'we can't just do nothing!'

'But what can we do?'

'I'll have to see Marjorie, and speak to her myself.'

'Yes,' he responded vacantly, glad that someone else was taking the responsibility.

'I'll see if I can reason with her. Get her to see how wrong Graham's course of action is.'

'Perhaps I should do it,' her father said unconvincingly.

'They won't let you anywhere near her,' she said firmly. 'I'll do it, Daddy, but best not to tell Maria if she rings, not yet.'

He looked at her, gratitude and relief apparent in his moist eyes. 'Lucy dear, you're my angel, you really are.'

*

At 8.20 a.m. the following Saturday, a tall woman, wearing a black trouser suit and red silk blouse, boarded the Oxford Tube at Gloucester Green station in the centre of Oxford and walked to the back of the bus – for despite its name, a bus was what it was. She sat down at the back, on the driver's side just in front of the toilet. She took the window seat for herself, but placed her handbag and mackintosh on the one next to her. She was, to all intents and purposes, a woman determined to ensure her own privacy.

At Queen Street, in St Clement's, and at three different stops in Headington, the bus steadily collected more passengers, the majority paying their money and then making their way past her and up the stairs. The last pick-up in Oxford was on the very outskirts, at the Thornhill park and ride stop. Four people got on there, the first three being an elderly couple and a girl of maybe eight or nine. Behind this grandparental trio, there trailed a middle-aged woman. Her round face was framed by straight, fake-blonde hair that almost brushed her shoulders, and she wore a black three-quarter-length mackintosh and a blank expression that flickered only once as she made her way laboriously down the aisle. She needed, Geraldine Payne thought unkindly, to lose some weight.

'Hello,' Geraldine said suddenly, her voice a study of surprise. 'Fancy seeing you here!'

'Geraldine,' came the equally amazed reply. 'Are you going to London?'

It was, of course, a fatuous question. Where else would she being going on the Oxford Tube? But Geraldine played along. 'I thought I'd have a day's shopping.'

'Me too!'

'Why don't you sit down here,' Geraldine said, moving her bag. It was, she thought, ridiculously dramatic, this public display of surprise, especially when she was sure there was no one on the bus who knew her, but her fellow traveller had insisted, and she had agreed to play along.

'Looking for something in particular?' The woman had fought

her way out of her mackintosh, and had slumped heavily down into the seat.

'Not really.'

'I took two bags to Oxfam yesterday, so I need to fill the gaps in the wardrobe. You can't go wrong in John Lewis.'

'No, I guess you can't.' Reluctantly, Geraldine forced herself to continue the game. 'I've got a civil partnership coming up next month, so I need something for that.'

And so they chatted, two acquaintances, casually met, who were determined to make the most of their unexpected encounter. Only when the coach had passed Lewknor and forced its way up the steep cutting that took them out of Oxfordshire, did their voices grow silent, as each of them drifted off into sleep, oblivious of the red kites that wheeled above, searching for prey along the borders of the motorway.

Geraldine Payne's sleep was the deeper, and it might easily have lasted until they reached their destination had she not been woken by a sharp jab in the ribs.

'Are we there?' she said, a moment before her eyes told her that they clearly weren't.

'I need to talk.'

'God, you could have waited. I was having such a nice sleep.'

'I need to talk,' her companion reiterated, but her voice had dropped down to a confidential, but intense whisper. 'I've done something stupid.' She paused, and looked up, checking that there was no one who could possibly overhear her. 'Something really stupid.'

'What are you talking about?' There was still irritation obvious in Geraldine's voice, but she too had dropped several decibels.

'I'm being blackmailed.'

CHAPTER 2

Maria Tull died shortly before 10.00 p.m. on the Monday following her return from Venice. No one – with one possible exception – knew the precise time, though later the general consensus of her shocked students was that she had left the St Aidan's Hall in St Clement's round about 9.45 p.m., give or take five minutes. She had been giving the first of six planned lectures on the history of Venetian art, and it had gone well. Those who knew her modus operandi would have expected her to join her students in a local pub or bar at the end of the evening. Socializing was part of her make-up, and she was shrewd enough to know that if she established a personal bond on that first night, then her students were much more likely to stay the course. In the event, the weather put paid to any such plans on that particular Monday night. Round about 9.15 p.m., it had begun to rain. Not the soft refreshing rain celebrated in the old hymn, but a driving, torrential downpour of such primeval fury that it caused the flood-conscious residents of the lower-lying parts of Oxford to twitch curtains, peer nervously out of windows, and wonder if sandbags would need to be drafted into action again.

These were the weather conditions that greeted Maria's students as they prepared to leave, and it was therefore inevitable that they left at a run, in ones and twos, heading for the bus stop, the car or the pub. Maria was the last to leave. John Abrahams, a tall, old-fashioned man in his late sixties, later confirmed this to the police.

He had waited for her to lock up, and then he had walked hurriedly to the bus stop twenty metres to the east, while she scurried off in the other direction, towards town. After some seventy metres, she very likely turned right, down a passageway that led into the St Clement's car park. That, at least, would have been her most direct route to her car, which was parked in the corner at the back of the car park. And it was by the car, as she was scrabbling around in her handbag trying to locate her keys, that she felt a sudden and unutterable pain in her side, before collapsing on to the tarmac. The knife which had caused this searing agony struck again, this time into the neck area, but she felt nothing, for she was already dead – or as good as.

Despite the fact that this untoward event occurred in a public and well-used car park, it was not until shortly after 10.30 that evening that a middle-aged couple, Mr and Mrs Martin Barnes, who had been enjoying a leisurely anniversary supper at the nearby Thai restaurant, returned to their car and almost literally stumbled over her body.

It took an ambulance approximately six minutes to arrive. Martin Barnes had reported the prone woman as a possible heart attack victim, for the darkness in that area of the car park had hidden the telltale blood, and the intensity of the rain had discouraged him from any close inspection. Mr Barnes knew he needed to ring 999, and that was enough. But when the paramedics arrived they quickly realized (a) that the woman was irredeemably dead, and (b) that she had been stabbed. Within another six minutes, three other vehicles had arrived, out of which emerged two uniformed policemen in the first case, then two plain clothes detectives (both female), and finally another non-uniformed woman who was obviously well known to all four members of the police.

'Sorry to spoil your evening, Karen,' DI Susan Holden shouted, as the latest arrival clambered down from her four-by-four.

Dr Karen Pointer flashed a grim smile through the darkness. 'What's there to spoil on a Monday night?' she called back, as she walked to the back of her car, opened the boot and pulled out a squat, black case.

Both the wind and the rain had eased somewhat, but water was still beating down furiously from the black sky with a power that gave the unfortunate group of figures no sense of relief. Umbrellas had been found, however, so as Dr Pointer knelt down to examine the body, she did at least receive some protection from the remorseless elements.

'I can confirm that the subject is dead,' she said. 'There's a stab wound in the neck.' Her eyes made their way methodically down the body, until they came to rest on a darker patch. 'Can I have more light?' she snapped, and began to unbutton the sodden fawn mackintosh in which Maria Tull had died. She pulled it open. A dark red patch on the white blouse told its own unequivocal story. 'There's a stab wound to the heart as well,' she continued. 'At least death would have been quick, maybe instantaneous.' She peered closer, unbuttoning the blouse to get a proper look at the wound. 'You should be looking for a narrow-bladed knife,' she concluded, before rebuttoning the blouse and standing up. 'If it's OK by you, Detective Inspector, I'd rather continue my investigations in my lab, in the morning.'

Holden nodded. 'There's nothing to be gained by you catching pneumonia,' she said, wishing that she too could escape into the dry, but there were things they had to do first. 'We'll take a look round for the weapon.' Holden now knelt down herself, not to take look at the wound, but check the woman's coat pockets. This yielded a mobile phone, which she passed to her young colleague, Detective Constable Jan Lawson. 'Bag this, will you.' Then Holden stood up. 'There must have been car keys, and probably money, and she's wearing lipstick, so the chances are she was carrying a handbag. So let's get looking for them. If we don't find one, we can always check the car's registration to get an ID.'

While Holden and PC Hughes began a methodical sweep of that end of the car park, Lawson and PC Wright followed a footpath which exited at the back and dropped down into Angel and

Greyhound Meadow which separates this more modern area of East Oxford from the medieval city. Wright went left and Lawson right, but it was Lawson who found the handbag where it had apparently been tossed, half hidden under some bushes behind a fallen tree trunk. It was large and brown with black patches, like a crocodile. The leather was soft and expensive, and the name PRADA was positioned, discreetly but prominently, just under the lip of the bag. Lawson could only dream of owning something like this, assuming it was genuine, and no reproduction rip-off. Despite the circumstances she felt a brief flash of envy. The dead woman had clearly possessed both money and style.

The bag had not been ransacked. The only item obviously missing was a wallet or purse. Of the knife which killed the woman, there was no sign. All of which pointed to a mugging, a druggy wanting cash for his next fix, Lawson volunteered much later, as she drove her boss home. This was after they had made the necessary but unpleasant visit to the Tull household, to tell a husband and two adult children about the death of their wife and mother, Lawson was determined to put that experience behind her by focusing upon the practical detail of the case. Holden made no response to this speculation. 'Don't you agree?' Lawson pressed. She wasn't someone who found silence comforting.

'Concentrate on getting me home in one piece, Constable,' Holden replied brusquely. Her mind was on practical detail too, but for her there was a whole raft of it floating around in her head. What staff would she need? How early should she get Lawson to collect her in the morning? What were the chances of finding forensic evidence? (Might the killer's clothing have snagged somewhere as he or she fled the scene?) Was there any chance of finding the knife? It could easily have been tossed into the river; and then again the killer could have taken it home, washed it clean, and put it back in the kitchen drawer, if that was where it had come from. A thin knife, Karen had said. How thin? And why had the killer stabbed her? She hadn't been a tall woman, and if the killer had been an addict desperate for a fix, he could surely have done so with just a clout round the head. Or did he threaten her with a knife, and did she refuse to surrender her bag? In any case, it would be instructive to check out in the morning if anyone had actually tried to use any of the woman's cards. Maybe Lawson was right: drugs were the obvious answer, but somehow it didn't quite feel like it. The killing was clean and quick, as if someone knew what they were doing, not a messy desperate assault by someone driven half-crazy by the need for the next fix. Anyway, whatever, it was far too bloody early to go jumping to conclusions.

Lawson had gone obediently silent, allowing her boss's thoughts to go where they would, and she said nothing else until she pulled up outside Holden's house in Chilswell Road. Holden was relieved to be home. She liked her little house, tucked away here in the middle of Grandpont in south Oxford, protected by its position from the noise of the Abingdon Road to the east and that of the railway line to the west. It was raining harder again, battering against the windscreen of the car, but she wasn't concerned. She had survived the floods of July 2007, so what was there to worry about?

'Here we are, Guv,' Lawson said, trying again. 'I expect you'll be glad to get to bed after all that.'

'I doubt I'll be able to sleep,' Holden said firmly.

'My mum always swears by a cup of cocoa,' Lawson continued, her optimism undimmed.

Holden gave a snort, and immediately regretted it. Lawson was only trying to have a normal conversation, trying to deal with the brutality of what she had encountered that evening. But she, Holden, was being a right cow. She knew that. And it wasn't just about the dead woman. She had other things on her mind. The relief at returning home was not an unalloyed feeling. Coupled with it came another feeling, an unnerving sense of loneliness that would sometimes lie in wait for her and leap out as she shut the front door behind her. What was it? Two years since that bastard Richard had walked out on her. Yet there were times when she found herself missing even him. Bloody hell, what was happening to her?

'Sorry,' she said, trying to make amends. 'I'm sure your mother is wonderful, Lawson. But I doubt I will ever be a cocoa person. Or even, before you suggest it, a herbal tea person. In these circumstances, a slug of whisky is more my line.'

'Oh!' Lawson replied. She was, untypically, lost for a suitable response.

'But I appreciate your concern.' Holden paused, and switched modes again. 'Anyway, can you pick me up at 7.45 in the morning?'

'Of course, Guv.'

'Good.' Holden opened the car door, but didn't immediately get out. She twisted round to face her colleague again. 'Mothers are a good thing, Lawson, and it's important you have someone you can talk to. But remember that mothers worry about their children, so sometimes they also need protecting. They don't need to know everything. Are you with me?'

Lawson nodded after a pause. 'I think so Guv, yes.'

'Good night, then, Lawson.' And with that, the detective inspector got out of the car into the unrelenting rain and shut the door firmly behind her.

At 8.30 the following morning, DI Holden was sitting at her desk facing Lawson, Detective Sergeant Fox and Detective Constable Wilson. Fox was by some distance the oldest of the quartet, and the biggest. Being seated seemed, if anything, to accentuate his bulk, stretching his shirt and jacket tight across his chest and shoulders. Wilson, sitting next to him, seemed small by comparison, though in reality he was less than an inch shorter. Wilson was, however, a slight man, and his hunched posture merely underlined that slightness. He lacked confidence in himself, and not for the first time Holden wondered fleetingly if there wasn't something she should be doing about it. Lawson, by contrast, sat bolt upright, her face open and eagerly watching her boss. She would, Holden had no doubt, go far if she chose to put career in front of domestic bliss.

'So,' Holden said, her eyes flicking between the two men, 'I dare say you're up to date on last night's events. A stabbing in the St Clement's car park. The victim is one Maria Tull, married to a GP in Bainton Road. He confirmed last night that she had been giving an art lecture at St Aidan's Hall. The thin-bladed knife that killed her is missing, so Fox I want you to put together a search team and see if you can locate it. We found her handbag abandoned in the Angel Meadow, so that was clearly the killer's escape route. Lawson can provide more details,' she concluded, switching her gaze.

'I've marked up a map showing where I found it, Guv,' Lawson responded. 'I turned right, so was heading towards Headington Hill. There's quite a spread of trees and bushes there, along the edge of the grass. So I guess that's the place to start.'

'Don't worry,' Fox said firmly. 'I'll sort it.'

'As for you, Wilson, see what CCTV coverage there is of the car park. Of course, given last night's weather conditions, you may see a lot of umbrellas and hoods and few decent mug shots, but we might get lucky.'

'No probs, Guv!' This was only his second murder case, and Wilson, who had not had the experience of seeing the body, was thrilled to be part of it.

'We also recovered the victim's mobile. The last phone call she made was about 6.00 p.m.' Holden faded to a stop. The wide grins on the faces of the two men made it apparent that Lawson had not only told them about the mobile, but had shown them the photo she had found on it too, a photo of a naked, as yet unidentified man. But Holden had no intention of indulging them. 'So the next thing, after you've tracked down the car park's CCTV, will be to track down who exactly was there at St Aidan's and try to tie the details down tight.'

'Yes, Guv,' Wilson said, still grinning.

'Well, bugger off then.'

Holden waited for Fox and Wilson to leave her office, and then cast a quizzical frown at Lawson. 'What is it with men?' she said in a tone that suggested she found them a rather quaint and alien species.

Lawson laughed. 'As my mother always says, men are just overgrown schoolboys.'

Holden smiled back. 'Well, I'm sure my mother would agree on that!'

Half an hour later, Holden and Lawson were outside the Tulls' front door in Bainton Road. The ring of the bell was answered almost immediately by Lucy Tull.

'Oh,' she said. It was a single word, the shortest greeting that she could have offered, yet the intonation of her voice and her body language spoke volumes. Their arrival, Holden realized, was certainly not welcome to her.

'Do you mind if we come in?' Holden asked politely. 'We need to ask you all a few questions.'

'Questions?' came the sharp reply. 'What sort of questions?'

'It's routine procedure,' Holden continued, still resolutely polite. 'It won't take long, I hope.'

'So do I!' And only then did the young woman yield ground and open the door wide so they could enter. 'Follow me!' she said firmly, turning on her heel. 'And shut the door behind you.'

Holden and Lawson waited in silence for three or four minutes in the large sitting room in which they had sat less than twelve hours earlier when giving the news of the death of Maria Tull to her family. Heavy steps on the stairs heralded the arrival of Joseph Tull, who walked over to an armchair and slumped soundlessly into it. Holden made no attempt to engage him in conversation, and instead looked out of the French windows and watched two goldfinches pecking fiercely at a bird feeder. She turned only when more footsteps presaged the arrival of Alan Tull and his daughter Lucy. He had the appearance of a man who hadn't slept much, but his eyes nevertheless looked eagerly across at the two detectives. 'Have you found the killer?' he asked urgently. 'Tell me you have!'

'No,' Holden said. 'Not yet. I'm sorry to bother you, Doctor. We just need to ask you – each of you – a few questions.'

'Why us?' he said plaintively. 'Shouldn't you be out checking the

CCTV cameras, and bringing all the local druggies in for questioning?'

'Really, Dad,' Joseph broke in angrily. 'You've watched enough bloody crime dramas on TV. They want to ask us questions because we're family. And because we're family, we're prime suspects too. Isn't that right, Inspector?'

'We do need to ask you where you were last night, yes,' Holden acknowledged. 'Your son is quite right. So if you just sit down, we'll try to get it over with as quickly as we can. My colleague, Detective Constable Lawson, will take notes.'

'Come on, Daddy.' Lucy led her father over to the sofa, and there sat down with him, her hand gently resting on his arm.

'I was out at a party,' Joseph volunteered loudly. 'Freddie Johnson's. In Southfield Road. It was his birthday. Lots of people there. Lots of witnesses.'

Holden turned and faced him. 'What time did you arrive?'

'Oh, about nine o'clock, I should think.'

'Did you arrive with someone? Did your friend Freddie let you in?'

He paused, as if in thought, and then made a face. 'The answer to that is no, and no. Is that a problem?'

Holden smiled. 'Not for now. But as it stands, without corroboration, it's not exactly a watertight alibi if you need one.'

'In that case,' Joseph replied cheerfully, 'I'll find some witnesses, don't you worry.' As if finding witnesses was the easiest thing in the world. Like buying fags at the local corner shop.

Holden turned back towards the sofa. 'Dr Tull, would you mind telling me where you were last night?'

'I was at home. I got back from work just after six o'clock. Maria was still here. I had a whisky while she finished her supper. Let me think.' He paused, and gave an impression of a man thinking. Holden too was thinking. Dr Tull had asked why they weren't pulling in the local druggies. Why had he said that? She herself had certainly said nothing along these lines the night before, so where had that idea come from?

'Ah yes!' Dr Tull now gave the impression of a man suddenly remembering a vital detail. 'I made a couple of phone calls, and then ate supper in front of the telly. I think I fell asleep for a while. After that I did a few chores. I was a bit worried because of the rain, and I went out to check the drain at the back hadn't got blocked, but my trousers got soaked, so I went and had a bath, and then sat and read in bed, but I think I must have fallen asleep again.'

'He did,' Lucy said, taking up the baton. 'I found him asleep with his glasses still on and his lights blazing when I got in.'

'So where had you been, Lucy?'

'The Raglan Hospital, in the Woodstock Road. I was visiting someone.'

'We need a name.'

'Marjorie Drabble. She's dying of cancer.'

'When did you leave the hospital?'

'Hell, how should I know? You don't worry about time when you're visiting someone. You try to give them your full attention.'

Holden gave a slight shrug and smile. 'I appreciate that, but we do need to know,' she insisted. 'Did you stay to the end of visiting hours?'

'It's a private hospital. They don't throw you out on the dot, but I guess I must have left by 8.45.'

'And then what?'

'I went and had an ice cream in Alfredo's in Little Clarendon Street, and then because it kept raining I had a coffee, and then when it didn't stop I caught a taxi home. I guess I must have got in between ten-fifteen and ten-thirty.'

'Which taxi firm?'

Lucy gave Holden a look of utter disgust, as if she couldn't believe the nit-picking pedantry of her questioner. 'Oxford Cabs,' she said finally, and stood up, placing her hands truculently on to her hips. 'You can check with them if you want to.'

'We will,' Holden replied, unwilling to concede any more sympathy to a young woman whom she was finding it hard to like.

'Is that it then?' Lucy snapped back brusquely.

Holden nodded. 'Joseph and you are welcome to go. However, I do need a couple more minutes of your father's time.'

'Why?' she demanded. DC Lawson, sitting there taking it all in and writing brief notes, decided that Lucy had already taken over the role of matriarch in the house.

But Holden was not deflected. 'Lucy,' she said firmly, 'Constable Lawson will come with you. Because one practical thing we do need are some photos of your mother.'

This request had the most surprising effect. Lucy, who had briefly turned her baleful gaze upon Lawson, twisted back round towards Holden. 'Maria Tull is not my mother,' she snarled. 'My mother died over twenty years ago, in a car crash. Maria is my stepmother,' she continued, her tone now so stressed that Holden feared for what she might do next. 'So if you want photos, Joseph is the person to ask. If it's all right by you – or even if it isn't – I'm going to go to my room now, as I need to make a phone call.' With that, she stalked out of the room, and up the stairs.

'I've got lots of photos,' Joseph said triumphantly. 'Come on, Constable, I'll show you them all and you can choose as many as you like.'

Lawson followed Joseph out of the door, closing it carefully behind her, for she knew what Holden wanted to do next. Behind the shut door, silence descended. Holden hadn't quite decided how to ask what she had to ask. In her head, as Lawson had driven her to Bainton Road, she had rehearsed three different approaches, but she had failed to be satisfied by any. While Lawson was parking, she had torn up her mental notes and decided to play it by ear. In the end, she decided, how she said what she had to say probably wouldn't matter that much. What would be important was Alan Tull's reaction.

It was Alan Tull who broke the silence. He had been slumped back in the sofa all the time Lucy was in the room, but now he sat up, shook himself slightly, and leant forward. 'So,' he said, politely, as if addressing a new patient in his surgery, 'how can I help you?'

Almost without realizing it, Holden took a deep breath in and then slowly let it out. She put her hand into the small black bag she

31

was carrying and pulled out a mobile phone. 'We found this in your wife's coat pocket. Does it belong to her?' She spoke casually, and held it up to show him, but he glanced at it only briefly, as if it had no interest to him. 'Well, if it was in her pocket, I dare say it is. It certainly looks like hers. Why do you ask?'

Holden studied the mobile, and her fingers quickly flicked across the keypad. Then she stood up, walked over to the sofa, and held it in front of Tull. 'Can you tell me who this is?' she said quietly. She kept her own eyes on Tull, and she saw shock – or what she certainly believed to be shock – flash across his features.

'God!' was all he said.

Holden continued to watch him for clues. The picture on the mobile was of a naked man, sprawled on his back on a bed, but apparently raising himself with one arm. The look on his face suggested he was not expecting to be photographed at that moment in time. Was it just a bit of fun, or blackmail? That was the question that Holden had debated with Lawson when her constable had discovered it while checking the mobile for recent phone calls. And that was what she was trying to divine now.

'I appreciate this may have come as a bit of a surprise,' Holden said gently, 'but I do have to ask you about it. Do you know who the man is?'

'Yes,' he croaked. 'He's the plumber.'

'I need a name,' Holden pressed.

Tull cleared his throat. 'Jack Smith. He put a new shower in for us only a few weeks ago, and redid our bathroom last year. Several of our friends round here use him. He's very handy.'

'Have you seen the photograph before?'

Tull looked at Holden as if she'd just asked him if he'd ever run naked down the High Street.

'It must be a joke, a big joke. One of Maria's friends must have taken it and sent it to her for a laugh. He does tend to charge a lot. I bet they wanted to cut him down to size.'

'We think the photograph was taken with this mobile!' Holden responded.

'Rubbish!' he exclaimed, his voice now shrill. 'Anyone could have taken it.'

'But the most likely explanation is that your wife took it,' Holden insisted. However unpleasant it was to pressurize like this a man whose wife had just been murdered, she had no option. Unless Maria's death turned out to be a mugging gone wrong, then this photo made her husband suspect number one. There was no room for sentiment.

'She wouldn't have,' he protested, though Holden detected a buckling of confidence in his voice. 'I mean, how could she?'

Holden removed the mobile from his eye-line and put it back into her bag. 'I appreciate this is a difficult time for you, but you will understand that I have to follow this up.'

'If this comes out. . . .' Tull began, but his words dribbled to a halt.

'I can assure you, Dr Tull, that I will be as discreet as I can. Only time will reveal if this is relevant to your wife's death. For the meantime, if you could give me Jack Smith's address and phone number, we'll leave you in peace.'

He looked at her in astonishment. 'Peace? Do you seriously think you'll leave me in peace when you walk out the door? Are you absolutely deranged, Detective?'

It took Fox, four uniformed constables and a dog an hour and half to do a sweep of the southern side of the meadow, and of the bushes and shrubbery along the northern edge of the St Clement's car park, an hour and a half in which they found precisely nothing. Although DC Lawson's discovery of the handbag had earmarked the likely escape route of the killer, there was no sign of the weapon. Not that this surprised Fox. There were plenty of established waterways around here, he ruefully told himself, and if anyone had been intent on getting rid of the evidence, they would surely have used one of them, rather than just toss it into the nearby bushes. In addition, the rain of the previous night had continued for so long after the incident that any footprints made at the time had been greatly degraded, and indeed, early morning joggers had already squelched their way along the area, further reducing the chance of getting anything useable from the scene.

When the sky darkened, and more rain began to fall heavily from the low, grey clouds, Fox called off the hunt and returned to the Cowley station. There he found Wilson in a state of equal disgust. The CCTV had yielded nothing, because the CCTV in the car park had failed at approximately 7.00 p.m. the previous evening, and no one had been inclined to go out to see why. The only bright light in the gloom was a sheet of paper he had located in Maria Tull's designer handbag, a list of all the people who had been due to attend her lecture, complete with contact phone numbers.

'It was tucked away in this little zip compartment,' Wilson said eagerly, demonstrating the zip as he did. 'Lawson missed it.'

But Fox was more interested in the list than the intricacies of the handbag.

'Maybe there is a God,' he muttered, as he slumped down at his desk.

CHAPTER 3

After leaving the Tulls' house, it was for DI Holden the work of a single call to Jack Smith's mobile to track him down, and barely more than a single minute of conversation with him to establish that he would prefer to come down to the station rather than be questioned in the house of Mrs Anderson of Beechcroft Road. Jack had already realized Mrs Anderson was one of those women who liked nothing better than a good gossip, and the idea of being quizzed by the police anywhere near her was not one that appealed to him. How long would it take for her to ring his wife and casually mention that it had been such a surprise when detectives knocked on the door and insisted on questioning Jack while he was meant to be installing a new hot water tank? Hell, that was the last thing he needed. So, he made his excuses, telling her that he needed some extra piping in order to complete the job. With a bit of luck, the police wouldn't want him for long, and he would be able to return to work with neither her nor his dear wife finding out anything about it.

About twenty minutes later Jack Smith was sitting in an interview room at the Cowley station. He declined DC Lawson's offer of a coffee, insisting he just wanted to get the interview over and get back to his job, but Holden deliberately waited for ten minutes before making her way down. It wasn't that she was sadistic – well, no more so than her job demanded – but it made sense to probe any weak spots, and if playing on Jack Smith's anxiety to be out of the station meant she got better answers out of him, then that was what she would do.

When Holden, accompanied by Detective Sergeant Fox, did finally put in an appearance and sit down at the table opposite Jack Smith, she opened a file and begin to read through the first sheet of paper in it.

Smith gave a snort of impatience. 'Look, why don't you bloody well get on with it. I've got work to do, you know.'

'And so do we, sir,' Fox growled back, leaning his considerable bulk forward as he did so. He was pleased to be alongside his boss again. He hadn't exactly minded leading the hunt for the knife in the rain, but he did resent the fact that Lawson had been the one to accompany Holden to the Tull's house. Holden, he couldn't help thinking, favoured Lawson, saw her maybe even as a protégé, and he wondered where that might leave him.

Jack Smith flinched instinctively before the sergeant's aggression, and muttered something inaudible under his breath. But when Holden continued to read her file, he tried again, this time less aggressively. 'Anyway, what is this all about?'

Holden looked up from her papers, and smiled thinly at him. 'I'm sure you know, Mr Smith.'

'Why should I?'

'You do know that Mrs Maria Tull was murdered last night?'

' 'Course I do!'

'Who told you?' The quick-fire question came from DS Fox. It was a technique they often employed, changing the line of attack, first one then the other, throwing the interviewee off balance.

'It was on the news,' he replied uncertainly. 'Radio Oxford.'

'We didn't release the name to the press until about half an hour ago,' Holden said mildly.

'So who the hell told you?' Fox barked.

Jack Smith shifted uneasily in his chair. 'Sarah Russell. She's a friend of Maria, and I rang her about some money she owed me, and she told me.'

'I see,' Holden said, nodding slowly, and frowning as if deep in thought. 'In that case, we've only two questions to put to you. The first is, where were you last night between nine and ten o'clock?'

'I went out to price up a job about eight-thirty. A Mr and Mrs Knight in Harpes Road. Then I went home. About ten, I guess.'

'Can anyone confirm that you were at home?'

'My wife works at the hospital as a nurse. She's on nights this week, so no, there's no one to confirm when I got home. The Knights will confirm I went to them, of course.'

'We'll need their details,' Holden said, 'but there is another question. We found a photograph on Maria Tull's mobile phone. Her husband told us that the photo was of you. Perhaps you can explain it?' And with that she removed a photograph from the bottom of her thin file and slid it across the table. 'This is a copy.'

Jack Smith had been pondering how to respond to this question when it was asked – as he had known it surely would be – but even so he found himself hesitating. Should he tell the truth? And how the hell was he going to square it with his wife if it came out?

'It was just a bit of harmless fun,' he said finally, trying hard to sound unconcerned.

'Really?' Holden said in a tone that signified disbelief. 'What do you think, Sergeant,' she continued, turning to Fox.

'I doubt Mrs Smith would see it as harmless fun,' Fox replied instantly. 'But maybe she's more broad-minded than my missus.' Not that Fox had a missus. Not any more.

Smith reacted with alarm. 'I don't see what it's got to do with my wife!'

Fox grinned broadly. 'It doesn't,' he said cheerfully, 'but if you don't explain it to our satisfaction, then maybe we'll have to ask her if she took it and then sent it to Maria as a laugh.'

'She didn't,' he replied quickly. 'Maria took it.'

'You were lovers then?' Holden had taken up the baton again, and leant forward as she asked the obvious and crucial question.

'We had a fling. A one-off.'

'And that was when she took the photo?'

'Shit, aren't you a smart cookie!' he snapped back, spitting sarcasm in self-defence.

'Careful!' It was Fox who growled the warning, and like a guard dog bristling in defence of its mistress, he half rose from his chair. Holden gestured him down, but her eyes were fixed on Smith. She pointed at the photo. 'And this one-off took place at her house?' she continued, her eyes firmly fixed on his face.

'No. It was a house I was working in. She came round to chase me up about a problem with her shower, and it just happened.'

'A bit of a ladies' man, are you! One look at you in your dirty overalls, and they can't wait to tear them off?'

'Are you taking the piss?'

'How many of your clients have you slept with?'

'What's that got to do with anything?'

Holden leant back, turned to Fox and shrugged. 'Maybe you were right, Sergeant. I think we'll have to keep him for a few hours while we pursue other enquiries.'

'Sure, boss.'

Smith's panic was palpable. 'What do you mean, keep me here? I've answered your questions, and I have to get back to work.'

Fox gave a brutal laugh. 'You think a few half-arsed lies are enough? If you want to get out of here any time soon, you'd better start answering the inspector's questions properly. And she asked you how many of your clients you've slept with? Mind you, personally I find it hard to imagine how any woman in her right mind would want to get jiggy with a tubby creep like you.'

Smith half-opened his mouth, but said nothing. He looked across at Holden, but if he was hoping she would call her sergeant to heel, the hard set of her face told him he was out of luck.

'We want a list of names!' she said firmly. 'Then we might let you go.'

He swallowed, and licked his lips uncertainly. 'Honestly,' he said quietly, 'she was the only one.'

'Liar!' Fox bawled.

'I'm not,' he yelped back. 'She was the first, the only one. Christ, I wasn't expecting it. I wish it hadn't happened, but it did.'

'And then she took the photo?'

Smith paused before he spoke. The fight appeared to have gone out of him, and when he replied he did so in a resigned monotone. 'Yes.'

'What was she blackmailing you about?'

He looked up sharply. 'I never said anything about blackmail.'

'So why did she take the photo?'

He shrugged, and gave a sheepish grin. 'Maybe to show her friends?'

Holden turned again to address Fox. 'Well, I suppose if we asked around we could soon find out. Get a dozen copies printed off. Ask them to blow them up nice and big so that there can be no confusion about identity—'

'Hey! Just a minute! What are you playing at?' Smith squealed desperately. 'Do you want to wreck my marriage?'

'We aren't playing at anything,' Holden said flatly. She knew instinctively that Smith had cracked, but she had no intention of taking the pressure off. 'We are investigating a murder. And given that the dead woman appears to have been blackmailing you, you are currently a prime suspect. So I will ask you for the second and final time: why did Maria Tull photograph you in the nude?'

Smith felt his throat tighten. 'I wouldn't call it blackmail exactly. I found a painting in the house.' He paused, wondering quite how to describe what happened. 'She offered to help me sell it. Well, she knows a lot more about that sort of thing than I do. We haggled a bit about the split, and then we had sex, and after that she took the photo to make sure I didn't cut up rough about it later.'

Again Fox interrupted. 'So it was her idea, the sex?'

Smith turned his head to face Fox. He said nothing, but he had the look of a cornered rat, Fox reckoned, only he didn't look half as dangerous.

'Tell me about the picture,' Holden asked quietly.

'Well, it looked old to me,' Smith said quickly, relieved to be talking to the woman about something less embarrassing. 'That's all I can say. An oil painting, maybe two foot square. There were two women standing up, and a man lying on a bed. Maria said it needed a damn good clean.'

'So how much was it worth?'

'I've no idea. A few hundred, a few thousand, who knows? But she was interested, all right, so I knew it must be worth a fair bit.'

'And you trusted her to give you a fair price?'

'God, no! I wouldn't have trusted her further than I could spit. But I reckoned anything was better than nothing.'

Holden nodded her head slowly up and down, and then leant forward, as if to pass on a secret to Smith. 'It seems to me that you've got a pretty good motive for killing her.'

'What are you talking about?' His voice was strident with alarm. 'I don't even know where the bloody painting is now. And I told you I was pricing a job up last night. Ask Mr and Mrs Knight. They'll confirm it.'

'For your sake, I do hope so.'

'Can I go now?'

Holden pursed her lips and half closed her eyes, as if pondering – all at the same time – the meaning of life, the likely winner of the 4.30 at Kempton, and what on earth to wear to the police charity ball. Eventually she closed the file in front of her, looked across at Smith, and nodded. 'You can go as soon as you have given my sergeant Mr and Mrs Knight's details. But make sure you stay around.'

Tracking down and interviewing everyone who had attended Maria Tull's first, and final, lecture on the art of Venice was not entirely straightforward for Detective Constables Wilson and Lawson. Maria had done her best to make their task easy: she had left inside her handbag a printed list of sixteen persons. Alongside each name had been written, in a variety of different biros and pens, phone numbers and, in the majority of cases, email addresses. No doubt, Maria had requested her students to do this in case she needed to contact them. In addition, a single hand-written name – Dominic – had been added at the bottom of the list, but with no surname and no contact number or email address

There is no easy way to tell someone their tutor has been murdered, and telling someone this baldly over the phone is not ideal, but in the circumstances it seemed to the two of them the only way to proceed. They reasoned that few, if any, of her students would have met her before that lecture, so her death might be a shock, but hardly an emotional trauma. So the pair of them began the process of investigation by making eight phone calls each. In point of fact, they managed to contact only thirteen at this stage, but such was the willingness to help – or maybe the novelty of being asked 'to come down to the station to help us with our enquiries' – that within three hours ten of them had come and made a statement.

One thing the statements made clear was that the Dominic who had been added to the list was someone known to Maria. This Dominic, it transpired, was some sort of antiques and fine art dealer. He stayed only for the first half of the evening, and for the coffee and socializing in the interval when he seemed keen to introduce himself around and hand out his business cards. John Abrahams, the third witness to arrive, had one of these business cards in his wallet, and it confirmed that the Dominic was a Dominic Russell, the proprietor of D.R. Antiquities.

'He was a nice enough chap,' Abrahams confirmed, 'if a little overdressed for the occasion – navy blue pin-striped suit, yellow shirt and bow tie. Mrs Tull obviously knew him, though I'm not sure she was entirely pleased that he had turned up.'

'What makes you say that?' Wilson's interest was roused.

Abrahams pondered the question. 'Just an impression,' he conceded. 'I can't say they argued or anything like that, but there didn't seem to be any warmth between them. Maybe she felt he was queering her pitch, if you know what I mean.'

Despite the patronizing comment and tone, Wilson nodded politely, and then moved the conversation on to the end of the evening. Abrahams stated that he had left at the same time as Maria, after all the others had gone. 'I don't believe in leaving a woman on her own at night, so I waited while she locked up, and then I headed for the bus stop. She had a car, she said. Maybe I should have accompanied her to it, but it was a terrible night, wasn't it, and I'd have got wetter.'

When Wilson and Lawson compared notes, it was Abraham's statement which stood out as being useful. Only one other student, a middle-aged woman called Dorothy, commented on what she termed a 'frosty atmosphere' between Maria Tull and Dominic Russell.

'Could you elaborate on that?' Lawson had queried. 'What did they say to each other?'

But the flustered Dorothy couldn't remember. 'It was just that he kept talking about her as if she was a great friend, and she pretty well ignored him.'

'So was there anyone else that Maria seemed to talk to in particular?'

'I'm not sure. Just let me think.'

Lawson had let her think, patiently waiting for her to remember something, anything, but it was to no avail. 'Oh dear!' Dorothy had said finally. 'I'm not sure I'm being much help.'

'Don't worry,' Lawson had replied politely. But she took it as her cue to terminate the interview.

Holden and Fox arrived at the pathology laboratory just after three o'clock. An officious receptionist whom Holden had not encountered before insisted they don white coats, and then shepherded them through to a large white-walled room, in the middle of which Dr Pointer was leaning over a naked female body.

'Ah, talk of the devil,' she exclaimed brightly.

'Good afternoon, Doctor Pointer,' Holden replied, unsmiling, conscious of the po-faced receptionist hovering at her shoulder.

'Thank you, Maureen,' Pointer said. She waited until her human guard dog had retreated from the room. 'Nice of you to come, Susan.' She spoke as if it was a social call, the pair of them popping round for tea and cake. 'And you too, Derek,' she added, looking at Fox. 'We like to use first names here, in case you've forgotten, Susan.'

Holden acknowledged this rebuke with a slight upwards movement of her head. 'Any progress on Mrs Tull?'

'She's as good as finished, Susan,' came the reply. 'Not that there's a lot to be said. As you know, there were two stab wounds, one to the heart and one to the neck. The stab to the heart would have brought about almost instantaneous death.'

'What about the weapon?'

'The weapon? Ah, Susan, that is the one interesting thing about this case. It was a thin blade, and over 14 centimetres in length. Probably the killer plunged it as far as it would go.' She paused, waiting for a reaction.

'Karen,' the detective inspector said, finally using her name, 'what sort of knife should we be looking for. I presume from what you are saying that it's not something snatched from a kitchen drawer?'

'Absolutely not,' she said emphatically. 'In my judgement, Maria Tull was killed with an Italian-style stiletto. A switchblade, perhaps, so that it could be easily and safely hidden in a pocket or handbag even. We're looking at a thin blade, maybe as much as 15 centimetres in length, and a very strong one. A good-quality stiletto like this would generate very little resistance, and wouldn't run the risk of bending. That's what the killer would have needed. It pierced her coat and blouse, causing minimal damage – to the clothing that is. There is no sign that the killer had to twist the knife or force an entrance. One stab, straight in and then straight out. Instant oblivion. Not that the killer would have known for certain, especially not in those weather conditions. Hence, perhaps, the second stab to the neck. Just to make sure. Job done.'

'Job done?' Whether consciously or not, Holden used exactly the same words as Pointer had when she returned to the station, though whereas Pointer had used them as a statement, in Holden's mouth they became a question. Both Lawson and Wilson swivelled to face her.

It was Wilson who responded first. 'We've got as far as we're likely to get. Ten statements so far, out of the sixteen students printed on Mrs Tull's list. They all pretty much agree on detail. Nothing out of the ordinary happened except for the foul weather. Mrs Tull locked up round about 9.45 p.m., according to John Abrahams, that is. He insisted on staying behind. A rather chivalrous, military type. Mind you, his chivalry has its limits. He went to catch the bus while she went to the car park. Otherwise, the only interesting thing was Dominic; you may remember his name was hand-written at the bottom of Mrs Tull's list—'

'I do remember,' Holden cut in testily. 'I am not senile.'

'No, Guv,' he replied, trying not to mind the sharpness of her tone. 'Well, we have established that this man is Dominic Russell. He deals in fine arts, antiques, architectural antiquities, and so on. He has a business out on the ring road, near the Pear Tree roundabout. Anyway, he was clearly well known to Mrs Tull, but by all accounts they weren't on best-buddy terms the other night.'

He paused, as if to get his breath back.

'What do you mean by that? Not being on best-buddy terms.'

'Well, Mr Russell stayed only until the interval, about half eight or quarter to nine. He did a bit of sales patter, handed out his business card to anyone who was prepared to take one, and then he left. The only thing is, Mrs Tull didn't seem to be very happy about him being there.'

'I see.' Holden raised her left hand, and began to massage the lobe of her ear. It was itching. It was always her left ear, never the right one. But she did like wearing her studs. 'Anything to add, Lawson?' she asked suddenly. 'Any observations?'

'Yes!' Lawson was quick to take her opportunity. 'I think we're agreed that Mrs Tull may have felt he was encroaching on her ground, turning a lecture into a sales plug if you like. If not, well, the fact that Mrs Tull hardly said a word to him all evening? There must be some reason for it.'

D.R. Antiquities occupied three old farm buildings just inside the Oxford ring road. Had they not been uncomfortably within earshot and exhaust range of both the A34 and the main exit road from North Oxford, they would no doubt have been converted into rather pricey country homes. 'I moved the business here five years ago,' Dominic Russell explained, as he escorted Holden and Fox into the largest of the three buildings. 'I used to be in Jericho, but the landlord was desperate to develop the plot into canal-side apartments, so I negotiated a very generous deal to give up my lease early, and Bob's your uncle, here I am now. D.R. Antiquities. If you fancy a nice statue for your garden, a bit of stained glass as a feature in your hall, or a nice little Victorian genre scene on your dining room wall, then Dominic's your man!'

DS Fox gritted his teeth as he listened. Holden had asked him to accompany her while she left Wilson and Lawson to chase up on Maria Tull's unresponsive students, and he had appreciated that. But already he was wondering how much of this garrulous git he could stand. Indeed, he thought he already understood only too well why Maria resented him turning up unannounced and buttonholing her students. In fact, if anyone had deserved a knife in the gut that night, it was surely Dominic bloody Russell.

But Dominic was alive and well and talking. 'This used to be the cowshed,' he said with a flourish of his hand. Even Fox found it hard not to be impressed by the collection of items through which they were now passing. There were stained-glass windows of various saints, and of Jesus holding a lamb; busts and statuettes of classical figures; a set of six gargoyles; dark oak pews from a church; oil paintings of castles and seascapes, sour-faced gentry and still lifes; old street lamps; and even a row of Foden lorry radiators. Fox paused despite himself to peer more closely at one of them, and then whistled at the price on the tag.

They had come to a glass door, through which Dominic now led them. 'My office,' he announced, 'and my wife Sarah.' The woman at the computer looked up briefly from her computer, and then down again, as if the visitors were beneath her interest. 'She helps out from time to time. Minette usually mans the post – nice girl, French-Canadian, but her parents are over here so I've let her have a few days off.'

'Do you really think the police are interested in Minette?' Sarah Russell said tartly, and without even the pretence of looking up. 'Perhaps you should invite them to sit down and ask their questions, and then they can go.'

'Please,' her husband said apologetically, and with another wave of his arm towards the two plastic green chairs ranged against the right-hand wall.

Holden and Fox sat down, while he plonked himself down at the other desk, opposite them.

'Was it quick?' he said leaning forward, the effusive manner suddenly abandoned. 'I mean, did she suffer?'

Holden registered the fact that this was the first time he had shown any sympathy for – or indeed interest in – Maria Tull. 'Yes, it would have been quick,' she said simply, not wanting to give out too much information.

'Well, that's something.'

'We understand you attended Maria's lecture last night.'

'Yes.'

'Venetian art is an interest of yours?'

He laughed. 'All sorts of art are of interest to me, as you have seen.'

'So why did you leave at the interval?'

'Ah!' he said, 'you have done your homework.' And he wagged his finger at Holden.

Holden wondered if this was the way he was, or whether he was playing for time. She kept her eyes on his, and said nothing. Fox noticed that Mrs Russell had given up pretending to be busy and was now watching her husband with considerable interest.

'It was a long day, yesterday, and I was tired. I wanted to support Maria, of course I did, and she certainly knows, or knew, a lot more about Venetian art than I do, but I was there to network, essentially. Of course, half of them were there just because they wanted a reason to escape from the house and the wife or husband, but you only need to make one good contact and it's been worthwhile.'

'How would you characterize your relationship with Maria Tull?'

The question, fired in low, caught him amidships. 'What do you mean?'

'You said you wanted to support her. I guess that implies a relationship of some sort.'

'Ah, spot on, detective,' he blustered, as he fought to regain his equilibrium. 'I've known her husband since we were at Keble together, and her almost as long as Alan has known her. And until someone stuck a knife in her, she and I worked together. Not in any formal sense, but if she found something that I could shift I'd give her a commission, or vice versa if she found a buyer for any of my stock. It suited us both very well. So to answer your question, that was the sort of relationship we had. A business one. All right?'

'Can you tell me what you did when you left St Aidan's?'

'I went home.'

'What time would that have been?'

The reply to this question came not from Dominic, but from Sarah Russell. 'He came in just as I was settling down to watch *Waking the Dead*.'

'And he stayed in, did he?'

'As I recall, he got himself a whisky and then fell asleep in the chair. It was very peaceful, apart from the snoring!'

'Is there anyone else who can verify this?'

Sarah puckered her lips together while she considered the question. Then her eyes brightened. 'There's Charlie!'

'And who is Charlie?' DI Holden replied.

'Charlie is my cocker spaniel.'

Mrs Jane Holden laughed when, much later, her daughter recounted this to her. 'She must have a sense of humour, that Sarah!'

Mother and daughter were sitting at the elegant mock-Georgian dining table in Mrs Holden's spacious retirement flat in Grandpont Grange. They had just eaten a three-course meal courtesy, Susan was fairly certain, of Marks and Spencer, and in deference to the older woman's bad back they were still sitting at the table as they sipped their coffees.

'I'm not sure I thanked you for the supper,' Susan said absent-mindedly, ignoring her mother's comment. She was looking down at her cup, which she held in her two hands as if cradling something small and precious.

'I'm used to that,' her mother said sharply.

Her daughter looked up. 'Sorry!' It was the automatic reaction of a daughter to a demanding mother.

'Your father never said thank you for a meal. He would clear away the dirty dishes, and stack them on the side in the kitchen, but he never said thank you.'

Silence descended. Perhaps if Susan had been a perfect daughter, she would have pondered the implications of this exchange, and then sympathetically explored the issues and feelings that underlay her mother's words. But she wasn't, and she didn't, for her mind was on other matters. And they were much more pressing. At least, as far as she was concerned, they were. She frowned. 'That's the last thing I would have said about her.'

Her mother looked at her in bewilderment. 'About whom?'

'Sarah Russell. Serious, controlling, contemptuous even. But I wouldn't have described her as having a sense of humour.'

'Oh?' Her mother was back on track. 'You didn't find it funny, what she said about Charlie the cocker spaniel?'

Again, her daughter's response was not an answer. 'He's the hilarious one in their relationship. The life and soul of the party. Like daddy was. The perpetual naughty little boy. Sarah is stuck with being his mother.'

'But that doesn't mean she can't sometimes be funny.'

'I think she was trying to distract me.'

'From what?'

Her daughter didn't immediately reply. It was something that had occurred to her only as she had been sipping at her coffee, and she needed to give it one more whirl in her head before she gave life to it by expressing it in words. Eventually, however, she shrugged.

'From the fact that she is his alibi.'

Shortly after making this observation, Susan Holden pecked her mother on the cheek, thanked her again for the meal, and left. Or at least she would have left, except that her mother, who had gone to the front door of the flat as if to let her out, had turned and was leaning against it, blocking her exit. If Holden had not been so preoccupied, she would perhaps have sensed trouble.

'You ought to go out more,' she heard.

'I thought that was what I was doing this evening,' she replied. 'Going out.'

'Supper with your mother does not constitute going out.' Her mother spoke firmly, as mothers do when squaring up to their children. In her case she had got only one daughter, but that made her well-being all the more precious. And she was worried about her. 'We are sociable beings, designed to have a partner in life.'

'Ah!' Susan knew where this was going. It was a surprisingly long time – two or three months maybe – since they had had a conversation like this. But not long enough. Susan was tempted to answer back, but the single glass of wine over her supper had mellowed her mood. So she fought the urge.

Her mother was still leaning against the door, looking at her daughter, and there was sadness in her eyes. 'Just because Richard was a bad one doesn't mean every man is.'

Susan glared at her mother. There was no sadness in her eyes, only fury. That was forbidden ground as far as she was concerned, a no-go area dotted with unexploded mines. Bloody Richard. Bastard Richard. Richard who slapped her around, Richard who cheated on her, Richard who eventually ran out on her, thank God! Why the hell hadn't she walked out on him first?

'Were you happy with my father, then?' If her mother was going to mention the unmentionable, then so would she.

'Yes.' Sometimes only a lie will do.

'Oh yeah. Not from where I was sitting.' Why not be aggressive and nasty? She would give as good as she got.

Her mother wrenched the door open. The words had done their

job, and some. 'I can see I shouldn't have started this conversation.'

Her daughter strode past, and only when she was outside did she throw back a reply, but it was lost in the slamming of the door.

It would typically take little more than two minutes to walk to her house in Chilswell Road, but once she was in Whitehouse Road, she stopped under a street lamp, removed her mobile from her bag, and made a call. She needed someone to talk to. About the case. That's what she told herself. She had talked to her mother, of course, before the evening had disintegrated, but she hadn't been able to talk to her about the photo of the naked Jack Smith or the painting he had found. Apart from anything else, this wasn't information she wanted getting gossiped round the neighbourhood. So she still needed to talk to someone else, someone she could bounce her thoughts off, someone she could trust. At least, that was what she told herself as she searched for the number. Which was why and how she came to ring Dr Karen Pointer at 9.25 that evening.

'It's Susan Holden,' she said when her call was answered.

There was the briefest of pauses. 'Hello, Susan. What a lovely surprise.'

'I've just had supper with my mother.'

'That's nice.'

'No it wasn't. Well, it was OK until we got on to the subject of me, and then it all went tits up.'

'Oh dear.' Again there was a pause, though less brief. 'Would you like to talk about it?'

'I'm just walking back to my house.'

'Would you like me to come round, Susan?'

There was a pause. What did she want? Across the road, two students walked past. She recognized the woman as living up her end of Chilswell Road. They were talking intently, apparently oblivious of her scrutiny, and they were holding hands. 'Yes, please,' Holden replied.

'Now?'

'If you don't mind.'

'I don't mind at all.'

CHAPTER 4

'So, where are we, Sergeant?' In truth, DI Holden should have had a pretty firm idea herself of where they were, but at 9.05 that next morning, as she sat in her rather frayed but ergonomic office chair, facing the three members of her team, her mind was having a struggle to stay in the present and not drift back to the previous night.

Karen Pointer had arrived at her house in Chilswell Road within fifteen minutes of their brief phone call. Holden had seen her arrive, and had opened the door before the bell had rung. For several seconds they had stood unmoving, one outside, one inside. Was either of them conscious that this could be or might be or should be a defining moment in their relationship – crossing of the Rubicon or maybe a Pandora's box moment? Perhaps. It was Karen, eventually, who had broken the silence.

'You look exhausted.'

Susan had smiled and looked down at her feet almost bashfully, as if the other woman had told her how beautiful she was. And maybe that was exactly what Karen Pointer was saying.

'Thanks for coming,' Susan had replied, finally looking up.

Only then had Karen moved forward into the narrow hallway, where for some thirty seconds they had hugged each other before finally, tentatively kissing. Then they had gone into the kitchen and talked and talked over mugs of tea – about life and work, and the past and the future, and mothers. And Karen had insisted Susan ring her mother, even though it was ridiculously late. And then they had gone to bed, though not initially for sex. They had lain together fully clothed, Susan facing the wardrobe as she always did, and Karen tucked close behind her, her left arm curled protectively around her companion's body, and they had talked desultorily until they had both fallen asleep. Only much later, just after the clock on the landing had chimed four o'clock had Susan woken up and turned round and moved into territory that was for her scary and thrilling and unknown.

'Wilson and Lawson have chased up the rest of Maria's students.' Fox was summarizing where they had got to. Holden forced herself back to the present. 'But to be honest there's nothing to add to what we had already found out. Dominic Russell left at the end of the interval, and the last person to see Maria was John Abrahams. She received no phone calls, and there is no reason to believe she was planning to meet anyone. One thing several witnesses agree was, that there was ill feeling between Maria and Dominic that evening.'

'But that doesn't make him a killer,' Holden insisted. 'He was home by nine o'clock and fast asleep in front of the TV when Maria was killed, according to his wife.'

'She might be lying,' Fox stated.

'So who else have we got in the frame? Jack Smith? Maybe he thought he was being cheated out of this painting.'

'Maybe. If you ask me, his alibi sounds a bit thin. He said he was pricing up a job earlier in the evening, but how long would that take? And his wife was working the night shift, so there's no saying when he got home.'

'What about the family?'

'The husband was at home, supposedly asleep, but Lucy didn't get in until 10.30, so he doesn't have a real alibi. She says she was at the hospital till 8.45 – that should be easy enough to check – and then she claims she had an ice cream and a coffee in Little Clarendon Street, before catching a cab home. I guess that all needs checking out. Joseph was at a party, but how easy would it be to slip out of that. What with drink and drugs, who would have noticed?'

Holden didn't reply at first. Her mind had skipped to the weapon. A very sharp, thin-bladed knife, Karen had said. Maybe a stiletto switchblade. Easy to carry, and as easy to use for a woman as a man. Which meant no one was ruled out.

'What do you think, Lawson? And you, Wilson?' Holden was aware that she had been leaving them out of the discussion. But they never got the chance to join in because at that moment the door opened and through it burst an angry woman, behind whom there trailed the despairing desk sergeant, John Taylor.

The woman was tall and slim, with short black hair, dangling earrings, and oval, rimmed glasses. Her white blouse, dark slacks, and neat jacket would in normal circumstances have conveyed a message of smart professionalism, but the anger that seemed to rise from her, like steam from a geyser, sent out other signals, as did her first words, emitted as they were in harsh strident tones. 'Are you Detective Inspector Holden?' she demanded.

Wilson, Lawson and Fox had all risen to their feet, but Holden remained in her chair, apparently calm. She nodded. 'Yes. And who are you?'

'I'm Geraldine Payne. I want to know what you're doing to find my bloody painting. That scumbag Jack Smith has told me all about it and how he gave it to that Italian bitch, and I want it back. It was found on my property and so it belongs to me.'

Holden stood up slowly, conscious she needed to get the situation under control. 'We're investigating a murder,' Holden said firmly. 'That is our priority. Obviously, the painting may be relevant.'

'Well, of course it's relevant!' Geraldine's face was flushed and her right arm was waving angrily in the air. 'The woman stole a valuable painting, and now it's gone. Obviously someone killed her to get their hands on it.'

'Nothing is obvious at this stage.' Holden too had raised her voice, though she was still speaking less noisily than her opposite number. 'We have several lines of enquiry ongoing, and that is one of them.'

'Christ, did you learn that answer on some media communications course?' Her voice changed into an uncannily accurate copy of Holden's: 'We have several lines of enquiry ongoing.' She laughed aggressively. 'It sounds like a load of bloody flannel to me. The sort of official shit you spout when you're getting nowhere.'

If Geraldine was trying to provoke an angry reaction from Holden, she failed. In fact, Holden's response was to laugh loudly back, as if she found the other woman's words ridiculous. This had the desired effect of temporarily silencing the intruder, and in that interlude Holden stood up. She rested her hands lightly on the desktop and leant forward. 'Tell me, Ms Payne,' she said softly, so softly that the furious woman was forced to concentrate to hear her. 'Did you know Mrs Tull?' The question threw Geraldine metaphorically off balance, as it was meant to. For a moment or three, she said nothing.

'Well, yes. What's that got to do with anything?'

'You called her an Italian bitch.'

'Would you rather I called her an Italian cow?'

'How do you know her?'

'I'm a dentist. I used to do her teeth.'

'Used to?'

'Well, she's not going to need dental surgery now, is she?'

'But you didn't like her?'

'Those are your words, not mine, Inspector. We were different from each other. But as long as she was prepared to pay, I was prepared to look after her teeth.'

'And what do you know about the painting? You say it's valuable. But for all I know, it might be worthless.'

'If that Italian bitch wanted it so much she was prepared to be fucked by that bloody plumber, then you can be sure it wasn't worthless.'

'It seems a bit unlikely, finding a valuable painting under the floorboards,' Holden continued with a smile.

'Do you know who owned the house before me?' the other

woman snapped. 'Miss Eliza Johnson. Ring any bells, Inspector?'

Holden nodded, for the name did ring bells. Eliza Johnson was an eccentric recluse who had leapt to prominence after her death the previous August, when it hit the news-starved media that she had left her house and her collection of fine art to a cats' home, much to the disapproval of her only remaining relation, a niece. Which meant, Holden admitted silently, that any painting found there was likely to be a genuine and valuable work.

'It does ring bells, Ms Payne.'

'Well, find the painting, and you'll find the killer.'

'And did Jack Smith enlighten you on the subject of the painting. Because—'

But Geraldine Payne cut across her bows savagely. 'You're the detectives, aren't you? That's your problem. All he told me was that there were two women standing over a man who was lying on a bed.'

'As a description, it's not the most precise.'

'Well, go and get a better description, then, Inspector. I've got a root canal to sort out. So I'll go and do my job, and I suggest you do yours.'

Geraldine Payne turned and walked out, brushing past Sergeant Taylor, who shrank back before her despite the fact that he had at least 10 centimetres and 25 kilos advantage over her. He cast a final apologetic look at Holden, and then he retreated, hurriedly following the dental surgeon down the corridor.

As their footsteps receded, Wilson got up and shut the door, and then returned to his seat. 'Maybe she's right,' he volunteered.

'And maybe she's not!' Holden said with brutal force.

Wilson flinched, but he had learnt from experience that ducking out never won any Brownie points with the inspector. 'I merely meant,' he continued, 'that it seems like a good motive. I mean, if it was a really valuable painting. We know Maria Tull was an expert on Venetian art, so she would have known the difference between the real thing and a dud.'

'It seems reasonable,' Fox said, coming out in support of Wilson.

55

'But shouldn't we be looking a bit harder at the alibis?' Lawson interjected. 'What with a wife who was in the habit of sleeping with the tradesmen, rival siblings seeking the favour of their father, and a stepdaughter who may have hated her stepmother, there's plenty of scope.'

'Hated her stepmother?' Fox countered. 'Isn't that just your guess?'

'Based on the way she behaved when we interviewed them, it's more than a guess. It's a reasonable conclusion.'

'All right, that's enough.' Holden stood up, conscious of the tensions in her team. 'What we need to do is cover all the bases. I'll check out Lucy Tull's alibi. Dr Tull doesn't have one, but if he knew about his wife's infidelity, he's got to be a prime suspect, so we need to test out his story as far as we can. Check with his neighbours. Maybe they saw him return home after work. Maybe they saw Maria leave for her evening class. Maybe he went out afterwards and isn't telling us. I want you, Wilson, and you, Lawson, to deal with that. Sergeant Fox, you look into the son, Joseph. Find out a bit more about this party he went to. Who are his friends? Is he heavily into drugs, because he sure as heck looks like he uses. As for Jack Smith, let's pay him a visit at the end of the day – when he's home with his wife. That way, we'll be able to apply some pressure. We need to know exactly what this missing painting looks like. All right?'

'Yes, Guv,' came the chorused reply. The session was over.

Marjorie Drabble smiled at her unexpected visitor. 'Sit down, won't you,' she said softly, and with a wave of her hand.

'It's good of you to see me,' Holden replied, sitting down in the proffered chair.

'There's not much else to do here, except to watch wretched daytime TV. Anyway, it's not every day one is visited by a senior detective.'

The nurse had obviously briefed Marjorie Drabble in the five minutes during which Holden had had to wait in the reception area, as well as preparing her for her visitor. She was, Holden couldn't help but notice, obviously very well cared for. As she noted the general smartness of the room, the brushed hair and spotless nightie, the side-table ordered with fresh water, cards, and a photo frame of a bride and groom, Holden felt her vaguely socialist principles wilting. If, God forbid, her own mother ever needed hospital care, this surely would be the quality she would deserve too.

'Even so, I'll try not to take too much of your time.'

'Did they offer you a coffee?' Marjorie replied, conscious that this was her room and that despite the circumstances she was the hostess.

'I'm fine, thank you.' Holden paused, and ran a hand through her hair. She knew of no set of protocols that had to be observed when interviewing a terminally ill hospital patient, except perhaps to keep it short and low-key. So she smiled what she hoped was an encouraging smile, and said simply: 'I am investigating the death of Mrs Maria Tull.'

Marjorie Drabble smiled back from the pile of plumped pillows against which she lay. 'I thought you must be.'

'We are required to follow up everything and double check statements, so all I need to do is ask you to confirm that Lucy visited you on Monday night.'

'Lucy?' She sounded genuinely surprised. 'You surely don't think she's involved!'

'No,' Holden said firmly and quickly, conscious of the alarm apparent in Mrs Drabble's voice. 'Of course not. It's just standard practice to establish the movements of all the family. Then we can rule them out. And Lucy told us she was visiting you.'

'Yes, she was.' The reply was controlled, and if Holden had had an emotional thermometer to check, she would have found it registering something close to normal. It suddenly occurred to Holden that there was more to Mrs Drabble than met the eye. Before she had been reduced to this bed-ridden state – a prisoner on a medical death row – she might have been a rather formidable woman.

'Can you remember what time she left?'

'I expect they keep a visitors' book in reception.' It was a fair point, Holden acknowledged silently, but she realized too that Mrs Drabble was not going to freely offer up information at the drop of her detective's hat. Not that female detectives were prone to wear hats on duty.

'Visiting hours end at eight o'clock, don't they?' Holden said.

'I'm sure you know that they end at eight thirty!' The answer was instant. 'Either that or you are a much less competent detective than you appear to be.'

'So Lucy left at eight thirty, then?'

'I never said that inspector.' The smile was back on her face, though it was a smile devoid of warmth.

'Do you mean she left later?'

'They aren't strict on visiting hours here. And Lucy wasn't a clock watcher when she visited me. In fact, I usually had to remind her that time was more than up. So I'd guess it was more like eight forty-five when she left.'

'So she visits you regularly, does she?'

'Three or four times.'

'That's very good of her.'

'Yes, she's very kind.' Marjorie shut her eyes, and made a grimace. Holden took this as her cue to stand up.

'Thank you,' she said. 'I've intruded enough on your kindness.'

The ill woman's eyes opened again. 'Lucy likes to talk about her mother. You see, Christine and I were friends before she was born, and when she was born of course. Lucy was only one when her mother died, so she likes to ask me about her. What was she like? What sort of young woman was she? What did she like wearing? Indian skirts or Laura Ashley, miniskirts or jeans, stilettos or flats? What was her favourite perfume? She couldn't talk to her father about her, not after he had married Maria. So I think maybe that was why she liked visiting me. We could sit here in absolute privacy and say anything and everything. It was liberating – for me as well as her.'

Holden swallowed. She had been prepared to leave, yet now the woman lying so pale and drawn in the bed had become animated. So she took her chance. 'Did Lucy get on well with Maria?'

'Oh, Inspector!' Mrs Drabble grinned up at her. 'Never one to lose sight of your goal, I can see. Ask the key questions come what may. A very admirable quality, though not perhaps one that will win you many friends.'

'I'll go in a minute,' Holden said quickly.

'Just as soon as I've answered, eh?' She laughed, but the laugh was followed by a cough, and then a bout of coughing that had Holden on her feet and hurrying to pass her a glass of water. She gulped at it desperately, and then lay back as she regained control of herself.

'I'll go now,' Holden said firmly. She had found out as much as she was going to about Lucy's timings that night, and some other information besides. Best not to push any harder.

But Marjorie Drabble hadn't finished. 'Considering they were stepdaughter and stepmother, they didn't get on too badly, as far as I could see. Mind you, perhaps I should explain that I didn't see a lot of either of them. When Maria came along and took Christine's place, I didn't approve. It had all happened too quickly. Alan and Maria must have sensed it, because none of us made any attempt to keep in touch socially. Alan was my GP, so I kept in touch with him that way, but it was as if a glass wall had come down between us. We saw each other when I had a medical problem, but we never really communicated.'

'So how was it that Lucy started to visit you in hospital?'

Again, Marjorie Drabble shut her eyes. Holden could see that she was tiring, but some part of her brain refused to be convinced. To be too tired to answer this question would be very convenient for Mrs Drabble. Could Lucy really have come and visited her in the hospital just because she felt sorry for her? Somehow, she couldn't believe it. It didn't add up.

But she wasn't going to get an answer out of Marjorie Drabble, not now. For the hospital patient had pressed the bell to call the nurse. 'I need to rest,' she said firmly. Immediately the door opened, as if the nurse had been waiting outside with nothing else to worry about except meeting Marjorie Drabble's every need instantly.

'Time's up, I think, Inspector,' she said.

Holden nodded, thanked Mrs Drabble, and got up to leave.

Cornforth College is situated on the western side of the Woodstock Road, three or four hundred metres to the north of what used to be the Radcliffe Infirmary. The building had started life as a pair of semi-detached family residences, though of a size and magnificence that ruled them out of the reach of all but the most affluent of Oxford families. Their ownership had passed from senior university academics to businessmen, and then finally to Gerald Cornforth, a former public school headmaster who had grown frustrated with the irksome interference of a board of trustees and decided to set up his own educational establishment. DS Fox had driven past it on a number of occasions, and had noticed the blue and white board outside it which proclaimed its name, but beyond that he knew nothing of Cornforth College. This was not his part of the city, and he was certainly not a man who had ever felt the need or desire to seek out a private education establishment. A lack of offspring and a determinedly working-class outlook had ensured that.

Fox had parked the car in a side road, shortly after dropping Holden outside the Raglan Hospital, for their destinations were only a few hundred metres apart. He had then walked back down to the Woodstock Road, and turned left. Inadvertently, he found himself following two young women, with uniform blonde hair, white blouses and short dark skirts. They themselves turned left when they reached the college, walked up to the arch-shaped green door on the left-hand side of the building, and entered. Fox followed them, but once inside he stopped. The female students were already half-way up the wide wooden staircase which dominated the entrance hall. He looked around, and immediately saw someone he knew.

'Mrs Russell!' The administrator, who had been making her way from her office to try to locate the senior tutor, looked at the man looming in front of her.

'You haven't come to see me, have you?' she said defensively.

'No,' Fox said, noting the alarm in her voice.

'That's just as well,' she said quickly, 'because I am very busy at the moment.'

'I need to speak to Joseph Tull,' Fox said mildly. 'Perhaps you can track him down for me?'

'It's not very convenient, coming at this time of the morning,' the administrator replied acidly, her poise recovered.

'To be quite frank with you, I don't actually care how convenient it is for him or indeed for you,' Fox retorted. He had no intention of being pushed around, especially in a place like this. 'I need to speak to him, and I need to speak to him now. And I need a room to do it in.'

'I see,' she replied. 'In that case, I suppose you'd better use my office.'

She turned briskly on her heel, and without any further word led him back down the corridor from where he had seen her come, and ushered him through a door to the left. 'If you wait here, I'll go and see if I can find Tull.'

The task of tracking down Joseph Tull cannot, in the event, have been too difficult for Sarah Russell, because he appeared in the doorway little more than a minute later.

'What is it?' He spoke with an accent and arrogance that immediately pressed several of Fox's buttons.

'Well, I'm not here to enrol as a student, that's for sure.'

'I'm not sure they'd let you in. They are rather fussy.'

'So am I.'

'And it costs a packet.'

Fox said nothing back. He didn't like Joseph, but he knew from experience that he had to avoid getting sucked in if he was going to keep control of the interview. And besides, it was as plain as a pikestaff that Joseph was a clever little shit who'd always have a smart-arse answer up his sleeve. He went and sat down at the desk, gestured Joseph towards another chair, and waited for him to subside into it. Only then did he speak.

'The night your mother was killed, you were at a party. In Southfield Road as I recall. I need a list of people who can verify that you were there.'

Joseph put his hand to his head and pushed back the hair that had flopped across his face. 'That could be a problem,' he said.

'Why?'

Again the hand pushed at his hair, which had already fallen back across his face. 'Because I didn't go to it.'

'So you lied.'

'I had to. Because I had told my father that that was where I was going.'

'So where were you, and what were you doing?'

'I just went out. To the pub.'

'Which pub?'

'In town. Does it matter which one?'

'Of course it bloody matters. Which pub?'

'The Three Goats Heads, in St Michael's Street. But only for a while.'

'And is there anyone who can verify any of this? Because from where I sit, you've got an alibi that's worth bugger all.'

'My mate Hugo. Hugo Horsefield.'

'Just him?'

'Yeah.'

'And is Hugo Horsefield a pupil of Cornforth College, too?'

Joseph Tull said nothing at first. He chewed his lower lip, and looked apprehensively across at Fox, as if weighing up his options. Eventually he replied.

'He used to be.'

'What exactly do you mean by that?'

'He got expelled, two weeks ago.'

'Did he now! And why was that?'

'What's that got to do with anything?'

Fox smiled. He'd got the measure of this arrogant prick. 'Drugs, was it?'

Holden had just sat down with her pistachio ice cream and Americano coffee when Fox walked in. 'Treat yourself, Sergeant,' she said cheerfully.

'No thanks,' he replied, sitting down opposite her. 'Not ice cream weather, in my book.'

She made a face, and took a bite out of hers.

'Master Tull's alibi has gone AWOL,' he said.

'AWOL? In what sense?'

'In the sense that he wasn't at that party he claimed to have been at. He went out to score some drugs, and his only witness for the evening is a guy who has just been thrown out of Cornforth for selling coke to the other students.'

Holden took a lick of her ice cream as she considered this information. 'So he had the opportunity. What about the motive? Killing your mother is pretty extreme. Drugs I can believe, but. . . .'

But Fox had had time to consider this, and had his reasoning ready. 'Suppose he hadn't got enough money. Suppose he was desperate for a fix, so he went to meet her after her lecture, got into an argument, and when she refused him money he stabbed her.'

'It's possible,' Holden admitted, 'but it's all speculation. What exactly do we know about him to support that idea?'

Fox made a face. He knew it was speculation, but as a theory he felt it wasn't a bad one, so to hear Holden dismiss it so casually was irritating. God, she could be a pain up the arse at times. He had just blown a suspect's alibi wide open, and her reaction was to play devil's advocate. Thank you, ma'am!

'We know he takes drugs,' Fox said. 'And we know he can lie.'

Holden took another lick, but made no comment. Fox wished that he had had something now. A woman had sat down behind Holden in his direct eye line. She had a round face, frizzy hair and oval glasses that made her look rather academic, and she had in her hand a cornet of dark-brown ice cream. He wondered how old she was – maybe mid-thirties he reckoned – and then his eyes drifted from the ice cream to her left hand and he suddenly realized that he was looking to see if she had a wedding ring. She didn't, not that that necessarily meant anything nowadays.

'Is there someone you know over there, Sergeant?' Holden's words broke into his brief introspection, and he shook his head in answer.

'Sorry. I was miles away.'

'Do you want to know about Lucy Tull's alibi?'

'Yes, of course.'

'Because I find it disconcerting, in fact bloody rude, when you stare over my shoulder to check out the talent.'

Fox bowed his head slightly, as if in apology. 'So what did you fmd out about her?' he asked dutifully.

'Well, she was probably at the hospital till maybe 8.45 p.m. At least that's what she wrote in the visitor's book, and Mrs Drabble supports that sort of timing. But even so I reckon she could have made it to St Clement's in time to kill her stepmother. So time isn't an issue. I rang Oxford Cabs. She was picked up from here by a private hire car just after 10.00 p.m. So the key question is, was she here in the intervening period, as she claims?'

'You've asked, presumably?'

'Of course. But no joy. The manager can't remember. He says he thinks he's seen her in here from time to time, but there were a lot of people that night escaping the rain. And the two Poles who were working that night with him have just gone back to Krakow for a month.'

'Great!' Fox looked around the room, his eyes methodically scanning the four walls. 'No CCTV?'

'No.'

'So she's not got an alibi either.'

'And neither has her father.'

Fox laughed, remembering again the photo of Jack Smith, naked and startled. 'Well, the good doctor has certainly got motive. But maybe we're missing the obvious suspect. A druggie desperate for a fix, who saw her with her fancy bag, followed her into the car park, and stabbed her when she refused to hand it over.'

Holden said nothing. She was remembering the driving rain that night, and imagining Maria Tull walking as fast as her heels would allow down the St Clement's pavement, maybe even breaking into a trot as she hurried to reach the shelter of her car. She would have turned right, into the alleyway, then across the car park towards her car, parked in the far right corner. Had the killer been waiting for her, someone who knew her and knew her movements that night, and knew that sooner or later she would return to her car? Or had some random addict seen her in the street and followed, or been hanging around in the car park and decided she looked good for cash. If only the CCTV had been working, they might have got some hard evidence to go on. As it was, they had only hunches. She shrugged – temporarily resigned to the impossibility of knowing – took another lick of her ice cream, and glanced across at her companion. 'You really should take a chance one day, Sergeant, and try one of these. You might find you actually like it.'

When you're lying on your back, your mouth jammed wide open and your upper lip and left-hand cheek stuffed tight with cotton wool, it is hard to engage in any sort of conversation, let alone a meaningful one. That fact, however, did not deter Geraldine Payne, BDS, as she leant over her first patient of that afternoon, Dr Karen Pointer. The conversation, in reality more of a monologue, had begun with the hectoring tones which many a patient of the good dentist would have recognized.

'Now what did you have for lunch, Karen? A sandwich, I can see. Beef maybe?' It hadn't been beef, it had been roasted vegetables and humus, consumed messily in the car as she drove to her appointment, but that wasn't the point. And in any case, no answer was expected or required. But the dentist had located detritus that the pathologist's perfunctory brushing of her teeth had failed to dislodge, and the matter could not be allowed to go past without comment. The dentist followed up a few seconds later with a well-practised click of the tongue. 'Really, Karen! What are we going to do with you? At this rate, by the time you hit fifty, I'll be measuring you for dentures.'

The pathologist still made no comment, though she did wince with pain as the dentist reinforced her point by digging deeper with her instrument of torture. 'Don't you ever floss your teeth, Karen?' she asked in a tone which combined professional disapproval and personal disgust. Karen Pointer said nothing, in fact could say nothing in her current situation. Instead she focused her eyes beyond the dentist's face, on a children's mobile of prehistoric dinosaurs, and willed the session to be over.

'All right, you can have a spit now.'

Pointer pushed herself up, leant over the white bowl immediately to her left, and expelled the debris that had accumulated in her mouth. 'Sorry,' she said feebly, 'I must be your worst patient.'

Geraldine laughed, not entirely unkindly. 'It's people like you that keep me in business, Karen.'

'Well, that's something,' Karen replied, lying submissively back into her chair.

Geraldine leant over her again, and peered intently at her handiwork. 'Anyway,' she said, as she began a far from gentle flossing operation, 'you must tell me about you. About your love life. Because I've been hearing some rumours, and I was wondering if there could possibly be a shred of truth in any of them.'

Karen said nothing. Geraldine and her were more than dentist and patient. They had known each other several years, largely as a result of their sexual orientation. They had not been lovers, but they moved in overlapping circles, shared friends, and bumped into each other from time to time. Karen wondered what exactly it was that Geraldine had heard. She couldn't know about Susan and her, surely? Susan would hardly have started talking about it openly. They had admittedly been for a walk along the river the night before, but that was hardly compromising. More likely Geraldine had heard rumours, and she was just digging, saying something outrageous to see what response it provoked. That was just the sort of thing she would do.

When the flossing was over, Geraldine straightened up, but remained standing over her captive audience. 'Well, spill the beans. It's the least you can do!'

'I wasn't aware there were any beans to spill.'

'Oh come, come! A little bird told me you were in Chilswell Road the other night.'

'Really?' She tried to sound genuinely surprised.

'How is Inspector Susan?'

'Thank you for doing my teeth,' Karen replied.

Geraldine gave a grunt, apparently abandoning her inquisition, and pressed a lever which caused the chair to return her patient to a sitting position. Karen stood up, glad that that line of conversation had ended.

'I met her myself this morning. Went to the police station, in fact, and gave her the benefit of my opinion. I expect she'll want to tell you all about it tonight.'

'We try not to talk shop,' Karen said defensively, and then immediately regretted it.

'We!' She laughed. 'So my little bird was right.'

'It's early days,' Karen replied quickly.

'Well, tell her to hurry up and find my bloody painting, won't you, dear. Otherwise the two of you might be dropping off my Christmas card list.'

Karen smiled despite her best intentions. There was something about Geraldine that it was hard not to like, a sharpness of tongue and determination to get what she wanted that she almost admired. Mind you, she didn't recall ever having received a Christmas card from Geraldine, but that thought didn't make her feel any better at all. The fact was Geraldine wasn't someone you wanted to get on the wrong side of.

There was a knock on the door, but the person responsible for it had no intention of waiting for a reply. 'Hi!' a voice said.

Sarah Russell looked up from her laptop. She was reviewing the budgeted figures against the actuals for the term so far, and the last thing she wanted was to be interrupted. 'Oh,' she said, when she saw who it was. But there was not even the tiniest crumb of welcome in her voice. 'I'm busy.'

'Aren't we all?'

She looked down again, maintaining the pretence of being preoccupied with more important and interesting things. 'What is it you want?' She spoke with an irritation and sharpness that her colleagues and friends would have recognized as being absolutely normal, but buried somewhere within the layers of her voice was a frisson of anxiety that was by no means typical.

Her visitor looked at her with a smile. 'I need some more money.'

Reluctantly, Sarah Russell looked up again and considered her visitor. She had known this might come. She had talked about it with Geraldine, and they had discussed how best to handle any subsequent demands, but even so she found herself unwilling to concede. It wasn't so much the money. She could afford it. It was more the principle of it. She didn't like being pushed about. And besides, if she said yes, it would just happen again, wouldn't it? And again. But if she said no, what then? Was it a bluff? That was the big question.

'How much?'

Negotiate. That's what they had decided she should do. As long as the demands weren't too large, it was tolerable, because soon she would be able to say to hell with you. But right now, that would be too risky.

'Four hundred.'

Sarah Russell rubbed her nose as she considered this. It wasn't outrageous, but it was a hundred more than last time. Which meant that next time – for there would be a next time, she had no doubt – it might be five hundred or even more. 'I can let you have two hundred. But that's it. That's an end of it. No more, ever.'

'No it fucking isn't! I decide when it ends. Not you!'

Sarah said nothing. She didn't want to make things worse, but she was damned if she was going to lie down and roll over. She continued to stare at her unwelcome visitor, her face an emotionless mask (or so she hoped). She knew her position was weak, but she was damned if she was going to concede more ground than she had to.

'I'll call here tomorrow morning.' Her visitor had turned back towards the door, and had taken hold of the handle. 'Have it ready. Three hundred pounds.'

Sarah nodded briefly, and continued to watch until the door had slammed noisily shut. Three hundred pounds. No worse than last time. That was a pretty good result, she reckoned, as she returned to her spreadsheet.

Jack Smith heard nothing when the front door clicked shut, nothing when feet padded softly across the bare floorboards of the hall, and nothing when the kitchen door, which stood a few centimetres ajar, swung open. He didn't even hear the unoiled upper hinge, for its squeak was swamped by the cacophony which his hammer drill was generating. Only as he retracted the drill bit from the wall and eased his finger off the trigger did something – maybe a change in the light, maybe a sixth sense, maybe mere chance – cause him to swing round and see his unexpected visitor.

'Jesus! You made me jump.'

A laugh. 'I thought I might find you here.'

'You could have warned me, rather than sneaking up like that.'

A mocking gasp. 'Oh, it's less fun that way.'

'I'm not interested in your warped idea of fun. Just next time, don't bloody well creep up on me.'

'Don't worry, Jack, I won't.'

'Anyway, what is it you want?'

Jack's visitor stepped closer to him, but he had already turned away, to place his drill on the workbench. Which is why he was only infinitesimally aware of the flash of polished metal in his visitor's hand. His mouth opened slightly, revealing teeth yellowed by nicotine and neglect, and he gave a low grunt. And then slowly, almost in slow motion, he dropped gently on to his knees, as if overwhelmed by an all-consuming need to pray.

'You see,' the familiar figure was saying, by way of explanation, 'there won't be a next time.' This was, strictly speaking, accurate, but unnecessary. For Jack was already dead, and so completely incapable of hearing or comprehending anything. And presumably of praying too.

CHAPTER 5

Karen Pointer had rung Susan Holden and suggested that they have supper at her flat that evening. It was, in a sense, her turn, but it was the disconcerting conversation with Geraldine that had prompted her to make the phone call. So Karen arrived home – home being a brand new flat overlooking the canal in the north-western corner of Jericho – weighed down by two hessian bags bulging with the wherewithal to produce an easy but interesting supper, two bottles of rather expensive wine, and croissants and *pain au chocolat* for the next morning. She was not, she had realized, sure which of those Susan preferred. She unpacked, and made her way to the bedroom, where she began to discard her clothes in preparation for a shower. At which point, with the inevitability of Murphy's Law, the phone rang. She was tempted to ignore it, but only briefly, for the most likely caller, surely, was Susan.

And indeed it was Susan – or rather Detective Inspector Holden, as her tone of voice quickly made clear. There was no preamble. 'We've got another body, Karen.'

'Another one?' Pointer echoed.

'We think it's Jack Smith. Geraldine Payne, your dentist, found him, in a house he's doing up for her in Brook Street. Do you know where it is?'

'I was just about to prepare supper for you,' Karen replied, not entirely truthfully.

'Supper will have to wait,' came the answer. 'Go south over Folly

Bridge, first right into Western Road, and then first right into Brook Street.'

'I'll be there in 20 minutes.'

'I'll be waiting.'

'Love you,' Karen replied, but the detective inspector had already hung up.

'We think it's Jack Smith,' Holden had said on the phone. Pointer understood the reason for that note of uncertainty as soon as she walked into the kitchen area. Whereas the death of Maria Tull had been a remarkably tidy affair – two clean knife wounds and no huge emission of blood – the sight which greeted her was diametrically different. The body of Jack Smith, if Jack Smith it turned out to be, was lying twisted and sprawling on his back, and his blood was everywhere. It had spurted, splashed and run across the floor like some childish work of abstract art; in addition, a gigantic crimson rose appeared to have burst through his T-shirt, and two pools of blood had formed a macabre pair of oversized sunglasses on his face. For several seconds Pointer stood and looked, not because she needed that length of time to plan her strategy, but because she was trying to absorb the ferocity of what was in front of her and then cast it aside, so that she could get on and do her work. She knew she would never get used to brutal death. At least she hoped so, for if she did, what would that say about her own state of mind? She wanted always to feel, and yet her job demanded detachment. Perhaps, she told herself silently, this was not a job to do for life. But right now, this was what she did, so she put her black case down on a dilapidated work surface, next to a drill, and opened it with a click. 'I'll need a bit of time with this one,' she said firmly, 'and I could do with some extra lighting too.'

'Sergeant Fox will deal with that,' Holden said. 'I'm going to talk to Geraldine.'

Geraldine Payne was in the front room, sitting on the edge of a brown leather sofa, the only substantial piece of furniture in the room. An empty pine bookcase stood to the left of the chimney breast, and otherwise the only other pieces were two wooden kitchen chairs, on one of which Detective Constable Lawson was sitting. Lawson stood up, but Payne continued to stare fixedly at the Victorian fireplace, apparently unaware of Holden, who walked over to the empty chair, moved it nearer Payne, and sat down.

'Would you rather we talked later?'

There was no reply, though Payne's eyes did flicker briefly.

'Or shall we get it over with now?'

'Let's get it over with,' came the whisper.

'OK,' came the unhurried response. 'Tell me what happened.'

Again the eyes flickered, but this time with alarm. 'What do you mean? He was dead when I arrived!'

'I know,' Holden said firmly, mentally kicking herself as she did so. 'What I meant was tell me what you can about the circumstances. What time did you arrive? Was the door locked or unlocked? Did you notice anything unusual?'

In response, Payne emitted a sudden, hysterical laugh, and began to rock forwards and backwards on the sofa. 'You mean, apart from a dead body?'

'Just take your time.'

For maybe thirty or forty seconds, Geraldine Payne did just that, stumbling erratically from laughter to sobbing to silence, but when finally she did speak, it all came rolling out in the proverbial torrent, words crashing and bursting until there was no energy left. 'I left the surgery at five-thirty. I wanted to call in here and see how he was getting on. Well, I don't trust him any more, not since he fucked that Italian whore and gave her my painting. But I was damned if he was going to leave me in the lurch. He'd agreed to re-plumb the house, and he was damn well going to, and when he was finished I was going to withhold half his fee to teach the bastard a lesson. I didn't tell him, of course, but that was what I was going to do. It would have served him right. But first I popped across the road to the Playhouse and got a couple of tickets for the Chekhov, and then I walked here. It's not too far. Twenty minutes maybe, and I needed the exercise after a day bent over patients. When I arrived, the lights were on and the front door was unlocked. Well, do workmen ever lock front doors? I thought he must still be working, but when I got in the hallway and called him there was no reply. So I went through to the kitchen because I could see the lights were on through there.' She stopped and gulped, as she recalled the moment. 'And he was there, on the floor, and there was all this blood. Christ!' She shuddered.

Holden waited for a few seconds, allowing her time to recover, and then gently probed again. 'What did you do next?'

'What do you think I did?' There was sharpness in her voice, a sharpness which reminded Holden of their previous encounter, in the police station. 'I rang 999!'

'Did you touch the body? Check it for a pulse maybe?'

Geraldine Payne looked across as her questioner, with a look which made it clear that she thought the woman must be out of her head. 'It was patently obvious he was dead. I didn't need to check for a bloody pulse.'

'Quite,' Holden agreed. There was nothing more she was going to gain by prolonging the interview. 'Do you know his wife?' she said as she stood up.

'His wife?' There was a pause, then a short incredulous laugh. 'Why? Do you think she did it?'

Holden didn't answer the question at the time, but later, as Lawson drove her across town to Jack Smith's house, to break the news to his wife, she tossed the question around in her head. Her first assumption was that his death must be connected to the missing painting, but on the other hand Maria and Jack had had an affair, even if it had been the one-off fling which Jack Smith had claimed. But suppose his wife had found out, then that sure as hell gave her a motive to have killed them both. It would be interesting to see how she reacted to the news.

Dinah Smith was a big woman. When she opened the front door, her body filled its frame, blocking much of the light from within so that Holden and Lawson both stood in her shadow, briefly non-plussed. Everything about her was big, from her broad shoulders and her voluminous breasts to her bulbous hands and tree-trunk legs. She was a woman whom you could imagine mud wrestling or playing in the scrum in a woman's rugby team in her spare time, while in working life she was built for the role of prison warder, one who could control the most troublesome of female prisoners – or male ones too, come to think of it – with a single terrorizing glance. Which was why it seemed so incongruous to Holden that she took the news of her husband's death so badly. It wasn't that Holden expected her to react with indifference, but the wailing she emitted when she was told that her husband had been murdered was of extraordinary intensity. Holden felt herself almost physically engulfed by the blizzard of her grief. There was nothing to do except wait for the storm to pass. Eventually it did, but when Lawson offered Dinah Smith a handkerchief, she waved it away.

'Who on earth would have wanted to kill him?' she said, in an incredulous tone of voice. 'Do you think it was a thief?'

Holden's first thought was that this was a curious thing to say. She had told Dinah that her husband had been stabbed with a knife, but she had deliberately given no more detail. So why didn't Dinah ask more about how he died? That's what she would have expected someone in her position to ask, normally. Except, she told herself, this wasn't a normal situation. Being told that your husband has been murdered is in no sense normal. Holden knew that really, but even so she logged the woman's response away in her head for future consideration, and then answered her question. 'There's no sign of anything having been stolen. And to be honest, there's not much in the house worth stealing. A few pieces of furniture, but nothing in the way of ornaments or silver or electronic devices.'

'But who would have wanted to kill him?' She repeated the question in a voice that implied absolute incomprehension. 'Who?'

Holden cleared her throat. She ought to leave this till the next day, till the woman had had a chance to get over her shock, assuming it was shock, but this was a second death and there were no prizes to be won by being nice, or skipping awkward questions. 'We understand your husband had an affair with Maria Tull.'

Dinah looked at her, her mouth half-open in astonishment. Then, as if in slow motion, it began to close until the upper and lower lips met, compressing against each other until they had twisted into a snarl. At the same time, the wide-open eyes narrowed into the darkest of slits. In a matter of seconds, she was transformed.

'You think it was me.' The words hissed out of her mouth, and she stabbed a finger at Holden. 'You bloody cow! You think I killed my own husband. What sort of woman are you?' She was shouting now, and on her feet, and towering over Holden.

'I don't think anything.' Holden tried to speak in a calm, reassuring voice, but she wasn't at all sure she was managing it. 'I can assure you of that. I know this is difficult for you—'

'You know shit!' she snapped, cutting across Holden. 'You know nothing about me and Jack, nothing about our relationship.'

'I want to catch his killer,' Holden said firmly, fighting to regain control. 'That's my job. I want to catch his killer and Maria Tull's killer, and I need your help. But we can come back tomorrow—'

Again Dinah Smith cut across Holden's words, though this time with a laugh. 'When I feel better, you mean?'

'Do you have a relation or friend you'd like us to call?'

Dinah Smith didn't reply. Instead, she turned away from Holden, and walked over to a table in the corner of the room, from which she picked up a photo frame. For several seconds she stood looking at it, before placing it back down. Then she turned back round and looked across at Lawson. 'Would you mind making me a cup of tea, dear? Two sugars.' Lawson glanced briefly at Holden for guidance, and then nodded at her questioner. 'Of course.'

Dinah Smith waited for Lawson to leave the room, and then she returned to her chair, sat down, and apologized. 'Sorry. It's just been one hell of a shock.' She shrugged. 'I should know. I've seen enough of it in hospital.'

'I'm the one who should be saying sorry,' Holden said, relieved that the crisis had blown over.

But Dinah Smith's mind wasn't interested in politenesses and apologies. 'I wouldn't have called it an affair,' she said simply.

'No,' Holden responded, and waited.

'They only did it once. That's what Jack told me. I believed him then, and I believe him now. He was a good man, Jack. A bit weak. Easily led. And she led him on, the silly bitch. Because she wanted that painting he found.'

'What did he tell you about the painting?'

'Nothing. He just said it was old and dirty and quite small, so he was a bit surprised when he realized Maria thought it was valuable.'

'Did he say what it looked like?'

'No.'

'And what about Maria? What did he say about her death?'

'He was shaken up by it. I think he felt a bit scared. He slept with her once and now she was dead, and was he going to be next?'

'He said that, did he?'

'In so many words. And he was right to be scared, wasn't he?'

'Yes,' Holden replied, because there was no other reply to make. They relapsed into silence. Sometimes words just got in the way. From outside came the sound of an ambulance siren. Holden listened as it sped down the hill away from the hospital, on its way to what? Injury, illness, death – they were all around.

'Here's a mug of tea, milk and two sugars.' Lawson had appeared at the door, and now walked across to Dinah Smith.

She took it, and cradled it in her two hands.

'Do you need to ask me anything else, because I'd like to ring my sister.'

Holden held up her hand. 'We'll go if you want us to, but it would very helpful if – for the record, just for the record – you could just tell us where you were today.'

'That's easy,' she said. 'I was working last night, so I had breakfast with Jack when I got in, and then I had a shower and went to bed. I must have woken about four o'clock, and then I went out to the little supermarket at the bottom of the hill, and I came back, and I've been in ever since.'

'Thank you.' Holden stood up. She was ready to go. It wasn't exactly a tight alibi. In fact, it was no alibi at all. But that didn't make Dinah Smith the killer. But it didn't rule her out either.

Dinah Smith raised her mug, and sipped noisily at the tea. Then she looked up at Holden. 'Just make sure you catch the bastard,' she said.

'Ah, good morning, Susan. And good morning, Jan.' Dr Karen Pointer beamed at her two visitors.

Detective Constable Lawson replied brightly, but Holden merely nodded. The fact was that she wasn't interested in exchanging politenesses. Given that their plans to spend the evening and night together had gone so spectacularly up the spout, what she would really have liked to do is hug the woman, to hold her tight and smell her skin, but Karen Pointer seemed to be oblivious of her, and interested only in the corpse over which she now pored, like a philatelist over a stamp album.

'Well, it looks like the same murder weapon. The initial stab wound is not quite in the same place as it was on Maria's body, but the knife was either the same one or an identical one. However, he didn't die instantaneously. He may have lost consciousness. There's no sign of a struggle, but the blood from the neck wounds indicates he was still alive when those were inflicted. Then there followed the facial disfigurement. A single stab to each eye. The coup de grâce. Though that appears to have taken place after the heart had ceased to pump.'

'Time of death?' Holden was brusque, but if Pointer noticed she gave no sign of it.

'It's hard to be precise. The house wasn't heated, and so it was pretty cold. I'd estimate between maybe twelve noon and two o'clock.'

'Can't you be more precise?'

Dr Pointer looked up, and this time there was irritation in her voice. 'No, I can't.'

'Oh!' came the graceless reply.

Lawson, conscious of the tension between the two women,

forced herself to focus on the body, and to imagine, without emotion, what it must have been like. Lying on the slab, stripped of clothes, and bereft of dignity, it presented a very different picture from the image imprinted in her head, of the twisted blood-spattered, brutalized person she had seen on that kitchen floor. What sort of person could do that?

'At least,' Pointer said suddenly, 'it would be hard to tie the time down with absolute certainty. But maybe nearer two o'clock than one.'

'Right,' Holden grunted. Then, almost as an afterthought: 'Thank you.'

'That's unofficial, you understand.'

'Of course.'

Again there was silence, and into this Lawson now gently tossed the question which had been growing in her mind. 'Dr Pointer,' she said, before remembering the pathologist's preference for first names. 'Karen, there was a lot of blood. Do you think the killer could have avoided getting it on his – or her – clothes?'

'It's hard to be certain. The knife cut the carotid artery in the neck, so that might have sprayed, but the heart was already in crisis by then, so there would have been less pressure, and. . . .' She drifted to a stop.

'Thank you, Karen,' Holden broke in, apparently deciding that they had got all they could from the visit. 'You've been very helpful. If you could email your full report over when it's done, I would be most grateful.'

'Not at all,' came the reply. Formal politeness was suddenly back in vogue in the pathology lab. 'Oh, I nearly forgot. His possessions are over there.' Pointer pointed to a large grey high-sided tray sitting on one of the work benches. Lawson, looking at it, felt a sudden surge of queasiness. The tray was just like the ones in airport security, the ones into which you have to place everything you are carrying and half of what you're wearing. She had only flown abroad twice in her life, which made her something of an oddball amongst her friends. The first had been with friends to

Ibiza, and the second had been less than a year ago. It had started with a five-hour delay at Gatwick. This had been followed, on night number two, by her developing a horrendous bout of gastroenteritis. Three days later, when she could finally risk venturing out on to the beach, she overdid it, fell asleep on her towel, and got horribly sunburnt. And alongside and during all of this, her relationship with her boyfriend Tom had been deteriorating via angry outbursts (hers) and surly exits (his) until there was no part of it that was not in ruins. She hated flying.

Holden, oblivious to her constable's interior musing, had walked over to the tray and cast a brief eye over it, before turning away. 'That's your job, Lawson. Get it into the car, and while you're waiting for me, check out the mobile for recent calls, and all his contacts. Karen and I have one or two things to discuss.'

Lawson got the message, and hurried to collect Jack Smith's personal possessions and get out of the room. She was no mug, and had already wondered about her boss and Dr Pointer. Not that she had voiced her suspicions to anyone. But she was human enough – and nosy enough – to wonder what things Holden still had to discuss with the pathologist, and in private. Her guess was that it wasn't police procedures or new developments in post-mortem techniques.

However, by the time Holden had joined her in the car several minutes later, her idle speculation on her boss's private life had long since gone out the window. For all her attention had been hijacked by what she had seen on Jack Smith's mobile.

'We've got another one, Guv!'

Holden wrenched her mind away from the conversation she had just had with Karen Pointer. 'What was that?'

'There's a photo on this mobile too, Guv!'

'What? Of a naked Jack Smith?'

'No, Guv. It's a painting. You know, like an oil painting.'

Holden's interest shot up several points. 'Well, let me have a look then!'

It is not easy to appreciate the quality, or even the subject matter, of a painting on a screen approximately three centimetres square. Holden had to squint, and then to move the mobile's face around before she could get a decent grasp of what it was. Lawson's estimate that it was an oil painting seemed to be a good one. There were two figures. In the centre was a woman, lying back against a rock. She appeared, as far as Holden could see, to be in distress. Although clothed, her diaphanous dress was dishevelled, and her left breast uncovered. To the viewer's right, a male figure could be seen, moving away from the woman, but casting a glance behind him, though whether the expression on his face was mischievous or triumphant, evil or embarrassed, Holden could not divine.

'What do you think, Guv? Do you think it's the picture that he found?'

'No,' Holden said flatly. 'That one had two women and a prone man, according to Jack.'

'Maybe he was lying.' The words shot out of Lawson's mouth. Quite why she uttered them, she wasn't sure. It wasn't as if she had mulled the idea over for even a second.

'Why on earth should he be lying about the subject of the painting?'

Lawson pursed her lips, and said nothing. She felt foolish for not having remembered Jack Smith's description of the painting. She hadn't been there – Fox had been with Holden – but she had seen the notes of the meeting, and she really should have remembered.

'Well, come on, Lawson.' Holden was not going to let her off. 'Why? Give me a possible reason why Jack Smith might have lied. You're on my team, so I want you thinking, not playing the village idiot. Why might he have lied?'

'To mislead us, Guv.' Lawson's idea was only half-formed, and maybe only half-baked, but if Holden wanted ideas, she'd ruddy well give her one.

'Any chance of you fleshing that idea out, Detective Constable?'

'Yes, Guv,' she replied sharply. 'To make sure that we wouldn't recognize the painting if we came across it.'

'Hmm!' Holden leant back and shut her eyes briefly as she

considered the idea.

Lawson, pleased that her suggestion hadn't been dismissed out of hand, decided to follow up. 'In fact, that seems to me to be the obvious solution.'

Holden's eye opened – an owl wakened from its reverie, or more likely a hawk. 'Obvious!' she repeated with sarcastic emphasis. 'Well, well, well, Constable. Aren't you the clever clogs! The only problem is I don't see Jack Smith as being the smartest cookie in the jar. When Fox and I interviewed him, if he was lying, he was very good at it.'

'Maybe it wasn't his idea,' Lawson riposted. She was flying by the seat of her pants now, but there was no way she was going to bail out. 'Maybe it was the idea of his killer.'

Holden was sitting forward now, and her eyes were looking at Lawson with an intensity that made the constable uneasy. Eventually, she smiled. 'You'll make a good detective, Jan. A very good detective.'

Lawson, uncertain of her ground, smiled nervously back. 'Thank you, Guv.'

'But just for the sake of argument, Lawson, let's suppose Jack wasn't lying. Let's suppose there are two different paintings. What would you make of that?'

Lawson frowned. She was so set on her own idea that she found it hard to switch her thinking.

'Well?' The prompting was gentle, but insistent.

'Two different paintings?' Lawson spoke slowly, trying to buy some time while she thought of an answer. 'To be honest, I would have to say if they are two different paintings, then' – she struggled for the words – 'then it's one heck of a coincidence.'

'Is it?' came the reply. 'Is it really?'

Lawson shivered as a childhood memory resurfaced. It was one of those defining moments of growing up, which mark the progress from innocence to knowledge. She had been watching her cat, Flossie, playing with a mouse in the garden. She was lying on the lawn, and Flossie was toying with the mouse as she sometimes toyed with a ball of wool. Occasionally she would touch it, allowing it to move this way or that, but never once taking its eyes off its helpless playmate. Jan remembered feeling intensely uneasy. The cat was playing, but this was no toy she was playing with, this was a live, harmless little mouse. She did not fully understand what she was seeing, and yet she felt anxious almost to the point of fear. She called Flossie by name, but the cat ignored her. The mouse ran a little way to the left, and Flossie pranced effortlessly into its path, so it stopped, mesmerized. It was a bright sunny day, but at that moment a cloud drifted over, and a shadow passed across that familiar patch of grass, and next door's Jack Russell began to bark, and – all in an instant – Flossie the cat had pounced and snapped the mouse's neck with a single bite.

'What about Dominic Russell?' Holden said, her face a picture of innocence. 'He's got lots of oil paintings.'

'You think he did it?'

'Hey! That's a mighty big leap. But there's a painting or paintings at the middle of this business. And Maria had, at the very least, a business relationship with him. So I'd say Dominic Russell seems an obvious place to start looking.'

Two unmarked cars pulled up outside D.R. Antiquities just after 2.00 p.m. that afternoon. Dominic Russell, who was preoccupied with labelling a couple of garden statuettes he had just acquired, looked up, his hopes briefly raised that this might herald a serious bit of business. God knows, he needed it. But when the passenger door of the leading car opened and DI Holden got out, he knew it was not to be.

'You're not, by any chance, here to buy a retirement gift for the Chief Superintendent, because if you are I am sure I can do a very good deal.' He grinned as he said it. Mr Bonhomie himself.

'This is a search warrant.' Holden held up a piece of paper in front of his face. 'My colleagues and I would appreciate it if we could have your cooperation.'

'A search warrant?' Dominic Russell spoke with apparently

genuine surprise. 'What on earth are you looking for?'

'I am not required to answer that question, Mr Russell,' Holden replied. 'But we would like to see every single painting you have on the premises.'

'Well, you'd better be bloody careful! If you damage them—'

'We won't damage them,' Holden assured him.

The big policeman, whom Dominic remembered from their previous visit though he couldn't for the life of him recall his name, stepped forward in his role of polite enforcer. 'All the more reason to cooperate with us, sir.'

For an hour they searched, Holden and Fox in one team, watched by Dominic, and Lawson and Wilson in the other, escorted by Sarah Russell, who had again been working in the office. It didn't take long to see that the painting they sought was not on display, but Holden had hardly expected that it would. One of the two smaller buildings turned out to be an area for storage and repair, but careful examination of it proved fruitless. The third building stored mostly furniture, and despite Lawson and Wilson assiduously opening every door and drawer, no paintings were found.

'So that's that, is it?' Dominic said. 'Such as shame we couldn't help you find whatever it is you are looking for.'

The mocking tone of his voice did nothing to improve Holden's mood. She hadn't liked him on first acquaintance, and she liked him even less now, the patronizing self-satisfied git. But she wasn't ready to give up yet. They were back in the office, and she looked around again, scanning the room for inspiration. 'You have catalogues of your paintings, do you?'

'Nothing current.'

'When did you last produce one?'

'Well,' he said warily. 'I suppose that would have been a couple of months ago.'

'Can I see a copy, please.'

'I suppose so.'

'And maybe we could have four coffees, too?'

'We're not a branch of Starbucks, you know.' The arrogance was back in his voice, an arrogance which suggested he felt less threatened now. Maybe, for him, the danger had passed. Publicly available catalogues held no incriminating secrets.

'Would you rather my sergeant did it? I wouldn't. Because number one he's very clumsy, and number two he makes bloody lousy coffee.'

Dominic turned towards his wife who had taken up her guard dog position behind the desk. 'Sarah, would you mind?'

'Actually, I'd like to talk to her. Why don't you make it yourself? Constable Wilson will come and advise you on our milk and sugar requirements.'

For a moment it looked as though he was going to object. A grunt of disgust emitted from his mouth, and Holden prepared to resist, but his bluster was just that, and he turned and left the room, trailed by Wilson.

Sarah Russell meanwhile had stood up, and had removed a slim publication from the shelves behind her. 'Here you are!' She slapped the catalogue down on the desk.

Holden picked it up and passed it to Lawson. She had already given up on it as being of use, but you never knew. In the meantime, she was more interested in Sarah.

'You must be a very busy woman, Mrs Russell. We come here, and you're here. Sergeant Fox goes to Cornforth and you're there. We return here, and lo and behold here you are again.'

'Dominic is short-handed at the moment.'

'Yes, I remember you saying that last time we were here. A French-Canadian, wasn't it? Minette?'

'You've a good memory.'

'Her parents were visiting, weren't they?'

'That's right.'

'I'd like to talk to her.'

'Why?' Was there was a note of anxiety in her reply?

'That's my business.' Holden was giving nothing away, but something told her Minette was a sensitive spot. 'Can you give me her address and phone number.'

Sarah did something with her mouth that was half-way between a smile and a scowl. 'I could. But it may not be much use to you.'

'Why?'

'Because at this very moment she's on a flight back to Quebec.'

This time it was Holden's turn to be disconcerted. 'I thought you said her parents were just visiting.'

Sarah Russell smiled her broadest, most self-satisfied smile. 'I think seeing her parents made her homesick. Suddenly she realized what she was missing in Quebec – families, friends, the French language – so she insisted on going home with them. Rather touching, don't you think?'

Holden didn't say what she thought. Instead she turned to Lawson. 'Have you found anything of interest, Lawson.' It was a futile question. Lawson would certainly have interrupted if she'd found the painting. Holden knew it, and she knew too that she was running out of options. She could surely track down Minette's phone number in Quebec and ask her over the phone if she had seen the painting, but it was a long shot. Can the girl really have got homesick just because her parents had visited?

'Can I make a suggestion, Guv?'

Holden turned to Fox, absurdly pleased at his intervention. God only knew what he was going to suggest, but anything was better than nothing.

'Have you ever seen the Mona Lisa, Guv?'

Holden shook her head.

'Me neither. But my sister went last year. And you know what most surprised her?' Fox paused, though not because he expected an answer. He wasn't above wanting a bit of attention. 'It was so bloody small. She'd always thought it was this huge great canvas, and in reality it was tiny. So what I'm saying is, maybe this painting we're looking for isn't so big.'

Fox was pleased with himself, and even more pleased with his boss's reaction. She was nodding like one of those dogs that people put on the back of their cars. Like that Churchill dog. Almost dementedly. 'Right!' she said.

'So, my point is that it could be almost anywhere in this office. In Mrs Russell's desk drawers, for example, or up on those book shelves, or maybe tucked behind the catalogues, or. . . .' and then he stopped talking, for his eyes had alighted on some flat brown paper packages on the desk to Sarah Russell's right. He moved over and stretched out an arm.

'They're waiting to be picked up,' Sarah Russell said calmly, her hand moving protectively on top of the pile, as if daring Fox to touch them. 'In fact, if DHL don't arrive very soon, I'll have to ring them.'

'We'll have to open them first, madam,' Fox said bluntly.

She turned in appeal to Fox's superior, but Holden merely smiled. 'Lawson,' she said cheerily, 'perhaps you can help Sergeant Fox.'

Eventually, they found the painting, though not in the pile of packages that were due for collection. It was located by Fox on the topmost of the shelves, inside a plastic supermarket bag and wrapped in hessian. He reached it down just as Dominic Russell and DC Wilson walked through the door bearing coffees.

'What are you doing?' Dominic asked rather pointlessly. Given that four detectives had arrived with a search warrant, the answer was obvious. No one made any attempt to respond, however, for at that moment all their eyes and attention were on the painting that Fox had just unwrapped on the desk. 'Bingo!' he said, when he saw it.

'Is that what you were looking for?' Dominic tried again to elicit information, but again there was no answer.

'I presume this belongs to you, sir, does it?' Holden asked, ignoring his question, but asking her own.

'Well, sort of.'

'I'd like you to explain what you mean by that, Mr Russell. But I'd like you to do that down at the station in a more formal setting.'

'Is that really necessary?' This time the question came from Sarah Russell, riding belligerently to her husband's aid. 'He has a business to run. We've been very cooperative so far, and I really cannot see why—'

But Holden's patience was at an end. 'Enough!' She spat the word out like the exasperated teacher of a class of 11-year-olds, suddenly desperate for silence. 'Mrs Russell, your husband has three minutes to get himself ready, and then he will be leaving with us in order to help us with our enquiries. In the meantime, we will drink the coffee he has so kindly provided.'

'And while you are drinking our coffee,' Sarah riposted, 'I will ring his solicitor.'

'Perhaps you can explain to my client and to myself the precise reason why you have called him in for questioning.' James Turley, solicitor at law, spoke with a clipped diction that spoke volumes of his background. Public school certainly, Oxbridge probably. In fact his tie would have told Holden that he had attended Queen's College, Oxford, had she been interested in such collegiate details. But Holden had no interest in his tie, or his expensive suit, or his ostentatious gold cufflinks or even his rather poncy manner. They served only to irritate her.

'Certainly,' she smiled. 'Sergeant,' she prompted, briefly turning to DS Fox, sitting to her right at the table. Fox responded by removing the painting from its package and placing it on the table in front of Turley and Russell.

'We found this on the premises of D.R. Antiquities, the business run and owned by your client. When asked if it belonged to him, he replied: "Well, sort of." A photograph of this painting was found on the mobile phone belonging to Jack Smith, a plumber who was found dead yesterday in a house in South Oxford. He had been murdered.' She paused, for at this moment she was more interested in watching the face of Dominic Russell than engaging in verbal fisticuffs with Turley.

To be fair, as Fox later said, either Russell was genuinely shocked by this news or he was a bloody good actor. Certainly, his habitually flushed face seemed to pale, and his mouth gaped open in an impressively convincing display of surprise. His first verbal reaction was to address his solicitor: 'This is ridiculous, James.

Quite ridiculous!'

'So if you don't mind, Mr Turley,' Holden said, determined to keep the momentum going, 'I'd like to ask your client some questions. And then we can rule him out of our investigations, unless, of course, his answers lead us to rule him in.'

Turley shrugged at Russell, and then turned back to Holden. 'I am sure my client is happy to assist the police in any way he can.'

'In that case, Mr Russell, can you explain what you meant when you said you sort of owned the painting?'

'Well.' The fingers of his hands, which had been face down on the table, began to tap a rhythm on the table. It was the beat of something that Holden vaguely recognized, but couldn't place. Was that what he did, she wondered, when under pressure or playing for time or maybe telling a lie? Or all three together. 'I'm the temporary owner, if you like. The intermediary.'

'You mean, like a fence?'

Russell flushed back to his more normal colour. 'What are you implying?'

'There's no need to be alarmed,' Holden said with a smile. 'I'm implying nothing. I'm just trying to understand what "sort of" ownership means. Because of the job I do, I'm familiar with how a fence operates, and so I was merely seeking to clarify your terminology.'

'The hell you were, Inspector,' Turley broke in. 'One minute you say you want his help in connection with a murder enquiry, and the next you're implying he receives stolen goods without any evidence to support such a preposterous idea.'

'In that case, I apologize,' Holden said quickly, conscious she had pushed her luck. 'I didn't mean to, but that does still leave us with my original question unanswered. So perhaps I can rephrase it. Who owned the painting before it came into Mr Russell's possession? And can I see the paperwork?'

Russell swallowed, looked to Turley for support, but again got a shrug back. Russell looked back at Holden and knew that one way or another he had to say something. The truth or a lie. Whichever way he played it, there were risks. Lies had a nasty way of coming back and catching you out. And if Holden was half as smart as she talked, she would spot the least inconsistency in any story. It was a gamble. Heads I lose, tails they do. Hopefully.

'I'm in no rush,' Holden said cheerfully. 'Take your time.'

'Maria bought it. She saw it in Venice when she was over there a week or two ago. And she brought it home.'

'Who did she buy it from?'

'How should I know? She had her own contacts over there. She wasn't going to share them with me, was she now? She was born in Venice. You probably know that. I'm sure you've checked her out. Born Maria Scarpa. Came to Oxford to improve her English when she was nineteen, but before you could say "Grazie" she had got her hooks into Dr Alan Tull, grieving widower and newly qualified GP. Rather a good catch from her point of view.'

'So you were selling it for her?' Holden could spot distraction techniques from a distance.

'Yes. I have more contacts than her over here. And a lot more in the States. So if I find a buyer for her, I get a cut.'

'So why was it hidden on the top shelf?'

'It wasn't hidden. It just wasn't on display.'

'I'm not sure I understand the difference. But that's beside the point. Just tell me why it wasn't on display.'

'It's quite simple. It was there because I had a buyer lined up. He's due over here in a week's time. I sent him a photo by email, but he likes to see what he's buying before he commits his money. So I decided to give him first bite of the cherry. So I opted not to put it on display.'

'He pays in cash, does he? So the taxman doesn't have to know?'

'My client will not be answering that question,' James Turley jumped in. 'The painting has not been sold, so he cannot possibly be found guilty of anything to do with its possible future sale.'

But Holden had no intention of going any further down that route. 'So really, Mr Russell, as I understand it, the painting doesn't actually belong to you. It belongs to Maria Tull, and so now by default to her estate? So when we have finished with it as evidence, I can hand it over to Dr Alan Tull. I presume that is OK by you.'

'As you wish.' He spoke gracelessly, dismissively. 'Is that all then?'

'Not quite. You see, I have a bit of a problem here. I have two murdered people. The first victim bought this painting, and the second one happened to have a photograph of the painting on his mobile. Furthermore, this painting is found on your premises waiting to be purchased by some big-money private collector from the USA.'

'What are you saying? That I'd kill two people for the sake of one painting?'

'I didn't say that.'

'Christ, if it was a Canaletto or a Rembrandt, then maybe it would be worth killing for, but for crying out loud this is just a picture that Maria picked up for next to nothing and that I can help her turn a tidy profit on. End of story.'

'I suppose it all depends what you term a tidy profit. Because with Maria dead, I guess you weren't going to bring her husband in on the action.'

'Just a minute!' James Turley stood up, determined to assert his authority. 'There is no firm evidence of any wrongdoing by my client. He has answered your questions, so now I must insist that he be allowed to leave. Unless, of course, you are going to charge him.'

Holden remained seated. 'He is free to leave. But as I said, we will be retaining the painting as possible evidence. And we will also be having it valued by an independent expert.'

CHAPTER 6

'Welcome home, darling!' There was a time when these three simple words would have presaged for Dominic Russell a truly welcoming evening. A gin and tonic as he stretched out on the sofa in front of the TV; a candle-lit supper of rare steak washed down with a fine burgundy, followed by sticky toffee pudding and freshly ground coffee; then a glass of port, a shower *a deux*, and sex. But that time was long since gone, and on this occasion, the only things these words, uttered with icy coldness by his wife, promised was conflict.

She had heard him enter. How could she have not, when the front door slammed shut with such force? And she had heard him pad uncertainly down the corridor in a manner that immediately told her trained ear that he was somewhat the worse for alcohol. His first words confirmed it as he poked his head round the lounge doorway.

'James and I had a couple of dwinks together.'

'More than a couple by the sound of it.'

'I knew you wouldn't mind.'

'You getting drunk is the least of my problems.'

'It's just that the police were a bit of a botherkins, so James and I decided we needed to talk tactics.' He belched, and then giggled. 'Whoops!'

'Tell me about the painting.'

'What painting?' He scratched his head, and giggled again.

'The one the police took.'

'Oh, that painting! It's a nice little painting, don't you think. Technically, not from the very top drawer, but very pleasant.'

'I'm not interested in the painting's aesthetic qualities, you idiot. Is it stolen?'

'No, of course not.'

'So where did you get it?'

He looked down, as if embarrassed, though whether a man can be embarrassed while drunk is a moot point. What is certain, however, is that a drunk can very easily put his foot in it, especially with an already angry spouse.

'Maria brought it back from Venice.'

'Maria!' Sarah's screech lanced inside Dominic's skull, bouncing around like a ping-pong ball on speed.

'It was only business,' he said quickly, but too late. 'Absolutely only business.'

'Then why didn't you tell me. Did she buy it on the last Cornforth trip?'

'Yes.' He was sitting down now, his right hand on his forehead, playing the sympathy card. 'Do we have any paracetamol?'

'Behind my back. You and her behind my back, laughing at me. You bastard.'

'It was just business. I swear.'

'So why keep it a secret from your wife?'

He held up his hand as if this might somehow deflect her ire. 'I didn't tell you because it's safer that way. If you knew, then you would be involved. You've got to believe me.'

'So was the painting stolen?'

'No. I told you. Maria bought it in Venice. The guy didn't know what he'd got. No doubt Maria worked her usual charm, and he ended up selling it to her for virtually nothing. She brought it to me, and I made a couple of phone calls, and Bob's your uncle, we had a deal.'

'So if Maria bought it legitimately, how come the police were looking for it?'

He didn't answer immediately. Keeping up with the barrage of questions was proving difficult in his current state. 'The police found a photograph of it on Jack Smith's mobile.'

'You what? How on earth did it get there?'

'Maybe Maria showed it to him, and he photographed it. I don't know. Look, I need some water and paracetamol. Please.'

Sarah considered the request, and then walked off to the kitchen, returning shortly afterwards with a large glass of water and two white pills. He tossed the pills down the back of his throat, and drank deeply. Sarah took the nearly empty glass, placed it carefully on the oak coffee table, and turned back to her husband.

'Did you kill Maria and Jack?'

Dominic Russell looked up at his wife, incomprehension plastered across his flushed, sweaty face. 'You what?'

'Did you kill them?' she repeated, her voice sharper, louder, almost visceral in its intensity. Even through his drunkenness, Dominic could sense the danger signs.

'Of course I bloody didn't. Why would I have done? It was just a business deal, plain and simple. Why should I kill them?'

'Can't you think of a reason? Well, let me see if I can help.' Every word she spoke was infected with sarcasm and disgust, and even her sot of a husband could feel it. 'Because with both of them dead, you've got that nice little painting all to your nasty little self. And maybe others that I know nothing about. So then you could go off and make a sale without your dear little wife knowing, and then you could spend it all on yourself. How about that for a motive?'

He licked his lips. His head was still throbbing, but the pain was displaced by a sudden sense of panic. 'I didn't kill them, I swear,' he insisted.

Sarah looked at her husband again, trying to see into his head. Was he capable of murder, she wondered. She doubted it. When push came to shove, he was one of the shiftiest of shits, but a killer? That was harder to believe. Mind you, she had a theory that in the right circumstances anyone could commit murder. Absolutely anyone. And that would, by definition, include him.

'So, husband, what was your cut for finding a buyer for Maria's painting?'

He looked at her, puzzled. 'What does that matter? She's dead. She never paid me a penny. And the police have got the picture.'

'I'm interested to know how much you charged her?'

Again he looked at her, though this time his brain was trying hard to engage. What was his wife's angle? 'Ten per cent,' he said.

'Ten per cent! Is that all?'

'It only took two phone calls.'

Sarah Russell picked up the glass she had earlier placed on the coffee table, and surveyed it, as if inspecting it for faults. Then, in a single whiplash of her arm she hurled it across the room so it crashed against the marble of the fireplace, exploding spectacularly into fragments.

Dominic almost jumped in his chair. He struggled to get up, but she had advanced close to him and her left hand pushed him back down.

'Were you sleeping with her? Was that part of your business deal? Was that why you only charged her ten fucking per cent?'

Dominic Russell's red face had grown pale again. His head was throbbing like hell, his wife wouldn't go away, and all he wanted was to go to sleep. 'No!' he shouted. 'You know that was ages ago. That's ancient history, you know it is.'

'Too old for you, is she?' Her face was now close up to his, so he could feel her breath as she spat her words at him. 'You like them young, and pretty and foolish, don't you, Dominic. We're no use to you when we have to start dying our hair to hide the grey ones, and booking ourselves in for botox treatment. When the centre of gravity starts to slip south, you start to look elsewhere.' She fell silent then, still looming over him, but there was a coldness in her eyes as she assessed him and found him wanting. 'Tell me, Dominic, did you manage to get your grubby little hands inside Minette's knickers?'

'No,' he said very quickly, and truthfully. Though it wasn't for the want of trying.

'But you would have done, wouldn't you. I could see it in your eyes. Which is why I told her we could no longer afford to pay her.'

'You told her what?'

'Well, it's not entirely a lie. Besides, would you rather I'd told her all about you?'

Dominic shook his head, but that only made his head hurt more and he groaned feebly. 'I thought she was homesick.'

'Actually, she said she'd be prepared to take a pay cut. The last place she wanted to go was home. But that's her problem. I've got plenty of my own.'

Dominic was beyond protesting. The pain in his head had got worse, not better. The paracetamols had been absolutely useless. 'I need to go to bed,' he moaned.

'Just as long as it isn't mine, you can do what the hell you like,' came the reply.

At much the same time as this rather nasty scene was being enacted in the Russells' home in North Oxford, a rather different domestic get-together was taking place in Chilswell Road, South Oxford, where Susan Holden was giving supper to her mother, Mrs Jane Holden, and Dr Karen Pointer.

It was not Susan Holden's normal practice to offer her mother supper during the week. In fact, because of Susan's work, it was so rare as to be abnormal. Which is why Jane Holden was so surprised to get a phone call at 12.30 that lunchtime asking her if she would like to come to supper that evening.

'Tonight?' she had said, not sure that she had heard right.

'Yes, if you can make it. I've got someone else coming.'

'Who?' she had said eagerly.

'You'll have to come to find out.'

That, of course, had been the clincher. Whatever curiosity does to cats, it certainly gets its hooks deep into humans too, and Jane Holden was human enough to be fascinated with every facet of her only daughter's private life.

She was, if truth be told, disappointed to discover that the mystery guest was female. She had hoped that the third person would be a man. Indeed, by the time she had knocked on the door of her daughter's Victorian house, she had convinced herself that he or she was unequivocally a he. So when she found Karen Pointer already ensconced in the kitchen dining room, drinking a glass of white wine, her excitement took a brief nosedive. She hoped it didn't show. She accepted a small glass of the same wine, and soon recovered when she discovered that Karen was a pathologist, and moreover a pathologist prepared to share the more gruesome details of her work.

Later, after supper and teas all round – 'much too late for coffee for me' Mrs Holden had said, and the two younger women had tactfully followed suit – the three of them walked round to Grandpont Grange.

'Thank you so much for a lovely evening,' she had said, at the door to her block of apartments. 'No need to come up. I'm not that decrepit yet. And very nice to meet you, Karen.'

'Likewise, Jane.'

'I don't wish to lecture you, but you won't be driving after all that wine will you? My husband died in a car crash you see. . . .' She tailed off remembering. Despite everything, it was a bad memory.

Karen rested her hand briefly on her arm. 'Susan told me, and don't worry, I won't be driving.'

'Good.'

Susan leant forward and kissed her mother on the cheek. It was her chance to say something. 'Karen is staying the night, Mum,' she said quietly. 'So no need to worry.'

'Right!' Detective Inspector Holden sat in her office in the Cowley Station, and looked round at Detective Sergeant Fox and Detective Constables Lawson and Wilson. It was just gone 8.30 a.m. and she felt better than she had done for weeks. 'Time to assess where we are. We've got two deaths, two mobile phones with photographs and, as far as we know, two paintings. But so far, no answers and certainly no arrests. So, what do we know for certain? Wilson?'

Wilson wasn't exactly ready for the question, but he wasn't exactly unready either. He was getting used to Holden's methods, and firing questions from the hip was certainly one of them.

'Both murder victims were killed by the same person, or at least the same weapon.'

'Good. But if it was the same weapon, why not the same killer, or are you just hedging your bets?'

'The second killing was more frenzied. A thrust to the heart, then to the neck, and then into the eyes.' He paused, wondering how this was going down. 'The first killing was more clinical.'

'Lawson, any comments?'

Lawson hesitated, remembering the corpse of Jack Smith, and in particular the red holes where the eyes had once been. 'The second killing was certainly more frenzied. But in both cases, the first blow was one aimed at the heart, and the second to the neck was to make sure.'

'Fox.' Holden rapped out his name as if taking a role call. 'One killer or two. Put us out of our misery.'

Fox leant back in his chair and looked around, at Lawson and Wilson, and then back to Holden. 'It's a hard call, Guv.'

'Sergeant! I want an answer, not a philosophical discussion.' She slapped her hand down on the desk, not hard, but sufficient to make her point.

'One.' Fox leant forward and picked up the mug of black coffee that sat on the desk in front of him. He took a sip. He looked around. He had got their attention. 'The first killing took place outside in filthy weather in a public car park. The killer didn't have time for afters. A stab in the bodily mass, then one to the neck to make sure, and he – or she – took off. But Jack Smith was different. He was inside, in a private place. So the killer had time, to do what he wanted to do, to do what he would have ideally wanted to do to the first victim. So two victims and one killer.'

'Thank you, Sergeant. There's no certainty, I admit, but I think you're right.' She looked at Wilson and Lawson, curious to see their reactions, but there was no need to rub the lesson in. The bottom line was that experience wasn't something you were born with. 'So, what do we make of the two paintings? The one that Jack Smith found and the one we found on his mobile. Wilson. Your turn again.'

The young constable looked around nervously. Holden looked back, but said nothing. He was a nice lad, but she wasn't sure he had what it took. It was a sink or swim business, and she was afraid that sooner or later he would end up drowning.

'Either Jack Smith was lying, or there are two distinct paintings.' Wilson paused, trying to marshal his thoughts. 'The one he described was totally different from the one we found at D.R. Antiquities.'

'And what do we know about the one we found?'

'It is probably quite valuable – Mr Russell admitted that – but not hugely valuable.' Wilson paused again, uncertain what else there was to say about the painting. They had all seen it, after all, so they knew what it looked like.

'It's quite small, isn't it Wilson?'

'Well, yes,' he replied.

'So it could have been hidden under floorboards?'

Wilson frowned, in thought rather than perplexity, for suddenly things had started to slot into place in his brain. 'Of course, what with all the supporting beams, it would be difficult to hide a large painting under boards.'

'Exactly,' Holden said cutting in. She was impatient to push on. 'It's just that yesterday Lawson came up with the theory that maybe there was only one painting.'

'Did she?' There was irritation in Fox's voice. He liked working for Holden, and was more than happy to be a sergeant, taking orders, and supporting his DI, but he was not immune to jealousy. And right now the green-eyed monster was telling him that Detective Constable Lawson was usurping his position, and was becoming – had become even – the person with whom his Guvnor swapped ideas and theories.

'She may have been playing devil's advocate, of course,' Holden continued quickly. 'But even so, let's just suppose for a moment that Jack Smith lied, and that the painting he found under the floorboards was the same one as we found pictured on his mobile. Why would he have lied to us about what the picture looked like? Why say it had two women and a prone man, when it had one man and one woman in some sort of classical seduction story?'

'Presumably Lawson has a theory on this?' Fox was still sore, and it was apparent in his voice. He wanted his boss to know.

Holden pressed her lips together. She wasn't so dense that she hadn't picked up on the undercurrents, but she wasn't someone to back down from a challenge either, and this felt like a challenge.

'Did you get out of bed the wrong side, Sergeant?' She didn't wait for an answer. She didn't want an awkward silence – that might cause more damage within the team. But she did want to make her point. 'As far as I am concerned, any one of you can come up with any damn fool or not such a damn fool theory, and they can tell me any time. They don't need to check it out with the rest of the team first. I'm interested only in catching a murderer, not running a bloody democracy. So Lawson will say what she has to say now, and then anyone else is welcome to comment as long as they remember what our collective job is.'

Holden stopped, and took a deep breath. Saying all this hadn't helped. She felt even more bloody annoyed now.

'It just occurred to me yesterday in the car,' Lawson began. 'I can't pretend I had thought about it a lot first.'

'For God's sake!' Holden turned her irritation towards Lawson now. 'Stop taking out insurance, Constable, and get to the point. Why might Jack Smith have lied about the painting he found under the floorboards?'

'Because then we would be looking for a different picture, and there would be no chance of us finding it.'

'Right. And are there any problems with this scenario, Lawson? You've had plenty of time to think about it now.'

'I guess the main problem is Jack Smith himself. The theory implies that first he is a smart cookie, and second that he knew how to sell a painting of dodgy provenance.'

'He presumably knew Dominic Russell.' Lawson, Wilson and Holden all turned and looked at Fox. Whatever Fox was now feeling after his dressing down, he wasn't letting it show. 'He had done plumbing for the Russells, hadn't he? He was well known in the area. Maybe he knew from Maria that Dominic could handle sensitive art sales. So he didn't need to sell it himself.'

Silence fell. Fox took a sip of his coffee, and waited for Holden to respond.

'Thank you, Sergeant,' she nodded. 'So, if Jack Smith did lie, then we have to assume that he knew where Maria had taken the painting, namely to Dominic Russell. And that even after Maria's death he hoped to be able to get his cut of the painting's sale. But maybe Dominic Russell didn't see it the same way as him.'

'Sorry, Guv.' Fox had half lifted his hand in apology. Politeness was suddenly in vogue. 'But are you saying you think Dominic Russell killed them both for a picture that he claims isn't worth that much money?'

Holden shut her eyes, and for several seconds rested her head on her right hand as she tried to get a grip on her thoughts. The pressure she had been putting on her team was rebounding back on her. The connections were there, and yet somehow it didn't hang together. Two people dead, and no clear motive. Two photos on mobile phones. But very different photos. And two paintings. Or maybe one painting? Two people dead. Was that it? Was that the end of it, or would it soon be three? She opened her eyes and sighed.

'What we need is more information.' She looked at her watch. 'At ten-thirty, I've got an appointment with Dr Eleanor Bennett, and hopefully she will spread some expert light on this ruddy painting. Wilson will accompany me. As for you, Fox, and you, Lawson, you're on house to house in the Brook Street area.' It would be good for them to work together, and without her or Wilson around. If they had anything to say to each other, hopefully they would get it said and out of their systems. 'And when you've done house to house, from twelve o'clock stop everyone entering or leaving the road by the towpath, or riding along past it. If they're regulars or locals, passing that way the same time every day, then maybe they saw someone or something. We'll join you as soon as we can.'

Dr Eleanor Bennett lived in one of the terrace of three-storey houses which front the western side of the southern end of Walton Street. Unusually for central Oxford, the front gardens in this residential strip were more than perfunctory, some five metres in depth, and it was up the pathway of one of them that the two detectives advanced cautiously, brushing past the box tree bushes, still wet from the morning rain, which had been allowed to protrude unmolested across the path.

There was a long delay after Holden pressed the doorbell, and she was just lifting her forefinger to repeat the exercise when she heard the sound of a bolt being drawn on the back of the door. It opened, but only as far as the security chain would allow, and a pair of sharp steel-grey eyes looked up at them.

'Who are you?' the owner of the eyes demanded.

'Detective Inspector Holden, and this is my colleague Detective Constable Wilson.' Holden passed both their ID cards through the gap, and waited while the woman looked at them carefully. She was expecting some police persons to call, but she knew from her regular perusal of the local newspapers that imposters pretending to be all sorts of workmen, from men checking the electricity supply to women claiming to be social workers, were at large and older people like herself were their preferred targets. Only when she was satisfied did she release the chain and open the door wider.

'Eleanor Bennett,' she said. 'Do come in. But would you mind taking your shoes off at the door. I hate cleaning.'

She led them slowly along the corridor, slowly because she walked with a pronounced limp, and then through a doorway. There they found a large living space. To the right was the sitting area with a sofa, two arm-chairs, a child's rocking chair, and a television. To the left stood a dark, heavy dining table surrounded by six chairs. In its centre there sat a dark, fat candle. It was alight and it gave off a smell of sandalwood. A portable laptop was the only other object on the table, and it was open.

'I was just about to make myself some tea. Would you care to join me?' Eleanor Bennett spoke precisely and quickly. 'I'm afraid I can't offer you coffee. My doctor's told me off about it. But I can't trust myself, so I just don't keep it in the house.'

'Can I help?' Wilson had stepped forward, shoeless yet eager. He was warming to Eleanor Bennett already, not least because she reminded him of his Gran. His Gran had been petite too, and a sparky cheerful soul, and she had liked to talk without demanding an answer. She had smelt of lavender rather than sandalwood, and – sometimes – of urine too, and he had loved her terribly.

Eleanor Bennett looked at him. 'Thank you, young man. I don't need help, despite appearances. But only a fool would turn down such a kind offer. Maybe you can locate the chocolate biscuits. I'm sure I bought some the other day.'

Holden, who was clutching the painting to her stomach, placed it carefully on the table at the other end from the laptop, and looked around the room. It was then that she noticed the oddity, the strangeness. There were no pictures on the walls. She had assumed that an expert in art history would have her walls thronged with interesting original paintings, or if not originals then high-class prints of favourites. Yet there was nothing. There were various family photos deployed in a phalanx on a side table, but beyond that there was nothing.

'I've had the decorators in,' Eleanor said. She had re-entered the room, with Wilson behind her carrying the tea tray, and had spotted Holden observing the walls. 'The pictures are all in the spare bedroom. I had to take them down, and I just haven't got round to getting them back on the walls. To be frank with you, Inspector, I was getting a bit bored with them, so I thought I'd take a break from them.'

'I was merely wondering what sort of paintings an art historian buys for herself.'

She chuckled in reply. 'My collection is what my nephew's daughter calls a funny old mixture. I am sure there are smarter words for it, but I think she sums it up rather well. Anyway, it's time for tea, and for me to take a look at your picture.'

'Just a dash of milk in mine, Constable, and half a teaspoon of sugar,' she said, but her mind had moved on, and her delicate, unadorned fingers were picking up the package and beginning very carefully to unwrap it. When she had removed the hessian, she lay the painting back on the table, and stooped over, peering at it with intense concentration. 'Constable, would you mind turning on the overhead lights,' she said, without looking up. She stood poring over the painting for at least two minutes, and then limped slowly to the other end of the table where she sat down and began to press away at the keys of her laptop. 'I'll be a few minutes. Please, do go and sit in the comfortable chairs until I've finished.'

It was more a command than a request, and so Wilson and Holden went and sat down, Wilson in an armchair and Holden on the sofa, and sipped their tea from china cups. While Holden tried to focus her thoughts on the investigation, Wilson thought rather smugly of Fox and Lawson doing door to door (it had started to rain again), and then wondered whether to go to the United game – home to Altrincham – the following day, Saturday. They had had a great start to the season, so the chances were that he'd see a win. And that, after all, was what mattered if they were ever going to get out of this poxy league. Yes, he thought he would go to the game. Definitely.

'Finished your tea?' The sudden question made both Holden and Lawson start. Eleanor was back by the painting now. She drank thirstily at her tea as they got up to join her.

'It's an interesting little painting. Not exactly my cup of tea, though!' She laughed, waving her own cup in the air, as if to explain her joke. 'Very competently painted, though not out of the top drawer. It's a typical Greek mythological scene, with temple ruins looming out of the background to underline that fact. Sexual union has been achieved, and the male is leaving rather casually, having made his conquest. The male is doubtless Zeus, a singularly randy God who left his bastard progeny all over the Greek world. The female might be one of several poor maidens deflowered by him, but I'd put my money on—'

'Talking of money,' Holden interrupted, 'could you give us an idea of what this would be worth?'

'Ah, well, it's probably worth more than I would chose to pay for anything so unoriginal, but the artist has for some reason become quite collectable. He died in his mid thirties and wasn't that prolific, so the scarcity of his work has not done his prices any harm. Six weeks ago, a similar painting by him was sold in New York for $14,500. Even in these uncertain times, I think if this came up at auction it might easily reach ten thousand pounds.'

Ten minutes later, Holden and Wilson took their leave of Eleanor Bennett and walked briskly to the car. The rain was persistent, but not heavy, and a patch of blue sky promised better things to come.

'Brook Street is it, Guv?'

'I think we'd better nip back to the station first, and get this painting into a safe place before anyone nicks it off the back seat.'

'It's a fair whack, isn't it, Guv? Ten thousand pounds. With Maria dead, it's no wonder that he decided to keep it all to himself. That amount of money is one hell of a temptation.'

Holden looked at her constable, a disapproving frown written across her face. 'Just remember that temptation is there to be resisted, Wilson. Especially when you're in a profession where it can so easily present itself.'

Wilson looked back at her, and flushed. 'Sorry, Guv. It was just a ... I didn't mean to suggest....' But he couldn't think of how to finish the sentence.

Holden turned and looked forward out of the car. She knew she had sounded a bit schoolmarmish, but she felt she had to say it. Wilson was a good constable, but naïve and, she feared, too easily swayed by others. He was the sort of man who might easily succumb to temptation without realizing it, or go with the crowd because he wasn't tough enough to stand against it. So it was her responsibility to mark out the boundaries as best she could.

'The key question as regards this investigation, Wilson, is whether a man would kill for ten thousand pounds? What do you think?'

'People have killed for less, Guv. It depends on the man.' He paused. 'Or, of course, woman.' He wasn't sure where these words came from, and he was even less sure how Holden would take them. He had decided that he didn't really understand women, women like Lawson who messed his head up something ridiculous, and Holden who behaved like a very strict version of his Mum. Even his beloved Gran had sometimes seemed like an alien from another planet.

'Hmm!' The word was in itself meaningless, but the tone of voice told Wilson that his words of wisdom had been well received. 'That's an interesting answer, Wilson. I'll think about it while you drive us safely to Cowley.'

The house to house enquiries in Brook Street and the area around it proved to be, if not entirely fruitless, then in terms of hard evidence the next best thing. Brook Street is a short street running in a south-north direction, parallel to the Abingdon Road and some forty metres to its west. It can be entered by car only from its southern end, via Western Road, but is not in a true sense a cul de sac, for access on foot and bike at the northern end is not just possible, but commonplace. Indeed for many local residents, hurrying to get to town on bike or shanks's pony, Brook Street represents a convenient little rat run, enabling them to minimize the amount of time spent breathing in the exhaust fumes of the Abingdon Road.

For DS Fox, marshalling his team on a grey morning of persistent rain, this openness to all corners presented its own complications. Looking at it, as Fox did, from the point of view of the killer, there were several routes in and – even more important – out again after the deed had been done. A cyclist, for example, had several options: head back down to Western Road, and then either out on to the Abingdon Road and away out of town with traffic, or turn right along Western Road until it meets Marlborough Road, and then turn left and south, pelting along its length, then through Hinksey Park, and then via a few twists and turns into Wytham Street, running straight south along it until you choose to divert or reach the Redbridge park-and-ride. But a killer could also make his escape east along the towpath to picturesque Iffley. Or he or she could alternatively head west towards flood-prone Osney, and the unloved Botley Road. Or if they were a killer committing murder in a lunch break, they could nip back up to their city-centre office either over Folly Bridge or over the rather ugly footbridge some one hundred and fifty metres to the west, just beyond Marlborough Road.

The shortness of Brook Street was the one good thing about it, in Fox's view: knocking on the doors of all its residents wasn't an arduous task for the team of himself, Lawson and the four uniformed officers. However, getting useful information proved hugely more difficult. For a start, half the residents were already out – or possibly still in bed, or deaf, or merely perverse – and those who did open their doors had inevitably seen nothing. There was no improvement in their fortune as Fox extended their sweep along the river, knocking on the doors of Cobden Crescent and the northern end of Buckingham Street and of Marlborough Road.

When Holden and Wilson joined them just before noon, Fox was in the process of moving to plan B, namely intercepting locals as they passed along Brook Street and along the towpath, in the hope that someone on a regular commute to or from the city might recall someone or something of interest from the previous day. It proved to be a busy thoroughfare, and even on an increasingly wet and windy day, the eight of them found themselves constantly occupied in stopping passers-by and asking them questions. Had they come this way yesterday at this time? Did they notice anyone stopping at the house? Or anyone in a terrible hurry on the towpath? Or anyone – and this was surely a long shot – with blood on their clothes? Given that the weather the previous day had also been singularly nasty and wet, the answers given were generally short and unenlightening. One man, a beard on his face and a collie at his heels, said he had almost been run over by a cyclist speeding towards Osney round about 1.30 p.m. A tall Glaswegian, with an accent so thick Wilson could barely decipher what he was saying, gave a similar story, though he insisted it was round about 1.15 p.m.

'Did you manage to get a look at the cyclist's face?' Wilson asked hopefully.

'Naw! The bampot had a balaclava on. A black 'un. And he was wearing navy blue waterproofs.'

'Why do you say he?' Wilson fired back.

'Who kin tell, nowadays?' came the laughing reply.

They gave up at 2.15 p.m. and retreated to Cowley, where they dried off and warmed themselves with hot drinks in Holden's office. Outside, in the Oxford Road, the increased traffic levels signalled the end of school, and beyond their view the ring road was already clogging up, the result of the breakdown of a London-bound coach at the Headington roundabout. It was Friday, and Holden should have been looking forward to the weekend, but all she could feel was frustration. She began the meeting by briefing Fox and Lawson thoroughly on the visit to Eleanor Bennett, and concluded with a variation on the question she had earlier put to Wilson. 'Would Dominic Russell commit murder for the sake of a painting worth ten thousand pounds? Any offers?'

'Yes!' said Lawson. If truth be told, she was feeling a little resentful that Holden had taken Wilson rather than her to visit Eleanor Bennett. And now she was determined to show her worth.

'No!' said Fox firmly.

Holden turned. 'Are you playing devil's advocate, Fox?'

'No,' he said bluntly. 'I'm just saying it how I see it. You saw his business. Loads of expensive stuff. He may be a smarmy arsehole, but I don't see him as a killer prepared to risk all on a painting like that.'

'You're making two assumptions, with respect, Sarge.' Lawson had no intention of backing off, especially when Sergeant bloody Fox was in flat-foot mood. 'First, we don't know how well his business is doing. We've entered a recession, haven't we, and the stuff he sells is hardly essential for people's survival. So if ten thousand pounds was the difference between going bust and survival, why wouldn't he kill? Second, maybe there's a personal angle to it all. He and Maria have a bit of history. Who's to say this painting wasn't all that it needed to tip the balance.'

'Where's you evidence for that?' Fox spoke aggressively. He didn't much like Lawson. Fancied herself a lot. Thought she was smart as hell.

'We haven't got the evidence,' Holden snapped. She was angry that a brainstorming session was so quickly degenerating into a personal battle. Whatever their differences, they clearly hadn't sorted them out in her absence. 'That's why we're trying to bounce ideas around, preferably without you two scrapping like kids in the playground. But Lawson's first point is a good one. So let's run some checks against Dominic Russell and his business. See if there's any evidence he's got financial problems.'

She paused. She was tempted to bring the session to a premature close, but she was conscious there was other ground to cover. But in any event, Lawson had something else to say.

'Guv, we've also got the evidence of Jack Smith's phone calls.'

Holden looked at Lawson hard. 'What the hell are you talking about?'

'Sorry, Guv, but what with everything that went on yesterday, I only got round to going through his phone properly this morning.'

'But you got it from Dr Pointer yesterday morning!'

Lawson swallowed. 'Well, I suppose I got a bit distracted by the photo of the painting, and then we went to D.R. Antiquities, so I only did a thorough check this morning just before we went on the house to house.'

'OK, Lawson, that's enough excuses. So you've written your findings down, have you?'

'I sent them to you by email, Guv.'

'Do you think I've time to be checking my email every five minutes, Lawson. If there's anything important, you should tell me.'

'Sorry, Guv. It's just that I don't know if it's important, but it is evidence of sorts.'

'Lawson,' Holden said, with a suddenly – and dangerously – quiet voice. 'What is this evidence that you've emailed me? Do you think you could give us all a quick resumé or do I have to go and sit down at my PC in order to find out?'

Lawson flushed, and she replied with eyes not quite meeting her boss's. 'Jack Smith received a phone call from the Tulls' home number on Wednesday at 7.55 a.m.'

There was not so much a silence at this point as a hiatus. The world, or at least the room, stopped dead for several moments as the three other detectives in the room assimilated this news into their understanding.

'Hey,' Wilson piped up, 'that's only a few hours before he was killed!' On another day, or perhaps if they had been uttered from the lips of a less guileless person than Wilson, these words would have been petrol sprayed over a smouldering fire. But somehow there was no explosion. Fox jumped in, unusually sensitive to the currents swirling around in the room. 'To be fair,' he said in deadpan tones, 'it could be nothing. If your heating has broken down overnight, or something's leaking, that's the time you'd ring your plumber.'

'Or,' said Holden, 'it's the time you might ring on a pretext in order to find out where your murder victim is going to be later that day.'

'Agreed,' he replied instantly. It was the first thought that he had had. 'But we can easily check if the Tulls did have a plumbing problem.'

'We can and we will,' Holden concluded. 'In fact, the Tulls are due a visit. None of them had a watertight alibi for Maria's death, so we need to check their movements for the time of Jack's death. That way, with a bit of luck, we might be able to rule some of them out.'

'Do you want to do it here?' Fox said.

Holden looked at her watch. 'The chances are Dr Tull and Lucy are both at work, so why don't we see if we can call round when they are all at home later this afternoon. Wilson, can you fix that? Start with Dr Tull, see if it's OK with him, and then track down the others.'

In the event, Dr Tull turned out to have a 2.00 p.m. clinic that afternoon, and by the time Wilson rang there were only three patients waiting to be seen, so Dr Tull suggested the police come round to his house at 4.30. He insisted he would ring his children and make sure they were there too. He put the phone down with a sigh, conscious he had been slightly duplicitous; he had no intention of getting them home before 5.00 p.m. because he wanted to get his interview over and done with first.

'So,' Holden was saying, 'we just need to know where you were between 12.00 noon and 2.00 p.m. yesterday.'

They were sitting in Dr Tull's study – Dr Tull, DI Holden, and DS Fox, while the two detective constables waited in the hallway for Dr Tull's offspring to arrive.

'I see,' Dr Tull replied, rubbing his cheeks between the thumb and forefinger of his left hand. 'I had surgery from 9 o'clock till about 11.15. I then made a couple of phone calls, following up on a couple of my patients, and then made a home visit on Cumnor Hill. A Major Johnson. It must have been about twelve by the time I finished, so I decided to go for a walk. My only commitment on a Wednesday afternoon is paperwork, so there was no rush to get back.'

'Where did you walk?'

'Oh, I don't know. I just put my case back in the car – in the boot that is, out of sight – and I walked.' He paused, and then, as if realizing more was expected, continued. 'I just needed some time out. On my own.' There was another short silence. 'Time not to think, as it were. After Maria's death and everything, I just needed time out. Go walkabout. Isn't that what the Australian Aborigines do?' He took a white handkerchief out of his pocket and blew his nose.

'Wasn't it rather wet for walking?' It was a casually asked question, but not a casual one.

He looked at Holden with a look of slight bemusement. 'Probably. I'm not sure that was at the forefront of my mind. But I had my raincoat with me.'

'Did you meet anyone you know while you were walking?' Again a simple question, but with considerable significance. A significance that he would surely be aware of, Holden reckoned. She didn't buy this puzzled, I-don't-know-where-I-am-half-the-time act, not from a GP who was still attending his patients diligently despite his grief.

'No, I don't think so. I don't know many people in Cumnor, actually.'

'Sir,' Fox interrupted, 'what about any patients? I guess you must have a lot of those, and they'd always recognize their doctor.'

Again the look of innocent incomprehension as he tried to come up with a more satisfactory answer. 'Sorry, I really didn't meet anyone I know.'

'That's fine,' Holden said quickly, taking the reins back. 'There is just one other thing. Did you by any chance make a phone call to Jack Smith yesterday morning?'

For the first time that morning there was a look of genuine surprise on Dr Tull's face. He peered at Holden his eyes narrowing. 'No, I didn't,' he said firmly, before adding, 'though the shower is leaking.'

'It could be him,' Fox concluded tersely, after Dr Tull had asked to be excused and gone out of the room. 'No alibi.'

'It could be,' Holden replied. 'But who made the phone call?'

Joseph was the next of the Tulls to arrive home. His hair flopped across his face, and every gesture and word exuded the same disgruntled note, a young man at odds with the world and himself. He had been at college all morning the previous day, he insisted. He had had two classes, and the second had finished at 12.30, and then he'd gone home and played on his X-Box for a while and then he'd had to write an essay because it was late and he'd been given a bollocking about it by his tutor. And no, he hadn't rung the bloody plumber. If the shower was dripping a bit, so what!

It was rather a relief to Holden when Lucy Tull arrived. Fox intercepted her in the hall, and invited her straight into the study. She took off her black coat and scarf, hung them neatly on the coat stand in the hall, and went and sat down opposite Holden. Holden couldn't help but compare her with her half-brother. Whereas he had slouched in the chair and given every impression of total boredom, she sat upright and tense, her hands clasped tightly together on the table, and her eyes looking so directly at Holden that she might have been practising the pose. Look at me, she was saying, giving you absolutely one hundred per cent attention.

'I'm sorry if you've had to rush home, Lucy.'

'Our last appointment didn't turn up, so it didn't matter.'

'I'll try to keep it brief. We need to know where you were between 12.00 noon and 2.00 p.m. yesterday.'

'Work for some of it. I was in the surgery till about 12.45. We were running a bit late because we'd had to fit an emergency in. Then I went out, and I came back just before two o'clock.'

'That's a long lunch break.'

'Not really. You see, at least twice a week we catch up with the admin at lunchtime, so then it's a short break. So on other days I get longer.'

'And what did you do while you were out?'

'I went to get a new bell for my bike.'

'Where from?'

'There's a little shop on the Botley Road. I always use it. They specialize in Bromptons.'

'And then what?'

'Gosh, you do ask a lot of questions. Let me see, I put the bell on the bike, and I cycled back towards town, only it was really chucking it down so I stopped by that church on the right, near Osney, and sheltered in the porch while I ate my sandwich. Oh, yes, I nearly forgot,' she continued, with sarcasm now transparent, 'I read my book while I was waiting for the rain to ease off – Daphne du Maurier's *My Cousin Rachel* – and then I made my way back to the surgery.'

'So that all took you an hour and a quarter?' Holden had no intention of being distracted from her task.

'Roughly speaking.' She made a face, and Holden saw in it a flash of her brother's disdainfulness. Did they both get that from their father, then? Or was that the product of money and class. 'Maybe it was only an hour and ten minutes. I wasn't counting the minutes. But you can always check with Geraldine.'

Holden yawned. She too could play the 'I'm bored with all of this' game. But right now it was merely a distraction technique. The real game was altogether more serious. She ran her forefinger up and down the side of her nose, rubbing a non-existent itch.

'Did you ring Jack Smith yesterday morning round about eight o'clock?' If Holden hoped the suddenness of the question would throw Lucy off her guard, she was quickly disillusioned by the immediate and sure-footed response.

'Yeah!'

'Why was that?'

'Because the shower was leaking. Why else?'

'So you rang the man who had had an affair with your stepmother, in order to get him to fix a leaking shower?'

'Sure. He installed the damn shower, so he could fix it. You don't think I was going to call out another plumber who'd charge daddy at least fifty quid when it was Jack's responsibility to fix it for free. And besides, do you really think Jack Smith was the only person who'd slept with Maria? Because I don't.'

Holden nodded her head slowly. She's probably got as far as she could. But there was one more thing she wanted to ask.

'Why do you visit Marjorie Drabble?'

'Why? That's an odd sort of question. Why not? She's got cancer.'

'I'd like a better answer than that, Lucy,' Holden said, her voice now raised.

Lucy Tull looked down at her hands, which were still clenched firmly together. Her breathing was deep and noisy, so that Holden wondered whether she wasn't on the brink of exploding, but gradually the breaths grew quieter, until finally she raised her head and looked her questioner full in the face. 'To protect my father,' she said bluntly.

'Can you explain that for me?'

Lucy sucked in a deep breath and then let it out gently, as if preparing for a relaxation class. 'Daddy is Marjorie's GP. He's known her since way back when. She knew my mother. They were friends. But when Maria came on the scene there must have been a bit of a falling out. I guess she didn't approve of Maria or something. So although Daddy remained her GP, we rarely saw her socially. Marjorie contracted cancer, but it wasn't diagnosed till a few weeks ago. Graham Drabble blamed my father, saying he should have spotted the signs and sent her for screening sooner, and then he started threatening Daddy, and he said he'd accuse him of sexually molesting Marjorie if he didn't resign. It was all quite ridiculous, or would have been if Graham wasn't such a nasty piece of work, so I said to Daddy that I'd go and visit her in hospital and see if I could get her to stop Graham. We really hit it off, and she told me she would speak to Graham. So that's how we started, but really I like visiting her now because she remembers my mother, and we talk about her. For a few short years, they were really good friends, and I think talking about Mummy helps her to forget her own problems.'

She stopped, and took another deep breath. 'That's about it, really.'

'Thank you. I think that's about all.'

'I'm sorry if I was a bit late getting here,' Lucy said, as she got up.

'Don't worry,' Holden replied. 'We only had to wait five minutes or so. And that was because Joseph didn't have a lot to say.'

'No change there then.' She laughed. The social pleasantries were being observed. Despite the circumstances. 'Still, I would have been back sooner if Daddy hadn't rung my mobile when I was on my way home. He said you'd only just started quizzing Joseph, so I knew there was no mad rush. Now, did you have coats?'

*

'Bloody hell!' Holden slammed the palm of her hand down on to the dashboard. Her three colleagues – Fox in the driving seat, Lawson and Wilson in the back – jumped as one.

Holden turned round and gave her two detective constables a look that would have scorched a piece of granite. 'Why the hell did you let him near the phone?'

The looks of incomprehension on their faces only served to egg her on. 'When we were interviewing Joseph, Dr Tull went and rang Lucy as she was cycling back to Bainton Road.'

'I expect he was wondering where she had got to,' Wilson said innocently.

Fox, conscious that Wilson was now pouring petrol directly on to an open flame, tried for the second time that day to intervene, but he barely got his mouth open before Holden's hand again slammed down on to the dashboard. But this time Holden's voice was more controlled, if no less threatening. 'Let me explain, Wilson, in words of great simplicity. Someone rang Jack Smith from the Tull's house yesterday morning. Alan Tull said it wasn't him, but said the shower had been leaking. Joseph said it wasn't him, and said nothing about the shower leaking. And then we asked Lucy, who piped up very promptly that it was her who had rung Jack Smith because the shower was leaking. So now, Wilson, do you understand the importance I am attaching to the phone call Dr Tull made to Lucy Tull while Fox and I were talking to Joseph Tull?'

'Yes, Guv.'

'Praise the Lord!' Holden leant back in her seat and shut her eyes. 'Just get us home, Fox,' she added.

Fox started the car, but didn't immediately set off. 'To be fair, Guv, they weren't to know, and even if they had it would have been difficult to stop him making a phone call in his own house. He's probably got a mobile, and a land-line in his bedroom.'

'Thank you, Fox. So what you're saying is that it's actually all my fault for not thinking of it in advance, and planning accordingly.'

'No, Guv,' he replied quickly. 'I was just pointing out—'

But Holden had no interest in hearing anything else he might want to just point out on the subject. 'For God's sake, stop talking and drive us home, Sergeant!'

CHAPTER 7

Dominic Russell went missing the following day, Saturday. Quite when this occurred depends on your point of view. According to his wife Sarah, he left home at about 7.30 a.m. to make the short journey from his home in North Oxford to D.R. Antiquities. That was the last time she saw him, she said. Unless, of course, as Sergeant Fox later commented to Constable Wilson, it was she who killed him.

As far as Francesca Willis was concerned, Dominic didn't go missing. He just never arrived. She turned up for her Saturday stint at D.R. Antiquities at 10.15 a.m., nearly three-quarters of an hour late. In truth, she had already been running a bit late when she picked up her handbag and let herself out of her front door in the village of Marsh Baldon, but late became later when she discovered the front nearside tyre of her Mini was flat. By the time her husband had put the spare on, and she had returned the favour by chasing their twin sons off their X-Boxes and into their football kit, she was getting late enough to ring D.R. Antiquities to warn her boss she would definitely be in. But there had been no reply.

When she got to work there was no one there. This was not unprecedented. Dominic Russell was somewhat unreliable in his timekeeping, so she unlocked and made her way to the office without concern. When she found a hand-written note, 'Out on business. Back later. D', on the desk, she shrugged, powered up the

PC, and went to make herself a mug of tea.

By the time she had had her first sip of tea, the first of a steady stream of customers had arrived.

A few of these customers turned out to be silent browsers, not wanting to buy and not wanting to engage in a conversation either. But the majority were either chatty or there on serious business, and by noon Francesca had conducted four pieces of quite substantial business and was feeling rather pleased with herself, if not with her absent boss. At this point she rang Dominic's mobile, but it went straight to the answerphone service, so she left a message asking when he would be in, and explaining in slightly tetchy tones that she really could do with some assistance.

An hour and a quarter later, when there was still no sign of him, she broke an unwritten rule and rang his home number. Sarah Russell did not reply, so she left another message. Ten minutes later, Sarah rang back, and after a brief conversation, said she would come in and help.

'What the hell does he think he's playing at,' was Sarah's first reaction on reading the note that Francesca handed to her. 'Back later! How many hours is back later?'

'Where do you think he is?' Francesca asked anxiously. She was rather fond of her boss, and it did seem some way beyond his normal bounds of unreliability.

'If I knew that,' Sarah snapped, 'I'd not be here, now would I!'

But there was no more time for Sarah to snarl or for Francesca to worry about Dominic Russell – there were customers to humour and, besides, Francesca was in urgent need of a comfort break. For the next hour and a half, there was little respite for the two women, and it was in fact not until approximately 2.45 p.m. that they had a chance to revisit Dominic's absence.

'Wherever can he be?' Francesca asked in urgent undertones.

This time Sarah responded differently. 'I think,' she said unsteadily, 'I had better make a phone call.'

'Who to?'

'The police.'

*

'What is it?' Holden's response to the call she received shortly after 3.00 that Saturday afternoon was hardly gracious. But as she soon heard the words 'I'm sorry to be ringing you at this time, Inspector', she knew it could be only bad news, that is to say, news that was going to spoil her weekend.

'We thought you'd want to know, Inspector, that Dominic Russell has been reported missing by his wife.'

Ten minutes later and she was heading across the Donnington Bridge. Had she looked left or right, she would have seen eights, and pairs and single sculls out on the river as enthusiastic students and members of the city rowing club honed their skills, but her mind was focused on the new development in her case, not in her environment. Had Dominic done a runner? Was his wife panicking just because he'd gone off her radar for a while? Or had something worse happened? Time would tell, but for now she'd better go and see Sarah Russell and make a judgement. And fast.

Approaching the station, she almost ran into Lawson, who lived close by in Temple Road, and was hot-footing it across the Oxford Road. She'd asked control to try and contact her team. So that was one of them, at least. In fact, as she discovered inside the station, that was the only one of them for now. Neither Fox nor Wilson was contactable. 'I think Wilson's gone to the Oxford game,' Lawson told her. 'Maybe he'll switch his mobile on at half-time.' But of Fox's movements, she had no knowledge.

'No worries. You come with me to see Sarah Russell, and then we'll take it from there.'

They made it to D.R. Antiquities in double quick time, taking full advantage of the flashing blue light and the very light traffic on the ring road. As they pulled up outside, Sarah Russell and another woman tumbled out of the front door, both clearly in a state of alarm.

It took several minutes to calm them down, find out who the other woman was, move them back into the office of the building, and then get them to each tell their story. Though as Holden soon realized, in fact, it was Francesca Willis who was most voluble and was the most distressed of the two, and by some way. Initially, Holden made little attempt to interrupt or interfere. It was, she judged, better to let her say what she had to say, and then try and pick up on the missing details afterwards. All that dammed up emotion and anxiety – let it all flood out. Time wasn't that critical.

'So,' she said at the end, 'can I see the note Mr Russell left?' She looked at both of them as she spoke, but it was Sarah who responded, pushing her hand into her jacket pocket and pulling out a folded note. 'Here, I didn't want it to get lost.'

Holden tried not to look bothered by the contamination of the evidence. She read the note closely, as if examining it for a secret code, before passing it to Lawson. 'Mrs Russell, are you certain it is your husband's writing?'

'Yes, of course. I would have said so otherwise, wouldn't I.'

Holden ignored the sharpness in her voice. It was only to be expected, and her brief experience of Sarah suggested that her natural mode was sharp. The fact was that the note seemed unexceptional, whereas Dominic's disappearance was decidedly worrying. Either he didn't want to be contacted, or it was beyond his control. Holden turned towards Francesca.

'What time do you normally open up here, Francesca?'

'I only work here on a Saturday. We officially open at 9.30, but I try to get here a bit earlier, because more than once I've arrived and found people peering through windows, and if they make the effort you don't want to lose their business, do you.'

Holden turned back to the other woman. 'Sarah, was it unusual for Dominic to leave home quite so early?'

'He said he had a lot of paperwork to catch up on. You know how it is. If the office is empty and no one is bothering you, you can get on with things.'

'Yes,' Holden replied calmly. She didn't like Sarah, but she knew she mustn't let that get in the way. 'I do understand, Sarah, but I don't think you've quite answered my question. Did Dominic

121

usually leave for work at 7.30 a.m. on a Saturday?'

Sarah Russell looked back at Holden, as if weighing up her options. For a woman whose husband had gone missing, she seemed to Holden to be remarkably unflustered. 'Not usually, no,' she admitted finally.

'So typically, what time did he leave home on a Saturday? Because I can't imagine that it would take very long on a Saturday morning to get here.'

'Any time. I don't monitor him and I sure as hell don't get up specially to wave him off to work. I work too, as you may recall, and Saturday is my chance of a lie-in.'

Holden turned back to Francesca Willis. She might be a more cooperative witness. Not to mention more truthful.

'Francesca, you normally get in a little before 9.30. Was Dominic usually here when you arrived?'

'Sometimes, but sometimes not. In fact, he told me more than once that he liked the fact that I was always here in plenty of time. I think he felt it meant he didn't have to worry if he was running a bit late.'

'Look, what is this all about?' Sarah Russell was angry now. 'He left early today. He said he had paperwork to catch up on. I've told you. So why all the bloody questions?'

'If you spend Saturday mornings lying in, Mrs Russell, how come you can be so sure your husband left at 7.30 this morning?' Holden too was getting angry, and she wasn't convinced that Sarah Russell was being straight with them.

'God, you do ask a lot of questions!' came the snarled reply. 'He dropped a bloody glass in the bathroom, when he was doing his teeth, and he shouted when he did it, so I had to get up and see if he was all right.'

'And was he?'

'He was. The glass wasn't. Mind you, it was his bloody fault. I've told him not to take glasses in there.'

Holden nodded. 'Can you tell me the registration of his car?'

There was a sign of irritation. 'No, it's not the sort of information

I carry in my head, but all his documents will be in the desk at home, in his study.'

'Thank you, we need it now, if you don't mind.'

'Excuse me.' It was Francesca Willis. 'Actually, there's a copy of his car insurance here, just in case he had an accident.'

'Even better.'

Lawson, taking notes and watching from the sidelines, wondered if there wasn't some friction between the two women. Francesca was mid thirties, and attractive enough without having the sort of face that might launch a thousand ships. But from Sarah's point of view, she might be seen as a rival. She certainly had a better figure.

'Can we have his mobile number too?' Holden was talking to Sarah Russell again. A tactful move, Lawson decided. No doubt Francesca had that too – in fact she'd already told them she'd rung his mobile, so she must have got it – but there was no reason for Holden to provoke Sarah unnecessarily.

'Of course. Mind you, it's turned off, so I doubt it'll be much use. Anyway, what are you going to do?' Sarah demanded.

'For, a start, we can check what calls he made with his mobile since he left home.'

'And the car?' Anger and bitterness, or a very good impersonation of the two, were evident in every clipped syllable that issued from Sarah's mouth. 'You think he's done a runner?'

Holden didn't reply immediately. It was the question she had tried hard not to frame or even hint at. What had happened to Dominic? Was he dead or on the run? Why did Sarah think the latter? Was it because it was easier to think your husband had buggered off, rather than face the possibility that he had been murdered too? Or did she know, and was she playing games? 'I try not to speculate without good evidence,' Holden said. 'Whatever has happened, there is a good chance that his car was caught on CCTV somewhere. Unfortunately there's quite a wide time-frame during which he might have left here and driven off. And then, of course, there are several ways he could have gone from here. On to the A34 heading north or south, or the A40 towards Witney, or back round the northern ring road, towards London, or even under the A34 and off on the Eynsham road, or into Kidlington. Or if he wanted to avoid detection, maybe he used the lanes, through Wolvercote and Wytham. The chances are that he'll turn up somewhere on CCTV, but you can see our difficulties.'

'Here's one of Dominic's office cards,' Francesca Willis said, holding out her hand. 'It's got his mobile and the office phone number on it, and I've written his car registration on the back. It's a silver Renault Scenic, by the way.'

'A Grand Scenic, actually,' Sarah corrected.

If looks could kill, Lawson reckoned Francesca Willis's brains would have been spattered all over the magnolia office wall.

Holden and Lawson pulled into the station just after 5.00 p.m. and bumped into Fox in the corridor, near the hot drinks machine. 'Sorry, Guv, I left my mobile at home,' he said. 'What's going on?'

'Five minutes in my office. And mine's a black coffee, thanks.' Holden disappeared into the ladies.

'White tea, no sugar, if you don't mind, Sarge,' Lawson added, taking her chance, and then rapidly following her boss through the nondescript lime-green door.

Fox muttered ungraciously in response as she disappeared, and pressed the button for a black coffee.

The two women and Fox had barely sat down together before hurrying steps in the corridor announced the arrival of Detective Constable Wilson.

'Sorry, Guv.' His face was flushed, and his voice slightly hoarse. 'I was at the game. Had my mobile turned off.'

'Well, we won't hold that against you. Did we win?' The word 'we' popped out automatically. Holden had only ever been to watch Oxford United once, when they had beaten Swindon in the FA Cup, and she doubted she ever would do so again, but as a resident of Oxford she felt nevertheless it was her team. She had occasionally read a match report in the *Oxford Mail* or *Times*, in the hope that this might somehow offer her an insight into what drove people like Wilson and a number of otherwise sane people of her acquaintance to troop along on wet and cold Saturday afternoons to watch such a fatuous pastime, but enlightenment had failed to come.

Wilson, excitement still evident, was answering her question. 'Just. One nil. Last-minute goal. But three points for us, that's what matters.'

'Good!' Holden said firmly. 'Very good!' The football conversation was over. 'Sorry to drag you in on a Saturday, but Dominic Russell has disappeared.'

'What do you mean by disappeared?' Fox asked.

'He left for work at 7.30 this morning and hasn't been seen since. His wife was sufficiently worried to ring us, though not until three o'clock this afternoon. He had left a note at work saying he'd be back later. His assistant, Francesca Willis, found it when she arrived late, round about 10.15. His mobile is turned off. So what I want you to do is get a list of any calls to or from his mobile in the last couple of days. And were there any calls to his office early this morning? Second, we need to see if we can track down any CCTV images of his car after he left his office this morning. This might have been any time from 7.45 until 10.15.'

'Do you reckon he's the killer, Guv, and done a runner?' The adrenalin from the football had still not entirely dissipated in Wilson's body.

Holden made a face. 'Wilson,' she said, 'what I reckon is that we need some evidence of Mr Russell's movements. And then maybe, just maybe, we can start to draw some conclusions. So do me a favour and get on with it.'

Sarah Russell liked a drink. It wasn't that she had a drink problem, but she liked to have a sherry or a gin and tonic at six o'clock in the evening. And then a glass or two of wine over supper. There was nothing abnormal in that, she told herself, and there was nothing abnormal in having one just a little bit early tonight. After all, she'd had one hell of a day, so when she got back home just after half past

five, there seemed no point in waiting for the magic hour of six, that
sun-over-the-yard-arm hour that had so dominated her father's life.
Hell, what difference did half an hour make?

She poured herself a generous portion of gin, added the
obligatory ice and slice of lemon, and topped it up with slim-line
tonic. And then she took a sip, and then another. God, it tasted
good!

The phone rang, and she jumped, the clear cold liquid in her
glass lurching wildly with her, and splashing down her blouse. She
swore, put the glass down with a bang on the table, and reached for
the handset.

'Who is it?' she demanded.

'It's me.' There was a brief silence. 'Have you had a bad day?'

'Dominic has gone missing.'

'Gone missing?' There was a stifled laugh down the phone line.
'You mean he's left you?'

'I didn't say that. But who knows. Maybe.'

'I bet you're hoping he has!' Again there was a laugh.

Sarah Russell picked up the glass, and took another deep slug
from it.

'Are you listening?' the caller demanded.

Of course she was listening. Not that she needed to. She knew
damn well what the little bastard was going to say, and she knew
how she ought to react. She had discussed it with Geraldine. At
length. But after the day she had had, what the hell.

'No,' she spat back. 'I haven't the slightest interest in listening to
you, you little shit. In fact, you're the one who's going to listen now.
This is the last time you ring me. Never, ever do it again. Because as
far as I am concerned, our nasty little relationship is over. And if I
get so much as a look from anyone at college that indicates to me
that you have been gossiping about me, I'll come after you, so help
me God! And you'll regret the day you ever tangled with me.'

With that, she terminated the call, drained the rest of her gin and
tonic, and for the second time in three days hurled her glass across
the room so that it smashed extravagantly against the marble

fireplace. She smiled. That felt good.

The phone rang again. She glared at it, and after a second ring, as if it could sense her hostility, it stopped. A fly on the wall, if it had been so minded, would have seen the tension in her face dissipate, and the fury give way to relief. She picked up the handset, punched in a number, and waited.

'Hi,' she said as soon her call was answered. 'I'm so glad you rang.'

While Detective Sergeant Fox began the search for CCTV coverage of the roads around the northern end of Oxford, Detective Constables Wilson and Lawson took on the more immediate task of sifting through the phone calls. The calls to the office phone proved to be the simplest task. There were only two of them before 10.15 a.m., one just before ten o'clock and one just after. Lawson rang both numbers, and both claimed to be customers; a Mrs Jane Railton had rung to check the opening times of D.R. Antiquities, as she lived in Witney and didn't want to make a wasted trip; and the other was a Mr Keith Nelson, who had wanted to ask if they had got any new stained glass in. 'Well, not new,' he had giggled, 'old of course, but new stock. When I called a couple of weeks ago, the girl behind the desk had said they were expecting some in soon. Nice girl, but her English was rather French, if you know what I mean.' Again there was a snort down the lines. Lawson smiled to herself. He was a bit like her Uncle Simon. Thought he was a bit of a card.

Wilson meanwhile was going methodically through the calls to and from Dominic Russell's mobile. An emailed list from the mobile company revealed that he had received only one call in the critical period that morning, at 8.16 from what turned out to be a pay-as-you-go mobile. The call had lasted two minutes and twenty seconds. The next one had been a call from his office number which had gone straight to his answering service – that must have been Francesca's call just after noon – and then another one from his home number about 1.20 p.m., presumably Sarah ringing to see if she could get hold of him after Francesca had rung her. That all tied up. As for the previous day, there had been only two calls to his mobile, one from his wife and one from his solicitor, James Turley. Wilson scanned further back through the list of calls, but nowhere could he see a call from that pay-as-you-go mobile. So that, surely, was the key one.

Holden listened carefully to the reports of her two constables, but she recognized, as they had, that there was nothing they could get their teeth into. Someone, someone who didn't want the call to be traced, had rung him, and very likely it was that call that had led to Dominic leaving D.R. Antiquities, but beyond that there was nothing. A big blank dead end. Holden sniffed. She thought maybe she was coming down with a cold. 'You'd better go and give Fox a hand,' she said with a wave of her hand. 'His car has got to be there somewhere on the CCTV.'

Holden was right, but nearly three hours passed before they finally located it. It had had to stop at the lights on the A40 at Cassington at 8.41 that morning.

'Where was he going?'

It was the obvious question, but there was no obvious answer.

'Not the Channel, and not any of the obvious airports,' Fox said. There were several airports that an Oxford resident might use if he or she wanted to go abroad – Heathrow, Gatwick, Luton, Birmingham, even Stansted – but none of them was in that direction.

'Which suggests,' Lawson suggested, 'that he is more likely have been going to meet someone. Presumably whoever it was that called from the pay-as-you-go mobile.'

Holden nodded. 'I agree. The question is where did he go after Cassington. To Burford, to Cheltenham? Or maybe on to the M5 and then north or south from there?'

'We could get more CCTV from the A40 heading west,' Wilson volunteered. 'We know the timeframe, so if he did go as far as Cheltenham, it should be easy enough to spot him.'

Holden looked at her watch. 'Maybe, but I guess we all need

some beauty sleep. Let's call it a day.'

'Do you want us in tomorrow, Guv?'

Holden stood up, and arched her shoulder back, trying to loosen her tightened muscles. If Dominic had just done a runner with a woman, Sunday working was hardly justified. But if it wasn't that banal? If he was involved in the murders, or the elusive painting? She yawned. 'Let's sleep on it. I'll let you know in the morning.'

Glebe Barn stands about half a mile from the A40, up a narrow and easily overlooked lane which the eagle-eyed west-bound driver may spot shortly after passing through the Cassington crossroads. It is a lane known and used only by locals and keen map-readers. If you were to turn right off the A40 as you headed towards Witney, this single-tracked road would take you some 150 metres north before turning 90 degrees west, and then after barely 50 metres cutting back again on itself by some 120 degrees. By now, neatly cropped hedges will have given way to a dense deciduous woodland which presses on both sides of the road. The wood does not spread far from the road, but it provides a deep enough and thick enough cover to attract muntjac and roe deer. And it was in search of these that Jim Sturrock came that Sunday morning, and indeed of any other four-legged or winged quarry that he might come across. He came silently and stealthily, moving along the edge of the wood, every sense alert and on edge. For Jim Sturrock was an amateur photographer.

That morning, however, there were no deer to be seen or disturbed. Wood pigeon gave away their presence by their cooing, and a couple of cock pheasants took off noisily some ten metres in front of him, but there was nothing that caused him to even consider raising his camera. He proceeded along the edge of the wood, following it as it bent round to the right, until it came to an old Cotswold stone building. He had noticed it when he had been studying his map the previous evening. He had assumed that it would have by now been converted into an overblown country retreat for a city trader or celebrity chef, but in fact it had somehow managed to escape the intrusion of development, and it stood there, sheltered and half hidden by the lowering trees, almost apologetic in its isolation. Jim Sturrock's spirits lifted – it was, surely, ideal owl territory. A five-barred gate separated it from the field along whose edge he had been walking, but even at the age of nearly fifty he prided himself on his fitness, and he clambered over it with alacrity. It was then that he noticed the car, a Renault Scenic if he wasn't mistaken, which was parked away to the left. He froze, uncertain what to do. He hadn't bothered to track down the owner of the land to get permission to walk the area, because in his experience he was more likely to have been told to 'bugger off'. However, as he waited there, his anxiety receded. There was no sign of the driver of the car, and the several rabbits that he could see browsing the grass suggested no one had been wandering around the area for a little while.

In the centre of the barn wall that faced him were a pair of very substantial double doors. He advanced carefully towards them. A metal bar was firmly set in the horizontal position, holding the doors securely shut. Jim noticed this, and felt relief. The barn must be empty. The car's passenger or passengers could hardly have locked themselves in.

He lifted the bar with great care and pulled on the right-hand door. It opened with surprising ease, and he slipped inside. It took a few seconds for his eyes to adjust to the dim light, but when they had he saw the barn was largely empty. A single agricultural machine, a harrow, was stored there in the corner, and a few bales were ranged along the far wall. But the thing that caught his attention was the long ladder propped up against the loft floor above. He walked over to it, and started to climb, conscious that it might be a good vantage point if there were any owls around, and if not, at least a safe and undisturbed place for a sandwich and a cup of tea. In the event, however, Jim Sturrock did no tea drinking and no sandwich eating, for within seconds of reaching the top of the ladder, was hurrying down it and then across the barn floor, fighting with himself as he did so, for the bile was rising uncontrollably in his throat. With a gasp of effort he pushed hard at the door, hurled himself outside, and then vomited violently on to the ground.

CHAPTER 8

Dr Karen Pointer was in a foul mood. As if Susan's non-appearance the night before hadn't been bad enough, to be woken up at 8.30 a.m. by a phone call from Holden's eager-beaver sidekick Lawson was the ruddy limit. She knew as soon as she heard Lawson's bouncy voice that it wasn't just her Saturday night that had gone up the spout. Her Sunday was about to do exactly the same. There was another body, Lawson explained briefly, confirming her worst fears. It was just off the A40 on the way to Witney. Could she just come and take a look?

Could she just take a look? Well, it wasn't as if she could say 'no!' now was it? Not that she had expressed this thought to Lawson, but as she made her way out of Oxford and along the A40, she chuntered away to herself. Could she just take a look? What was Detective Constable bleeding Lawson talking about? The words of a conversation she would have liked to have had with Lawson began to bounce around the inside of her head, and then to reverberate around the car like angry hornets. Talking out loud to herself when no one else was around was a habit she had picked up in childhood, and clung to ever since, a way of letting off steam when there was no other safe way. Could she just take a look! Oh yes, of course, Constable! As if it'd only take ten minutes, and then she'd be heading back to Oxford in time for a mid-morning cappuccino! Yeah, right! In your bloody dreams, Detective Constable Lawson! She was driving faster than she should have been, but what the hell. If it was important enough to wreck her Sunday, then it was important enough for her to take liberties with the ridiculous speed limit. She put her foot down as her emotional temperature entered the danger zone, and flicked past a Morris Minor out for a Sunday morning crawl. What a shitty weekend this was turning out to be! Damn! Her right foot hit the brake. Fuck! The Cassington lights were, she suddenly realized, diminishing rapidly in her rear mirror, and the narrow lane which she should have been looking out for was about to flash past too. Her right foot hurriedly switched pedals, and she felt the brakes bite and the vehicle shudder, and for a moment it was touch and go. There was a squeal from her tyres, as they lurched through the 90-degree turn, but they gripped the road hard and tight. An oncoming white van flashed its lights, provoking an adrenalin-fuelled snarl from Pointer and a single-fingered salute. 'Fuck you,' she shouted, but the white van had already swung out of her line of vision, to be replaced by a pitted road surface and a fast-looming stone wall. But she had the car under control now. She twisted the steering wheel anti-clockwise as she followed the tight left-hand corner, and then sharply clockwise as an even tighter right-hander presented itself. She pressed the accelerator down to the floor as she came out of the bend, and then almost instantly had to brake as she realized, with sudden disappointment, that she had arrived. Some thirty metres in front of her, a uniformed copper was standing on the left-hand side of the road, next to an open gateway, a cigarette in his mouth.

Slowing down even more, she swung into it, acknowledging him with a barely visible nod, as if he too was at fault for everything that was wrong with her life. The short track on which she found herself was bordered to its left by thronging trees, and to its right by the towering side of a large stone building which Pointer, with all the insight of a townie out of her natural environment, categorized as a barn. Once past it, she swung right, bumping into the rough area which was now serving as a car park behind the barn. She was gratified to see four pairs of eyes turn expectantly towards her. But she made no acknowledgement, for – with the suddenness of a switch being flicked – she had entered work mode, and her brain had engaged with the process of a preliminary survey of the area. The people were not in themselves important, though she was glad to see that there was tape up, and that they were waiting this side of it. No doubt Susan had taken a look round, but she did hope the others hadn't been clod-hopping all over the scene.

Holden was moving forward towards her, half raising her hand in greeting – or maybe it was a sign of apology or peace. Pointer raised a hand in response, cut the engine, and climbed down.

'At least it's not raining,' Holden said with a smile.

Pointer moved to the back of her vehicle, opened the boot, and extracted some white overalls. Holden stood silently by, watching her as she kitted herself up, pulling on the overalls, zipping them up, adjusting the hood, and then turning her attention to her white wellingtons.

'Sorry to spoil our weekend.' Holden said this quietly, leaning closer to Pointer as she spoke, to ensure privacy. The comment made Pointer look up sharply, temporarily forgetting the job in hand. Our weekend, she'd said, not your weekend. Our weekend. One word – one letter even – made all the difference. She busied herself with her footwear again, pulling, and adjusting and tucking in the trousers, until she was satisfied, and she stood up.

'Is there any chance of you catching this bloody killer?' she asked, but there was a sparkle in her eyes. 'All work and no play. . . .' She didn't finish the sentence. There was no need, and besides, Mr Misery, a.k.a. Sergeant Fox, was advancing ominously towards them. 'Anyway,' she said, raising her voice, 'do you know who it is?'

'Yes. Dominic Russell.'

'Oh!' Holden had, of course, talked to her about both of the Russells. Not that she knew Dominic, but she had once bought a rather lovely Caughley blue and white jug off him when he was based in Jericho. She thought she remembered him from then, a rather florid, extravagant man. Anyway, she'd soon know.

'Mind your feet,' Holden said quickly, as they approached the double doors, which had now been propped open wide, allowing the improving morning light in. Her right hand pointed out the pile of vomit in front of them. 'That belongs to the man who found the body.'

'That's a shame,' Pointer said, thinking of the DNA possibilities that might have been.

'Well, the victim is a bit of a mess,' Holden said in explanation. Pointer looked around, but couldn't see a body, but Holden was continuing to explain. 'So it must have been quite a shock for the poor guy, when all he was looking for was a barn owl to photograph. He went up the ladder, and found rather more than he had bargained for.' Holden was gesturing towards a long ladder propped against an upper floor. This loft ran for perhaps one-third of the length of the barn. It was, Pointer could appreciate, a good vantage point for a man with a camera, but she wondered what had brought Dominic Russell out here and up the ladder. Or rather who?

She walked slowly across the floor, scanning it for anything unusual or out of place, and delaying the moment she would have to put her hands on the ladder and start to pull herself up rung by rung, pretending that she felt no fear. Don't look down, she said to herself, as she felt the metal of the aluminium ladder. It was cold to the touch, but her hands were clammy with sweat. Don't look down. Don't look down. She kept repeating the phrase under her breath, in the hope that like a mantra it would transform her to some other state of being for as long as it took her to get to the top.

When she got there, she eased herself carefully off the ladder and on to the loft floor, and then stumbled forward away from the edge, three or four steps. She steadied herself, straightened up, and stood still for several seconds as she looked around. At least that is what she told herself she was doing – looking round, familiarizing herself with the scene, and assessing what would need to be done. But in reality, she was trying to regain equilibrium. She forced herself to breathe deeply until the intense feelings of vertigo had dissipated, and she tried to banish from her mind the dreadful knowledge that she'd have to go down the ladder when she had dealt with the body.

But dead bodies were what she understood, and she turned to examine the outstretched corpse of Dominic Russell with a feeling that was almost elation. A dead man with, as she could immediately see, a gunshot wound in his head – that was the sort of thing she could lose herself in. And it was the man she had bought her jug off.

So successfully did she lose herself in her work, that it was only some quarter of an hour later, when Holden called up to her slightly impatiently – 'How are you getting on, Karen?' – that she stood up and noticed, a couple of metres away, an oil painting lying face up on the floor. Its canvas was disfigured by four slashes, two diagonally from one corner to the other, and two on the other diagonal.

'I need a couple more minutes,' she shouted down, 'and then I'll need some help to get this body down.' But her attention was now on the painting. She had already bagged a firearm, but where was the knife that had slashed the painting? Because that might provide some interesting forensics. She couldn't initially see one, but there was loose straw scattered across the floor, and soon, sure enough, she spotted it. Her sense of excitement grew as she crouched down to examine it. It had a plain wooden handle with brass fitting, and a slim steel blade about fifteen centimetres in length. It looked bloody sharp and it looked too, from its proportions, to be a strong contender for the blade that had killed both Maria Tull and Jack Smith. She'd have to do some careful measuring and testing, of course, but if her suspicions proved correct, this could be the bloody jackpot!

It was, Holden had decided in the car, becoming an all too familiar pattern, her turning up at the door of a stranger, or in this case not quite a stranger, and having to explain that someone very close to that person had been killed. She had met Sarah twice, and she hadn't exactly warmed to her, but that didn't make it any easier to be the bearer of bad news. Assuming, of course, that it was bad news to Sarah, or indeed news at all. For Sarah had to be a suspect too, surely, as the far from loving wife of this latest corpse. But one mustn't judge. That was what her mother would say, but didn't everyone make judgements all the time? And the bottom line was that, from what little she had seen and what she had heard, the marriage of Sarah and Dominic Russell hadn't exactly been made in heaven. Maybe it had, like most, started full of optimism and hope, but had long since degenerated into a thousand little resentments and bitter compromises. Not that you needed to marry, she reminded herself, to go through that.

The door opened almost immediately in response to Holden's ringing of the bell. Sarah Russell must have seen them arrive.

'May we come in?' Holden asked quickly, skipping the pleasantries. This wasn't something to be discussed on the doorstep.

Sarah Russell said nothing, retreating into her house and allowing Holden and Fox to follow her. Wilson and Lawson, who had followed them along the A40 and into this residential side street not far north of the Summertown shops, had been detailed to go and knock on some neighbours' doors. Sarah led her guests through to the living room and gestured towards the armchairs and sofa, offering them a choice of comfort. She, however, walked over to the fireplace and stood in front of it, legs astride, her left hand on her hip, while with her right one she rubbed intently on the side of her neck.

'Have you found him?' she said. Her tone was matter of fact, almost disinterested, as if she was asking visitors if they had a good trip and hoping they wouldn't go into any detail in their reply.

'We have.'

'And?'

It was a funny way to ask if your husband was dead, Fox reckoned. 'And?' Mind you, she was a pretty funny woman, was Mrs Russell. And a tough one.

'I'm afraid your husband is dead,' Holden said. It was a blunt statement, though she hoped it didn't sound too bluntly put. But how else do you say the unspeakable?

Sarah let out a gasp, and then turned away towards the fireplace, with the consequence that neither Holden nor Fox could see her face, or the emotion on it – whether fake or real.

'How?' she said, through what appeared to be a muffled sob.

'We found him in an old barn on the way to Witney.'

Sarah Russell turned back, and the only emotion visible was anger. 'Christ, I said how, not where. For fuck's sake, tell me straight. Was he stabbed like the others?!'

'Sorry,' Holden said involuntarily. Apologizing wasn't exactly second nature to her, but the ferocity of Sarah Russell's response had thrown her right off balance. 'He was shot,' she continued hastily, 'in the head at close range. Until the pathologist has had a chance to look more closely, we can't be sure if it was suicide or . . . or murder.'

'Do you want me to identify him?'

'At some stage, but there's no doubt, I'm afraid.'

'The stupid bastard,' she said. 'The stupid, stupid bastard!' And then, quite unexpectedly, her legs folded under her and she collapsed on to the floor with a whimpering cry.

The rest of Sunday was a write-off as far as Holden was concerned. As well as falling dramatically to the floor, Sarah Russell managed to crack her forehead on the edge of the marble hearth. Her blood had flowed red and messily on to the white rug – why the hell do people have white rugs, Holden asked herself irritably – and Holden and Fox had found themselves driving her up to the John Radcliffe Hospital at speed. Their rank at least ensured that they jumped the queue, but a diagnosis of concussion and shock for Sarah ensured there could be no further questioning that day.

While they were still waiting at the hospital, Holden had received a call on her mobile from Lawson, ringing in to report the results of Wilson's and her house to house. 'There's one interesting piece of information that you might want to follow up, Guv,' she had said, in a tone of voice that suggested that she was feeling rather pleased with herself. 'A Mrs Leighton, from just across the road, insists that Sarah left home yesterday morning shortly after Dominic. She saw her car leave round about 7.45 a.m. So no lying in that Saturday morning for Sarah. Despite what she implied when we talked to her yesterday.'

Lawson, Holden was fast coming to realize, had a very impressive head for detail. 'OK, Lawson, I think that's as much as we need do for now. We'll be taking Mrs Russell home shortly, but can you just call in on Dr Bennett on your way home? Wilson knows where she lives. If she's not there, leave a note. We need to get her to look at the damaged painting tomorrow. In the morning, if possible. Offer to pick her up in a car. After that, you can have the rest of today off.'

'Oh, thanks, Guv,' came the reply. There was, Holden reckoned, an unusual note of sarcasm in Lawson's voice, but that was hardly a surprise. It was already mid afternoon, and it was Sunday.

'My pleasure, Lawson,' she replied, but only when she heard the line go dead.

'So, was it suicide or murder?'

It was Sunday evening, and Mrs Jane Holden asked the question just after swallowing the last spoonful of fruit salad in her bowl. Both her daughter and Karen Pointer had already finished, and had gone into what Mr Holden would have called conversational reserve, had he been alive and sitting at the table with them.

Susan had been staring at her three-quarters empty wine glass since she had finished eating. She had insisted she didn't want to talk shop during the meal, but her mother had no intention of allowing that embargo to extend beyond the final mouthful of food. Susan suddenly raised the glass to her lips and drained the rest of its contents, before placing it down on the table with a clump. She leant forward, grasped the bottle of red wine, and refilled her glass. 'Anyone else?' she asked waving the bottle in the air.

'I've had enough,' her mother said pointedly.

'Just a little,' Karen said, stretching across and taking the bottle gently from her. She poured herself about a third of a glass, and then placed the bottle to her right, out of her friend's reach.

'Well?' Mrs Holden said firmly, looking at Karen. 'Which is it?'

'Well,' said Karen slowly, 'I'm not sure that's for me to say.' She turned to her left. 'Susan?'

'My daughter,' said Mrs Holden, as she wiped her mouth on her napkin, 'is not in a chatty mood. As you will discover, Karen, it is one of her enduring characteristics, learnt, I fear, from her father.'

'I don't mind silence,' Karen responded, and immediately realized she was defending Susan.

'Silence is one thing,' came the reply, 'but meal times should be social occasions.'

Susan Holden looked up from her glass, and smiled aggressively at her mother. 'I was thinking, Mother, not just being silent.'

'That's what your father used to say.'

'I know.' And she smiled again.

'And he used to drink too much!'

'For God's sake, Mother, I'm allowed to drink. I'm off duty, in case you hadn't noticed.' And to prove her point, she took a swig from her glass. 'Now, Karen, for God's sake just tell her all about it, while I carry on thinking.'

Karen Pointer took the tiniest sip from her glass, and then began to speak, slowly and methodically. She hoped that by doing so she might somehow cause the hostility between mother and daughter to dissipate. It was the first time she had experienced it, and she hated it. Because she loved Susan, and because she had already become fond of her mother too. 'Dominic Russell was shot at very close range. The gun must have been virtually touching his skin. You can tell by the powder burns on the skin, and the nature of the entrance wound in the head. Death would have been instantaneous.'

'So he could have shot himself?' Mrs Holden did not believe in keeping questions for the end.

'Yes. He could have. But there's no certainty.'

'What about fingerprints on the gun, or DNA or whatever?'

'If we could find traces of someone else, then that would be significant, because if someone else was there, then murder becomes the favourite. But so far the only traces we've got are from Dominic, which means that we can't tell conclusively whether it's murder or suicide.'

'Tell her about the painting,' Susan said loudly, before taking another swig from her glass. 'Tell her about the damn painting.'

'There was a painting near the body,' Karen said quickly. 'We don't know much about it yet. It looks quite old, painted in oils, and it had been badly slashed with a knife, diagonally both ways.'

'Why on earth would someone do that?'

'Maybe they didn't bloody like it!' Susan's loud interruption caused both her companions to look at her, and then at each other as if to gauge their next move. Susan was oblivious of the atmosphere she was creating, and she drained the last of her glass again, and again clumped it noisily down on the table.

'Was the painting valuable?' Mrs Holden asked, but not of her daughter.

'We don't know, yet,' Karen replied quickly. She hadn't seen Susan like this before, and she wasn't sure how to handle the situation, but she couldn't let it drift. She stood up, and turned towards Susan. 'We've both had a long day. Time to be going, I think.'

Susan looked up at her, and her eyes blinked. For a moment, Karen feared she was going to receive another blast of aggression, but the face that looked at her did so with a blank expression and a watery smile. She raised herself slowly to her feet, a naughty child suddenly realizing she has gone too far, and nodded towards her mother. 'Thank you for supper,' she said, and began to make her way uncertainly towards the door. She tripped, and half fell, but managed to right herself. Karen quickly moved forward, grabbing her arm. 'Steady!' she said.

'Christ, I feel sick,' Susan replied, just before she was.

When Holden walked into her office the next morning just after eight o'clock, her nausea of the previous night was a thing of

141

unpleasant memory only. Sometimes being sick is the best option. Throw it up and get it out of your system. Though she doubted her mother would have seen it like that. She ought to ring and apologize. She looked at her watch. Maybe later.

At half past eight, the rest of her team rolled in, gathering in her room with their first coffees of the day. Dr Bennett, she was told, had been hosting a family get-together on the previous day.

'It was her birthday,' Lawson chirped eagerly. 'Lovely lady, isn't she. She asked us in and showed us the cake.'

'We arranged to pick her up at eleven,' said Wilson, intervening. Sometimes he reckoned Lawson got a bit sidetracked by trivialities.

'It's a lovely house too,' Lawson continued enthusiastically. 'Even if it's a bit Bohemian.'

Holden nodded. She felt frustrated that Dr Bennett wasn't immediately on tap. It was vital to know more about this painting, and in particular how valuable it was. And she also needed Karen to shed some more light on Dominic Russell's death, and sooner rather than later. Not that she could fault Karen. She had left for work shortly before seven, waking her up just before she left with a hot cup of tea, a kiss on the forehead, and not a single word of reproach. God, she was lucky!

'Eleven is fine,' she acknowledged, shifting back to the present moment. 'We've plenty to do.' Which was true. For a start, she needed a proper chat with Sarah Russell. No, cancel that. Not a chat. What she needed, and was going to do, was her damnedest to get some straight answers to some straight questions, such as where had Sarah Russell been going to at 7.45 that Saturday morning when her typical Saturday started with a lie-in. In fact, she needed, they all needed, to take a close look at Sarah Russell. She wouldn't be the first or last – woman to kill her husband, and if the painting was very valuable, and he had been planning on selling it behind her back, well, it wasn't hard to imagine how – if she'd found out – that might have been enough to tip her over the edge. All this assumed, of course, that Dominic Russell hadn't blown his own brains out. Which brought her back to Karen.

*

Holden managed to resist the temptation to pick up the phone and start punching in the numbers until 9.45 a.m. She had originally decided she would wait for Karen to ring her, but she had spoken on the phone to Sarah Russell just after nine o'clock, and they had agreed that Fox and she would call round about ten thirty. It was, Susan had decided, a good time to arrive, as if they were old friends dropping in socially, at what her mother would have called coffee and chin-wag time.

'Sorry to chase up like this,' she said when Karen answered the phone. 'It's just that—'

'It's just that you've got three unexplained deaths on your hands and you need some help. No need to apologize, Susan. To be honest, I expected a phone call some time ago.'

'Oh!'

'I'm afraid I can't pretend that things have moved along very far. As we discussed, the injury is consistent with him having shot himself, but if someone had been able to get close to him, that person could have put a gun up close to his head and . . . bang!'

'How about the angle of entry? Doesn't that help. In terms of probability, which way does it point?' She was aware even as she spoken that a tone of desperation had entered into her voice. She heard a sound in her ear that might have been a sigh.

'I can't say for definite one way or another. And I can't give you odds, Susan. I'm not a bookie at the greyhounds. The way things are, unless or until we come up with something more at our end, you need to keep an open mind.'

'What about the time of death?'

'Ah, I thought that might be your next question. Again, I'm not able to be a huge help. Given that he wasn't found until Sunday morning and rigor mortis was fully established, the best we can do is make a judgement from his stomach contents. But assuming that he had breakfast no later than seven o'clock that morning, all I can say is that there is no sign of any more recent meal. Breakfast had been pretty much fully digested by the time of death, so I guess that leaves the time slot pretty wide. Let's say after nine o'clock, and before noon. Probably.'

'Probably?'

'Sorry!'

'Thanks,' she said, speaking without even a hint of irony.

'Thanks? I'm not sure I've been much help.'

'No, you haven't,' she agreed firmly. 'But I wanted to say thanks anyway, Doctor.'

'I appreciate it, Inspector.'

'Sorry about yesterday.'

For the second day running, DI Holden and DS Fox were seated in Sarah Russell's living room. This time, their host and interviewee chose, to Holden's relief, to sit opposite them rather than stand in front of the fireplace. The only obvious reminder of her fall was a plaster on the side of her forehead, and the livid swelling underneath it.

'I hope you're feeling up to this?' Holden replied. It was a politeness only. She wasn't about to get up and leave if Sarah said she wasn't.

'I've felt better.' Of course she'd felt better.

'I hope it won't take long.'

'In that case, why don't you get on with it?' The fall had clearly not knocked the aggressive streak out of her. 'You could start by telling me if it was suicide or murder.'

'I'm afraid we still aren't sure about that.'

'Great!' The fall hadn't damaged her capacity to do sarcasm either. Holden wondered if this was delayed shock, or a ruse to divert them, or just normal service resumed. She glanced at Fox, a pre-arranged signal. He was sitting with a notebook open on his knees.

'When we spoke to you on Saturday,' he said carefully, 'you said your husband left home that morning at 7.30. Is that correct?'

'As near as damn it.'

'And that was the last time you saw him.'

'Of course.'

'And you went back to bed till when?'

Suspicion raised its head in Sarah Russell's head. He knew something. This was not a detective going through the motions, ticking off the questions and counting the seconds until he could be out the door and off to the next interview.

'Who says I went back to bed?'

Fox looked down at his notes. 'What you said was: "Saturday is my chance of a lie-in". So I was assuming that meant that you went back to bed.'

'Is that what policemen do – make assumptions?'

Fox didn't rise. He wasn't going to answer her question because he knew from experience that when interviewees got aggressive, there is always a reason. Sometimes it was fear, but this woman showed no sign of that. So he smiled back at her, and deliberately paused. He never got to respond, however, because Holden cut in. She was not prepared to play softball.

'You clearly led us to believe that you had a lie-in on Saturday.' She leant forward as she spoke, and she stabbed her forefinger abruptly towards Sarah. 'That's a fact, not an assumption. And another fact is that one of your neighbours saw you driving off from here at approximately 7.45 a.m. So perhaps you would be kind enough to explain the discrepancy.'

'I went to the supermarket. I needed some things.'

'Which one?'

'Sainsbury's. In Kidlington.'

'What did you get?'

'What did I get?' There was a note of surprise in her voice. 'What the hell has that got to do with my husband's death?'

'Do you have the receipt?'

'Do you keep your receipts, Inspector?'

'Yes, I do. Did you pay with cash or by card?'

'What?'

'We're trying to establish your alibi, Mrs Russell. You're an intelligent woman, so I expect you've worked that out. Is there any person or any thing that can confirm that you were in Sainsbury's on Saturday, and the time you were there?'

'No!' Mrs Sarah Russell was indeed an intelligent woman, and she realized it was time to come clean, at least partially. 'But I do have an alibi for after that. I went to see Alan Tull.'

'I see,' Holden replied, though of course she didn't see. She didn't see at all. 'Can I ask why you visited him?'

'We're part of an amateur dramatics society. Alan is due to direct *An Inspector Calls* and I wanted to know if he was still up for it. In the circumstances, I thought he might want to pull out, and as the chair of the society I needed to check it out.'

'So how long were you with him?'

'I must have got there between half-nine and quarter to ten. He made us some coffee, and we sat and chatted until maybe eleven thirty, and then I went home.'

'And he'll confirm that?'

'Yes. Why shouldn't he?'

Holden nodded. It would be easy to check out, but if they were in some sort of relationship, they'd protect each other, wouldn't they? And if they were in some sort of relationship, what did that do to the investigation, not to mention their motives.

'Can you give me his mobile number then?'

Sarah looked at her inquisitor warily. 'If you want. But you must know where he lives.'

'It'll save time,' Holden said firmly. 'I could ring the police station, because we'll have it in the files, but if you give it to me, Fox can give him a quick ring, and if he doesn't answer we can try the surgery, and that way Dr Tull can confirm your alibi – for that period only of course – while we are still here.' And before you can tip him off, she might have added.

Sarah Russell shrugged, as if unconcerned. 'Be my guest, Sergeant. The address book is by the phone in the kitchen.'

It took Fox less than five minutes to get hold of Dr Alan Tull and to receive from him confirmation of Sarah Russell's visit, including the approximate timing of it and its purpose. Either they were very well organized, or she was telling the truth. Fox was disappointed. He disliked the woman, and had done since he had first clapped eyes on her. She was far too sharp and combative for his taste, and it would have given him the greatest pleasure to trip her up. The idea of her being the killer of her husband, not to mention Maria Tull and Jack Smith, appealed to his sense of justice. But they needed evidence. He made a face, and then scratched his cheek, realizing as he did so that he'd forgotten to shave that morning. Sainsbury's? Did she really go there? His eyes roved slowly round the kitchen, like a camera panning a long, slow shot, and they stopped only when they reached the fridge. The metaphorical camera zoomed in until only the fridge was in frame. Fox walked over and pulled the door open. He picked up the four-pint plastic milk bottle in the door, examined it and put it back. He did the same to a tub of dairy-free spread, briefly prising its lid off. There were two small pots of yoghurts which he also picked up, before shutting the fridge door.

Back in the sitting room, Holden and Sarah Russell turned as one when he reappeared.

'Did you get hold of him?' It was Sarah Russell who asked this, her voice demanding and impatient.

'Yes,' Fox replied. 'Dr Tull confirmed what you said. There was a little variance in his timings, but nothing significant.'

'Well, thank God for that.'

Holden stood up. She had spent the time probing Sarah about her relationship with both Alan and Maria Tull, but right now there was nothing more to be asked.

'In that case, we'll be off,' she said.

'Actually, I've got one more question, Guv.'

'Oh?' She was surprised. They hadn't pre-planned anything.

'All right, Sergeant,' Sarah Russell said, her voice dripping with the condescension she normally reserved for the students of Cornforth. 'What is it then?'

'With respect, madam,' he said calmly, 'I was wondering what precisely it was that you bought on your trip to Sainsbury's. It's just it certainly wasn't milk or soya spread, both of which are running very low in your fridge, and it wasn't yoghurts, because the only two in your fridge are now past their sell-by date.'

'Oh dear, what a shame!' Dr Eleanor Bennett's first reaction to the damaged painting was human rather than analytical. Lawson, standing in the proverbial wings, thought it rather quaint. It was the sort of thing her mum would say on discovering a snagged piece of wool in her cardigan, or a chip in the rim of one of her teacups. 'What a shame!' Dr Bennett repeated the phrase, but this time there was a stress on the first word, an indication that perhaps Lawson might have underestimated what the phrase might mean coming from the lips of someone other than her mother.

Lawson had picked her up at eleven o'clock, though not precisely. It was difficult to be anywhere in Oxford precisely at any time, unless you aimed to be early. And then, of course, every set of lights would be in your favour, every delivery lorry that typically obstructed the narrow streets whenever you were in a hurry would have magically disappeared, and you would arrive stupidly early. If you were an ordinary member of the public, you would then have to run the risk of an overofficious civil enforcement officer – as traffic wardens were now called in Oxford – slapping a penalty notice on your windscreen while you popped inside to discover the person you were picking up wasn't actually ready. That, at least, was one thing Lawson didn't have to worry about. And anyway, Dr Bennett was absolutely ready when Lawson rang her bell at 11.01 a.m. The trip to the laboratory had been straightforward in terms of traffic, and also in terms of social intercourse, as Dr Bennett and Constable Lawson chatted happily away. Once at their destination, they were ushered through a series of fire doors, until they came to a room in the centre of which stood a rectangular Formica-topped table. It was on this table that the object of their interest lay.

The painting was relatively small, no more than 60 centimetres square, and it had been slashed twice in a diagonal direction, from top left to bottom right. It had also been slashed twice on the opposite diagonal, with the result that where the cuts intersected a piece of canvas had been entirely dislodged.

Dr Bennett looked up at Lawson, peering over the top of her glasses. 'Why don't you go and find us a nice cup of tea, Constable, while I have a really good look. Black, no sugar for me.'

'Sure,' Lawson replied, though she wasn't sure at all. She would like to be there, watching and learning, and making sure. . . .

'Don't worry,' Dr Bennett smiled, as if reading her mind 'I know it is evidence. I won't touch it. I promise.'

Lawson nodded, and moved away. In that case, the sooner she got the tea and returned, the better. In the event, when she did return, Dr Bennett was bent over the picture, a small torch in her left hand, and she was moving slowly around the surface, as if taking in every detail.

'Here's your tea,' Lawson said, when Dr Bennett showed no sign of being aware of her return.

'Thank you.'

Lawson began to sip at her own polystyrene cup, but waited in vain for any response. Patience, she knew, was not one of her virtues and she had to fight the temptation to interrupt. Inactivity was alien to her, so she tried to think. Why anyone should want to damage this painting like this. She had no idea how valuable it would have been in pristine condition, but why do this to it? It must have been worth quite a lot. Maria Tull must have thought so when she wheedled it off Jack Smith. Because this was, no question, the painting that Jack Smith had described. And wouldn't Dominic Russell have known it was valuable? So why would anyone slash it so ferociously? Why not keep it? It was beyond reason.

'Ugh, it's cold.' Dr Bennett made a face as she belatedly sipped at her cup.

'It started hot.' Lawson wasn't going to be blamed for the temperature of the woman's damned tea.

The older woman smiled, and put it down.

'So, Constable, I can see you're a smart one, so why don't you tell me what you see in the picture.'

Lawson looked at her, and wondered if she was teasing her, the academic blue-stocking patronizing her because she was young and hadn't been to university and it showed.

'Let's start with when. Look at the clothes, look at the background. What sort of world are we in?'

Lawson paused, though not because she was uncertain. The clothing was a giveaway. 'The Bible.'

'Good. Have you any idea who the women are? How old are they do you think?'

Lawson leant forward and peered at them closely. The two women were standing close to each other, looking down on the man. The one to the left of the picture was resting her left hand on the other woman's shoulder, consoling her. That much seemed pretty clear, Lawson thought. The man was lying on a trestle, and appeared to be dead – or was he just ill? It was hard to be sure because one of the cuts had gone straight through his head. She looked back at the women. 'Quite old. Maybe late forties, or early fifties.'

'And the man?'

'Younger.'

'Young enough to be a son of one of them, I think.' This was a statement, not a question.

'Is it Jesus? Only he was put in a tomb, and this looks more like someone's house.'

'No, you're right, it's not Jesus. The clue is here, lying on the ground, in the corner. It's hard to see under the dirt, but I don't think there's any doubt.'

She stepped back, as if to encourage Lawson to lean forward and take another, closer look. 'But don't touch!' she added, a mischievous note in her voice.

'God!' Lawson said, and immediately wished she hadn't. Taking the name of the Lord in vain, that would have met with her father's loud disapproval. But there was no mistaking what the artist had depicted. 'It's a noose.'

'So?'

'Judas hanged himself.'

'Don't tell me I am in the presence of a policewoman who attended Sunday school. That would be unusual.'

Lawson was tempted to tell her that Sunday School was a rather old-fashioned expression, but she knew it wouldn't be polite. Children's groups was what they had been called where she had come from. Instead, she shrugged and merely said, 'My father was a vicar.'

'Ah!' Dr Bennett took off her oval glasses and rubbed them with a handkerchief that manifested itself as if by magic in her hand. 'You didn't want to become a woman of the cloth?'

Lawson made a choking noise that could have been a laugh killed at birth, and her faced flushed red.

'I doubt this scene is one you've ever come across in Sunday School, though,' Dr Bennett continued.

'No,' Lawson said. She was leaning forward again, her attention fully directed towards the painting. She would have liked to be able to answer the question, but she was stumped. She turned towards her mentor, and rather irritably admitted defeat. 'So if one of the women is his mother, who is the other one?'

'Ah!' Dr Bennett said again. She was looking, not at the painting, but at Lawson, a twinkle in her eyes. She liked the girl. She liked her enthusiasm, and intensity, and even her impatience. Her uncle had this expression that he would trot out: the wildest colts made the best horses. Well, it applied to fillies too.

'I believe,' Dr Bennett said eventually, her voice betraying her considerable excitement, 'she is Mary, the mother of Jesus.'

'That's not in the Bible,' Lawson said firmly.

'No,' came the soft reply. 'I don't suppose it is.'

Later, after she had returned Elizabeth Bennett back to her house, where she guiltily accepted the offer of a cup of tea with a piece of leftover birthday cake before returning to Cowley Station, Detective Constable Lawson brought her boss up to date. Holden listened without interruption, her concentration intense. Throughout it, her right hand fiddled incessantly with the left collar of her blouse. It was a mannerism Lawson had never noticed before, and she found it oddly disturbing. When Lawson fell silent, Holden nodded, fmally let go of her collar, and leant back, straightening her shoulders and stretching herself.

'You haven't said who the artist was?'

'Dr Bennett didn't know. Whoever painted it didn't sign it. Maybe, because of the subject matter, he wanted to be incognito.'

'Or she!'

'Or she,' Lawson repeated, accepting the correction. 'Technically, it's not of the greatest quality. Looking at the frame, she thought maybe nineteenth century.'

'To cut to the chase, how much does the estimable Dr Bennett think the painting would have been worth in its undamaged state?'

Lawson straightened herself in her seat, subconsciously mimicking her superior. 'She didn't want to be tied down to that. She's says she an art historian, not a valuation expert, but you're talking at least four figures, possibly five. Sterling.'

'I see. And in its current state?'

'Less, obviously. She said it's amazing what a top-notch restorer can achieve. To you or me, it could be made to look like it had never happened. But you're probably talking about five to six thousand for a top-quality repair job.'

Holden stood up and walked over to the window. The Oxford Road was surprisingly quiet. She placed her hands behind her neck, then pressed her elbows back, trying to release some of the tension in her shoulders. It was valuable enough for Maria Tull to have wanted some of the action. She could see that. But was it worth murdering for? Was it really valuable enough for someone to kill her and Jack Smith and maybe Dominic Russell too? She couldn't really see it. But what was the alternative? Dominic murdered Maria Tull and Jack Smith to get the painting, and then had such guilt that he slashed the picture and committed suicide? That seemed even less likely. Which left what? She turned round, to be confronted by Lawson, still sitting there, her hands gripping the hand-written notes at which she had been glancing throughout their meeting.

Holden looked at her watch. 'OK, bring your colleagues up to date will you, and remind Fox he's driving me to Geraldine Payne's later on. And ask him to allow time for a stop at a florist's on the way.'

'So you want to know about Sarah and me, do you? Well, I shouldn't be surprised. Everyone likes a bit of gossip, don't they!'

Geraldine Payne asked the question almost before they were sat down. Holden and Fox had agreed to interview her at her flat, or rather – as she had made clear – the flat she was renting just until her house in Brook Street was ready for her to move in. Last time, when she had wanted something from the police, she had stormed down to the Cowley station like a heat-seeking missile homing in on its target, but now that the boot was on the other foot, she had insisted on them coming to her. 'Not to my surgery!' she had stated, as if it was up to her to set the boundaries or what was and wasn't possible. 'I don't want you upsetting my patients. Come to my flat. Lucy can re-jig my appointments so I get off a bit early. Let's say 4.30 in St Thomas's Street.'

And so, here they were at 4.35 p.m. with Geraldine Payne doing her damnedest to call the shots.

'You could start by telling us about Saturday,' Holden replied evenly. She wasn't flustered by the woman, and she wasn't fooled either. Geraldine knew perfectly well from their earlier telephone conversation why they had come to question her. And Holden had no doubt that Geraldine and Sarah had spoken to each other, discussing tactics, agreeing times, and all that sort of thing. Even so, she still needed to interview her, and get her evidence down on the record. And you never knew what else might pop up. But that ironically was what Holden was worried about. Geraldine was part of the lesbian and gay network that Karen had long been part of, and Karen and she had even had a brief relationship. So Holden couldn't help but wonder if Geraldine might not exploit that if things got tricky.

'She came to see me,' Geraldine began. 'She arrived at about eight o'clock, and she left just after nine thirty. She said she was going to see Alan Tull.'

'And why did she come to see you?'

'Why not? We're friends.'

'Are you lovers?'

'Ooh!' Geraldine replied in a tone that was pure mock-horror. 'You don't beat about the bush do you, Inspector.'

'Yes or no?'

'No,' she said with a smile.

'Are you sure?' growled Fox. He shouldn't have interrupted. It wasn't part of the plan, but he was tired and he didn't like this dyke pissing his boss about.

Geraldine turned on him, all playfulness gone. 'Of course I'm fucking sure, Sergeant. I'd have noticed if I'd been having an affair with her. And I'd be happy to admit it,' she continued, turning back towards Holden. 'Only it's not true. I like her. I even tried it on with her once. But she wouldn't have any of it.'

Fox snorted. He wasn't that easily put off, and he sure as hell wasn't going to let the lesbian cow have the last word. 'So how come she came round so early in the morning, as soon as her husband had left for work. It looks bloody suspicious to me.'

Geraldine turned back to her male interrogator, and her face snarled with fury. 'Because, Mr fucking Policeman, her husband didn't like me. And because I'm a dyke, he wouldn't understand that Sarah and I might have a normal friendship. Like you, he'd have jumped to the conclusion that if we were seeing each other out of his sight, then it must be sex.' She paused. Her face was flushed and her breathing was fast and shallow. 'She just needed someone to talk to, that's all.'

'What if her husband had found out that you two saw each other socially behind his back?' Fox was leaning forward, a look of triumph in his eyes. 'And what if he had jumped to the conclusion that his wife didn't come round to see you just for a bit of tea and sympathy?' He spat the words out, so that Holden suddenly shuddered and wondered what the hell she was doing working with a man like him. 'Maybe they had a bust up and she blew his brains out?'

Geraldine Payne turned in supplication towards Holden. 'She wouldn't have done that. She's tough on the outside, but inside. . . .' Her words tailed off as she tried to martial her thoughts into coherence. 'Look, Susan,' she said, suddenly informal, 'if I thought Sarah had done anything like that, I'd tell you. I wouldn't protect a murderer. I know I'm not everyone's cup of tea, but I'm honest.' She paused, and then gave a sharp prod with her emotional knife. 'Ask Karen. She'll tell you.'

CHAPTER 9

She was on a train. It was the same one as always, just like the one in her grandmother's house. A bright red engine that careered along in front of her, while she stood in the front carriage – or maybe it was the only carriage, only she never dared to look behind her – unable to move. Her feet were glued to the floor, and all she could do was look forwards and watch the huge puffs of smoke which were emitted every few seconds from the funnel. It was like watching a cartoon, only she was part of it and it was real and she was terrified. The train seemed to be racing straight ahead, but they kept passing the same station, the same church, and the same set of signals, which stretched across the line just like in her father's Triang trainset, and she had to keep ducking every time the signals reappeared for fear they would decapitate her. At first these landmarks, the station, the church, the signals, occurred at regular, spaced-out intervals, but soon she realized the gaps were getting shorter. They were gathering speed and she had no way of getting off or stopping. And then the train let off a whistle, a terrible steaming whistle, and it got louder and louder until it wasn't a whistle any more. It was a scream of terror, and the scream was hers because right in front of the driverless train – for she had realized by now that it had no driver – there loomed a huge red wall and she was hurtling towards it and she knew she was going to crash into it.

Only she didn't. She never had done. This was the point at which she always woke. She sat bolt upright and shouted. It wasn't a loud shout, though it would have probably been sufficient to wake Karen if Karen had been there, but she wasn't. That had been Susan's own choice. She had spent the evening round at Karen's flat, but she'd insisted on coming back to Chilswell Road and sleeping on her own. She needed some time to herself, she had said, and Karen had said fine, as if she understood, but Karen had been hurt. Susan knew that, and she could have changed her mind, but instead she'd driven home to Grandpont and gone to bed alone. And now, at five o'clock in the morning, she wished she hadn't been such a self-centred cow. Because then Karen would be lying next to her and she could tell her about this stupid nightmare and then she could lie down again and Karen would wrap her arms around her and she would feel OK.

For a moment she considered ringing Karen, but shook her head at her own foolishness. Instead, she sent her a text 'Ring when u r awake' (as if one possible option for Karen was to ring when she was asleep!) and went downstairs to the kitchen. She placed her mobile in the middle of the table, checked the kettle for water, and switched it on. Next stop was the mug tree: there were six mugs hanging on it, each a different bright colour. She studied them for several seconds, and then chose the yellow one. It was a long time since she had drunk out of it. Next came the choice of tea. In the tin from France were the herbal teas – she ought to have one of them to help her sleep – but she wasn't sure she wanted to sleep and besides she kept them largely for guests. You couldn't live here in this left-leaning, Guardian-reading, healthy-eating, allotment-obsessed area of South Oxford and not have herbal tea for your guests. But she opted to open the white tin with the unequivocal hand-written label 'Builder's Tea' on it and pulled a bag out of that one.

She poured the boiling water in and let it stew for at least a minute before removing the bag and adding a dollop of milk. Then she sat at the table with her mug cradled in her hand, and tried to think. But nothing happened. Not a single constructive, analytical thought entered her consciousness. Not one. There was only feeling, deep and bewildering, a feeling of immense and intolerable panic, as if the very roof of the world was pressing down on her, squeezing and squeezing her until there was no space left for her and no breath left in her lungs. She gave a snort, releasing the air she had been refusing to let out, and then sucked the stale house air deep into her lungs. She slammed her fist down on the table and shouted at herself to ward off the panic. Get a grip, you silly girl, get a grip! They weren't her words, of course. They were her father's, rocketing back from the past, and as they had always done back then, they now acted only to make her more determined – or stubborn, depending on whose point of view you took. She stood up suddenly and went over to the small semi-circular table which stood between the door leading through from the front of the house and the half-glass door leading sideways out into the garden. The table was dark brown and Georgian, with elegant curved legs, and was totally out of place in the kitchen, but it had been her grandmother's and it fitted the space perfectly. The table was covered with a white lace cloth embroidered with delicate yellow flowers, and on this sat a silver-grey phone, a notepad, and biro. She picked up the notepad and returned to the kitchen table. She drank a slug of tea, revelling in its strong, ugly taste. Right, she told herself, it's time to get organized.

'Start at the very beginning, it's a very good place to start.' That was what Maria von Trapp would have said, prancing across her stupid Austrian mountains, but she couldn't do that. She could only start with Geraldine Payne, who seemed to be everyone's bloody dentist and had once slept in the same bed as Karen. Because the fact was that Geraldine Payne had invaded her head.

'Geraldine Payne.' She wrote the name down at the top of the blank sheet of paper in front of her. She paused, took another slurp from her mug, and continued to write. 'Dentist. Relationship with Sarah Russell. Sexual? Possibly! She denies it.' She paused, a prolonged pause which took in another slurp of tea and a desultory scratching of her armpit. She tore off the sheet of paper, placed it in front of her to the left, and started writing on a fresh sheet.

'Maria Tull.' She looked hard at the two words. The idea was that writing things down would help to lessen the confusion in her brain and allay the feeling of panic in her gut. But it didn't seem to be working. She picked up her mug again, and drained its contents. Concentrate, Susan! Concentrate!

She tried to recall the interview with Geraldine. In detail. It was easy to recall Fox's blundering aggression. She hated the way he had gone about it, and she hated the attitudes that had fuelled his questioning, but the fact was he had forced her to talk about her relationship with Sarah Russell. Holden had taken over from him at that point. She didn't feel she could walk out, job done, with the whiff of sexism and homophobia hanging acrid in the air. So she had changed the subject, moving it away from Sarah and towards the Tulls.

'I like Alan,' Geraldine had said firmly. 'He's a kind man, a gentleman. Just the sort of GP that anyone in their right mind would want. Of course, we both work in Beaumont Street, so we meet up occasionally for lunch. He always offers to pay, but I insist on taking turns. I think he likes being seen with me, a woman, but a totally safe woman. No chance of gossip or scandal, or anything getting out of hand.'

'What about Maria?' she had asked then.

'She was all right.' Holden had been struck by that expression. It was the sort of thing a child said about a teacher they liked or about an aunt who managed not to say embarrassing things in front of their friends. But in Geraldine's mouth it seemed incongruous. Especially in view of how she'd described her that time she'd stormed into the station.

'The first time we met,' Holden said unemotionally, 'you described her as an Italian bitch.'

Geraldine laughed. 'Yes, I dare say I might have. I was cross then, really furious in fact, so I probably said things I didn't really mean.'

'Do you make a habit of that?'

'Only when I want to.' She had laughed again, as if the very idea of behaving in any other way was too ridiculous for words. 'Look, we got on. We weren't best friends – far from it – but I think she found me interesting, what with me preferring women to men. She couldn't get her head round that.' Again, Geraldine had laughed. 'I liked to talk art with her. She was really interesting on it. Occasionally, we'd meet at the Ashmolean and have a coffee, and she'd take me to look at just one painting that had taken her fancy, and she'd talk about it. Endlessly!' She had laughed again. 'She liked to show off her knowledge.'

'Was she having an affair with anyone, do you think?'

Geraldine hadn't shown any surprise at her change of tactic. Perhaps, when you're being quizzed by the police, no question can be a real surprise. 'I wasn't her best buddy, Inspector,' she had said. 'I doubt she'd have confided in me. But actually, if you want my honest guess, I'd guess no. I'll tell you for why. She was a looker, was Maria. Not my type, you understand, but the men liked her. She always got looks. Hell, she encouraged them! She loved a bit of flirting, even if it was only with the pensioner standing guard in the pre-Raphaelite gallery. It was amazing the favours she could get if she put her mind to it. But it was always a game with her. The bottom line was she liked her life. She liked the financial comfort that her marriage to a GP gave her. She liked Oxford. She liked being able to dabble in the art market, and she liked her trips back to Venice. She once asked me about lesbian sex and what we got up to, and when I had finished, she made a face and said that personally she thought sex was overrated. So that's why I say I doubt she would risk it all for something she didn't much like.'

'Not even Dominic Russell?' Susan had asked, switching her line of attack.

But Geraldine had merely broken into peals of laughter. 'Are you kidding, Inspector. Especially not him. Rumour has it that he tried it on with her soon after she married Alan, and she turned him down flat. Dominic thought he was God's gift to women, but only the young and the naïve fell for his dubious charms. And the bottom line is, when Sarah cracked the whip he used to come running.'

'So when did you last see Maria alive?' She had intended it as her last question; she hadn't expected it to reveal anything interesting, but it had seemed like an easy way to wind the interview to a suitable conclusion.

Geraldine had frowned, and sucked in her lips. 'It must be two or three weeks ago. I bumped into her outside the Playhouse.'

'What did you talk about?'

She had shrugged. 'This and that. I admired her handbag. It was very stylish, just like her. And she asked if I'd been away on holiday. And she told me she was giving a series of lectures on Venetian art.' Geraldine had stopped at that point. Holden remembered noticing that something changed in her. 'I rang her about it,' she had said with intensity. 'On the night she was murdered, I rang her on her mobile to find out when she was starting her lectures.'

'You mean you spoke to her?' Holden had been suddenly alert. 'When was this?'

'No,' Geraldine had replied. 'She never answered my call.' She scratched her head, trying to recall the details. 'It must have been a bit after six o'clock. I had a feeling she had told me that her lectures were starting that night, but I had nothing written down, so I wanted to check. Her mobile rang several times, but she didn't answer. So I left a message, asking her to call me, and then I hung up. I never did speak to her.'

She had fallen silent then. They both had, as each wondered what might have been. If Geraldine had got hold of her and gone along that evening, would it have changed what happened?

Susan Holden yawned, and felt an almost physical jolt of tiredness sweep over her. She looked down at her piece of paper. Still only two words: 'Maria Tull.' She picked up the biro and started writing underneath. 'Missed phone call from Geraldine? [Check with Wilson, esp. time.] Why did Maria not answer? *Does it matter?*'

Then she put down the biro, picked up her mobile, and made her way upstairs.

*

161

It was the sound of her mobile that woke her. She scrabbled around on her bedside table for it, conscious that if she didn't pick up by five rings, it would go into the answering service. 'Yes,' she said, just in time.

'Are you all right?' It was Karen's voice. God, was it nice to hear her voice!

'I think I might be cracking up.' Susan hadn't meant to say anything as dramatic as that. But the words popped out as large as life and twice as unsettling.

There was an intake of breath at the other end of the call. 'Are you serious?'

'I had a nightmare. A pig of a nightmare.'

'Do you want to talk about it?'

'Have you time to listen?'

'For you, babe, all the time in the world.' It could have been a line from a cut-price B movie, and it was delivered by Karen as if it was, but cliché or not, it had a startling effect: Susan Holden burst uncontrollably into tears.

For twenty minutes they talked. Or rather for twenty minutes Susan Holden talked and Karen Pointer listened. And at the end of it Susan no longer felt like she was about to explode. 'Thanks,' she said simply at the end. 'I don't know what I'd do without you.'

'It's all part of the deal,' Karen said, trying hard to distance herself from her emotions. For a minute or two in their conversation she had feared she was in danger of losing the best person who had ever happened to her.

'I love you,' Susan said.

'I love you too.' And tears had begun to well up in Karen's eyes too.

'Can I come round and stay tonight?'

'Of course. Any night, or every night'

'Really?'

'Really. The only problem is I've lost a filling.'

'You've what?'

'I've lost a filling,' Karen said, more slowly and more loudly, as if talking to a call centre in Mumbai. 'From my back tooth.' She was louder now, fully into the part. 'I ate a toffee. Do you understand?' she said with exaggerated gaps between each word.

Susan laughed, and Karen laughed back, glad that Susan was reacting normally.

'So,' Karen continued, but this time in her sensible, organized voice, 'I'm going to ask Geraldine to squeeze me in at the end of her day. I might be late home. So I'll give you a ring when I'm finished and we can decide then what to do with our evening. OK?'

'OK. Love you.'

'Love you more!' Karen had replied, slipping into a cherished teenage game.

'Love you much more!'

'Love you the mostest!' Karen replied, terminating the conversation.

It was 8.31 a.m. when Lawson and Fox walked into Holden's office, Fox carrying two steaming polystyrene cups, and Lawson some cardboard folders. Holden looked at her watch. 'We'll wait for Wilson. He's just checking something out for me. In fact, since we're not quite ready, how about getting a coffee for him, and for me too. And tell him to get a move on, while you're about it.'

At 8.36 a.m., or near as damn it, the two of them returned with two more white cups and Wilson in tow.

'Sorry if I held you up!' Wilson said. Apologizing wasn't so much second nature to Detective Constable Wilson as hard-wired into his reflex system. Holden raised her head and looked at him. His skin was red and scarred by a ceaseless adolescent battle against acne, and his ears protruded too much. He would look a lot better if he grew his hair a bit, she thought, or if he used gel on it to provide a distraction. But she looked on him in the way that she imagined mothers looked on their gawky sons – the ones who were never going to make the football team or get the straight As – with a fierce and protective pride.

'You haven't held us up,' she said, gesturing towards a chair. She waited until they had all settled. Even now, she wasn't quite sure where to start. 'I need your help.' She paused. It was a ridiculously personal way to open the session. She should have gone straight to the detail of the case. 'Point one!' But she felt alone and exposed, and the anxieties of the night had begun to bubble up to the surface again. 'We aren't making fast enough progress on the case. Three dead bodies, and God knows how many more to follow if we don't pull our fingers out. So I want us all to start with a blank sheet of paper. Discard all your assumptions and look afresh at everything. OK?'

She stopped and looked around. Three heads nodded in acknowledgement. 'So let's start with Maria Tull's phone.' This startled Fox and Lawson. Simple observation told her that, and she felt glad. Whatever else, she had their full attention now. Wilson, of course, knew about her interest in Maria's mobile. He looked pleased.

'Fox, you were there yesterday when we interviewed Geraldine Payne. She told us she tried to phone Maria.'

'Sure. She said she tried to ring Maria on the night of her death. A bit after six, I think she said. She wanted to know when her lectures on Venetian art were starting. But Maria didn't answer, so she left a message asking her to ring back.'

'Accurate, but only in so far as it goes.' She spoke without malice, but the words were bound to hurt. Fox looked back at her, giving no sign. 'Wilson has been taking another look at this for me,' she continued, and turned towards her constable.

'She did ring. At 6.21 that evening. And she left a message. As Sergeant Fox said, she asked about—'

Holden cut in. There were no favours this morning, not even for Wilson. 'Let's have it verbatim, Wilson.'

Wilson looked down at his notes. His face was even redder that normal. He began to read. 'Hi, Maria. Geraldine here. How's tricks? I'm sure your famous lectures are about to start any day. Do remind me of the details. I completed failed to make a note of it. Byeee!'

'Thank you Wilson.' Holden took a sip of coffee. She looked around the semi-circle of faces again. She had got their attention all right.

'So why didn't Maria ring her back?'

'She never heard the message,' Wilson said. 'I was checking back in my notes. I went through the mobile in the normal way. Incoming calls, outgoing-calls, missed calls, text messages, and voice messages. This was the only unread voice message. I did write it in my notes, but—'

'We should have followed it up,' Holden said firmly. She believed in taking responsibility.

'We were distracted by the photo of Jack Smith,' Lawson said. The blame had to be shared. 'All of us were.'

'One missed phone call,' Fox joined in. 'It's not like it was a big deal.'

'Unless, of course, it turns out that it is a big deal.' Holden knew that now with absolute certainty. It was the biggest deal. Maybe the key, even. 'Maria didn't get the message and she didn't ring back. But she had the mobile on her. We know that because we found it in her coat pocket.'

'Maybe she had just turned it off,' Lawson suggested. 'She was starting a series of lectures. Maybe she didn't want to be bothered by anyone. I mean, she would definitely have turned it off before the lecture—'

'But it wasn't turned off when Geraldine rang her.' Fox had caught up now, and knew exactly where the Guv was going with this. No wonder she'd been so bloody sharp with him. 'Geraldine told us the phone rang several times before it went into the answering service.'

'Six times,' Holden said quietly.

'So it must have been turned on then,' Fox concluded. 'Or it would have gone straight into the messaging service.'

'If I can play devil's advocate for a minute?' This was Lawson's insurance, in case she was shot down in flames. 'Perhaps she was in the car, driving. That would explain why she didn't pick up at the time. And then, when she got there, she was too rushed or preoccupied to listen to it and ring back.'

'It's possible,' Holden admitted, 'but her car does have a hands-free kit. We checked.' That is to say, Wilson had checked. 'Which means, in the scenario you are sketching out, Lawson, she gets the call while driving to St Clement's, doesn't bother to answer it, and then doesn't bother when she has got there to check who had rung her and why.'

'That's a bit of a loaded way to put it.' Lawson didn't like her ideas been abandoned quite so obviously. 'To say that she couldn't be bothered.'

'I know, Lawson. But the bottom line is we have to make some judgements. Anyway, let's put Fox and Wilson on the spot. What do you two think of the scenario Lawson has proposed. Probable, possible, or unlikely?'

'Possible,' Fox snapped back. 'But on the unlikely side.'

'I agree,' Wilson chimed. 'I wouldn't want to put too much weight on it.'

'So Wilson, suggest an alternative scenario.'

The young man shifted in his chair. He didn't like being the centre of attention, but he had had more warning of Holden's thinking than the others, and he knew the answer because she and he had already discussed it. He spoke softly. 'Perhaps, when she was rung, she didn't have the phone with her.'

'Exactly!' Holden leant back in her chair, and sipped slowly at her coffee. She felt elated. She wasn't sure when the idea had first formulated in her brain, but she felt sure the seed must have been sown when she almost missed the call from Karen that morning. At any rate the idea had materialized by the time she'd pulled into the station car park, so she had been able to slip it into her briefing of Wilson. And now it was out there in the ring, fighting its corner.

She put the cup down, and looked around. 'Well? It is the obvious answer. Maria didn't answer the call because she never knew it had been made. We can't prove it, but let's run with it as an idea. OK?'

'OK,' Lawson nodded, though there was reluctance in her voice. 'So the next question would be where was the phone when Geraldine rang, and how come you found it in her coat pocket in St

Clement's car park?'

'I agree. But let's look at it from a different perspective, with a long lens and not a microscope. What, from the point of view of the investigation, is the importance of Maria's mobile phone.'

Lawson, typically, jumped in again. 'The photo of Jack Smith. It put us on to his affair with Maria Tull.'

'To call it an affair may be an exaggeration,' Holden said, remembering what Geraldine had said about Maria's attitude to sex. 'He claimed it was only a one-off, and I'm inclined to believe him. She wanted to get her hands on the painting, so she did what she felt she had to do to achieve that, and she took a photo to make sure he cooperated.'

'There was a photo on Jack Smith's mobile too.' Three pairs of eyes turned towards Wilson. 'Of a painting that had passed into Dominic Russell's hands.'

'And now Dominic Russell's brains have been blown out.'

'With the painting which Jack Smith handed over to Maria lying by his dead body.'

'Slashed with a knife, the same knife that killed Maria and Jack.'

'Whoa! Just a minute.' Holden raised her hands to emphasize her words. Her team were in danger of careering out of control. 'First of all, there is no certainty that the knife that damaged the painting is the weapon that killed Maria and Jack. We need to wait for Dr Pointer to confirm that. And second, you're jumping forward mighty fast. Maria's phone had a picture on it that pointed to Jack Smith. He is murdered and his mobile had a picture that pointed to Dominic Russell. Then Dominic is murdered or commits suicide, only there's no mobile, but there is a painting with him that we know Maria and Jack took possession of. So question one is: are these two mobile phone pictures part of the same pattern or are they coincidence?'

There was a silence. Holden's desk phone rang, but she ignored it. 'Well?'

Lawson volunteered again. 'I doubt it's a coincidence.'

'So what is it?'

'They're clues. Deliberately left by the killer.' Lawson's words were emphatic. 'Maybe to taunt us, maybe to lead us off the track.'

'So to go back to my earlier question, how come Maria didn't answer the mobile, yet we found it in her pocket in the car park?'

'It was planted,' Fox interrupted. He had just caught up. 'By the killer.'

'Quite. So where was Maria's phone when she rang? The answer is: in the hands of the killer, who naturally didn't want to answer it when it rang.'

'But if someone had stolen it and Maria had noticed, she'd have reported in stolen.'

Holden turned towards Wilson, who had now become the expert on Maria's mobile phone. 'Well? Was it reported Wilson?'

'No, Guv, it wasn't.'

She turned back towards the others, but her gaze settled on Lawson. 'How long would it take you to notice if your mobile was missing, Lawson?'

The features of her face tightened on concentration. 'It depends. A few hours at most, I'd say. Unless I'm really busy, and then I might not get time to check it. But normally, I'd maybe check it at lunchtime, and as soon as I get home, so I'd notice then if I couldn't find it.'

'So let's assume the killer took Maria's mobile off her sometime on the day of her death, either in the afternoon or early evening.'

'Damn!' Wilson, who had been scrabbling through the file of papers on his lap, swore as they suddenly slipped from his grasp and descended in a shower on to the floor. 'Sorry!' he said, the compulsive apology springing to his lips. Down on his knees he grabbed one piece out of the pile, and held it aloft. 'I was just checking. Maria's last call out on her phone was 13.35 that day. To Dominic Russell. So she had the mobile then for sure.'

'Not absolutely for sure.' It was Lawson again. 'Wilson is probably right, and I'm not saying he isn't—'

'Get to the point, for God's sake.' Holden had had enough of ifs and maybes and buts. They had to make assumptions somewhere along the line.

Lawson lifted her hands, palms upwards, as if in supplication. 'It's just that there's no certainty that the killer didn't make that call.'

Fox, conscious he was in danger of being sidelined, broke in. 'Well, we can't ask Dominic, can we!'

'Thank you, Sergeant.' Holden's reply was heavy with sarcasm. She sank her head in her hands and tried to think. Don't panic, don't let it overwhelm you! She could hear her heart pounding, reverberating between her hands and her temples. Faster than it should be. Don't let me be overwhelmed, she pleaded, getting as close to prayer as she ever did. Please don't!

She raised her head, and spoke. 'The people who most obviously had access to her mobile are her family. Namely Alan Tull, Lucy Tull, and Joseph Tull. Any one could have pocketed it in the house. None of them has a watertight alibi. So we could start with them, but we also need to find out what she did and who she saw that afternoon. Did she have any work appointments? If she rang Dominic Russell at lunchtime, maybe it was because she wanted to see him in the afternoon? Did she go to the dentist or the hairdresser, or to the Ashmolean for a last-minute piece of research on the art of Venice? Did anyone visit her at home that afternoon and pocket her mobile then? Otherwise, we're looking at the Tulls.'

She scanned the faces of her three colleagues. Wilson and Lawson shone with excitement, with the sense that they had made a breakthrough and the hunt was truly on. Even Fox had jettisoned his natural look of surly diffidence, and when her stare remained focused on him, he took the hint and responded: 'So we're going to interview them again?'

'Yes and no. I don't want to alert them. I'll give Dr Tull a ring and suggest I need to chat, make it sound more an update on the case than an interview. I can ask him what his wife did on that day easily enough. I can ask if she kept a diary or wrote appointments on a calendar? We play it as casually as we can. But I want us to turn up there with a search warrant in our proverbial back pocket. Because the bottom line is we need to check computers, hand-held devices, pen drives, mobiles, whatever they've got, for the photo of Jack Smith and the painting we found on Jack Smith's mobile, not to mention anything to do with Maria. So if the good doctor objects, out comes the warrant. Any other questions?'

'Yes,' Lawson said hurriedly. 'What about the Judas painting?'

'Ah, good point,' Holden said. 'Thank you for reminding me.' She turned towards Fox and Wilson. 'I assume you're up to date on this?'

They nodded.

'Any thoughts? It just that Lawson and I had a long chat yesterday and. . . .' She faded to a halt. Her right hand, Lawson noticed, was pulling at her collar again. 'Come on, Wilson. Any ideas?' It was unfair, she knew. If she was going to apply pressure, apply it to Fox. Hell, he was much more experienced.

'Maria got it off Jack Smith because she thought she could make money on it.' Wilson had clearly been thinking about it a lot, for he spoke carefully, as if he was recalling lines he had just learnt for a school play, but without having the confidence to apply any variation in tone or emphasis to them. 'She gave it to Dominic because she thought he could help her get the best price. The killer murders her, then Jack Smith, and then arranges to meet Dominic. Dominic realizes too late that the person he is meeting is the killer, and damages the painting to make it worthless and save his own life. But the killer shoots him because he knows too much.'

'Impressive, Wilson,' Holden said. 'And possible. However,' she continued, taking great care in how she phrased her misgivings, 'I do wonder if someone would have killed three people for a painting that might fetch at best ten thousand pounds.'

'Why not?' Fox countered with sudden force. 'If you need the money enough, why the hell not?' And he slurped noisily from his cup, as if the matter was well and truly settled.

'Why does it have to come down to money?' The question – or perhaps it was a challenge – came from Lawson.

Fox laughed dismissively. 'Money or sex. It's nearly always

money or sex.' And he laughed again, ridiculing the young woman's idea.

'Constable Lawson.' Holden deliberately looked directly at her protégé, ignoring Fox totally. 'Perhaps you can explain your thinking. Sergeant Fox doesn't have a monopoly on good ideas, at least not in this office.'

Lawson began slowly, feeling her way. 'Maybe what we should be focusing on is the painting's subject. It may not be of great artistic merit, but it is very unusual. Mary the mother of Jesus going round to visit the mother of Judas after he has betrayed her son. Now if that had been the work of an even moderately well-known painter, it might have been hugely valuable to someone. But even though it's by an unknown artist, who's to say that there aren't people out there who might want it very much, so much so in fact that they'd pay over the odds despite its technical limitations?'

'Ah!' Fox jumped in again, apparently unaffected by his superior's rebuke. 'So it is all about money.'

'Shut up, Sergeant.' This time she looked at him, and the acid in her voice and the thunder on her face finally caused his smirk to fade.

Lawson plunged on. 'I don't mean they would necessarily want to hang it on their walls. Maybe just the opposite. Maybe they'd want to destroy it because it contradicts the Bible. Do you know how Judas is described in St John's Gospel?' She paused, and realized that she'd got the attention of all of them, even the dismissive Fox. ' "Satan entered into him." That's what St John wrote. The same John who sat at the table with Jesus and Judas at the last supper. "Satan entered into him".'

'So what the hell does that prove?' Fox interrupted.

Lawson looked unflinchingly into his eyes. 'There was an artist who created twelve stained-glass windows of Jesus' disciples for a church in Dorset. He insisted on including Judas along with all the others. I'm not sure exactly what his point was, maybe to underline the fact that they all betrayed their Lord, and not just Judas, but the parishioners refused to allow Judas's image into their church. My point, Sarge, is that Judas is, and always has been, a controversial figure. Maybe Maria and Dominic realized that, and reckoned it might be worth a lot more than it deserved on artistic merit alone.'

Fox grunted cheerfully. 'So when push comes to shove, it is about money.'

'For Maria and Dominic, maybe,' Lawson conceded. 'But. . . .' She paused, determined to ensure she had all their attention for what she was about to say. 'For the killer, maybe the money was irrelevant. Maybe it was all about getting hold of and destroying a painting he or she saw as blasphemous.'

CHAPTER 10

They had to park some distance beyond the Tulls' house and walk back. Even at this time of day, when those who work are at work and the decreasing band of ladies who lunch are still prolonging their outings with a drawn-out coffee, there were few available parking spaces. The sky above was a uniform grey – cloud as opposed to clouds – a blanket of dampness that offered no hope of relief. Holden put her hand up to see if she could feel any actual rain, then touched her cheek. She grinned to herself, recognizing a behaviour left over from childhood. Please let it not rain today.

Dr Alan Tull opened the door. The smile of greeting on his face evaporated as soon as he saw them. 'Gosh, you have come in numbers.'

'We'll be quicker that way.' Holden tried to sound matter of fact, and upbeat. She didn't want to alarm him. 'Anyway, may we come in?' Tull was still standing in the doorway, and had been showing no sign of allowing them over the threshold.

'Sorry,' he said. Even under stress, he was courteous. 'I do apologize. Come in.'

'Thank you.' Holden led the four of them in. She felt bad. When she had rung him to arrange their visit, she'd made out that what she was proposing was merely a chat and a clarification of a few details, only one step up from a social visit to see how he was holding up. Now his decency and acceptance of the circumstances made her feel deceitful and cheap. He didn't deserve it. Unless, a little voice whispered in the back of her brain, unless he had killed his wife and her lover, and indeed her ex-lover if that is what Dominic Russell had been.

Holden tried to make it as non-threatening as possible. In fact, as they drove over the four of them had discussed where they should sit. When Alan Tull gestured towards the sofa, Holden moved towards it, and Fox joined her. Tull seated himself in an armchair opposite them, while Lawson and Wilson sat to the side, at a distance, in his eye-line if he chose to glance at them. 'Whatever you do, don't just hover,' Holden had insisted. 'It'll spook him.'

Alan Tull leant forward, his interlocked hands twisting slightly as he spoke. 'So, have you made progress? I take it you haven't arrested anyone yet.'

She nodded encouragingly. 'Yes, we've made progress, and no, we haven't arrested anyone. But there are a few details we need your help with.'

'Of course.'

Holden looked down at her notes. 'On the night your wife died, you came home just after six o'clock.'

'Yes.'

'Could you say what time she actually left the house?'

He scratched the crown of his head. 'She was finishing off her meal when I arrived. Mackerel salad. She was quite rigorous about what she ate. And about what I ate, in fact.' He sniffed. 'I poured myself a whisky and asked her if she was organized for her lecture, and she told me I had spilt some food down my shirt and I should give it a soak in cold water and salt.' Again, he sniffed. 'Then I went through to my study to make a phone call. I was still on the phone when she called through that she was leaving, and then the door slammed and she was gone.' He sighed, a deep, heavy sigh that seemed to Holden almost theatrical in its intensity. She remembered suddenly Sarah Russell's account of her visit to him on the morning of her husband's death, and she shivered. Was all this an act? The courteousness, the sadness, the sense of bathos wrung tight. Was he playing them for fools? He was keen on the theatre, after all.

'Could you give a time?'

'Maybe 6.15 p.m. I'm not sure, to be honest. But I do remember thinking she had plenty of time to get there and get organized, so it can't have been much after that.'

'And do you remember her receiving any phone calls before she left?'

He shook his head slowly. 'No, I don't think so. I'm sorry. I wish I could be more help.'

'Thank you.' Holden smiled. She too could do polite. A mobile phone rang. Damn. It was hers. She opened her bag, saw it was her mother, and killed the call. Then she powered the phone off. Her mother would only try again. 'Sorry!' she said sheepishly.

Tull smiled sympathetically back.

'Karen, my dear. What a pleasure!' Geraldine smiled broadly and directed her towards the chair with a wave of her hands.

'Not for me!' Karen Pointer hated dentists. Not personally. She and Geraldine still got on well when they encountered each other, as they inevitably did, on their social network. But the thought of going to the dentist, any dentist, made her shiver. Literally. There had been Mr Miller. That had been the name of her dentist when she had been a child. Miller the Killer, her brother had called him. For fun. At least her brother thought it fun. After the dentist they would always get a treat, a trip to the cinema or a visit to WH Smith with money to spend, but despite that she could never recall a time when, for her, visiting the dentist had been fun.

'You'll thank me afterwards,' came the cheery reply.

'Maybe.' Karen lay back in the chair and tried to pretend she wasn't there.

'Sorry I couldn't fit you in at the end of the day, but someone cancelled this spot only this morning.'

Karen said nothing. As far as she was concerned, the dentist was not the place for small talk.'So how is my favourite pathologist?' Geraldine pressed a button and the seat began to rise. 'Up we go!'

'Up we go! What do you think I am? A three-year-old?'

'At least five, my darling,' she replied instantly. 'Now, let's take a look at this filling. Ah, yes, now there's the hole! Still, it's nothing that can't be fixed.'

Geraldine Payne's chatter, designed to distract, continued as she got to work. She made the silent decision, based on her past experience of her patient, to skip the injection, and reached cheerfully for the drill as she recounted a recent and rather exaggerated incident involving herself and a traffic warden. She worked deftly and quickly, conscious of the mounting anxiety in Karen. She had had patients turn and walk out of the surgery at the prospect of a filling, so she took these feelings very seriously. She prided herself on making the experience as tolerable as possible. She knew she couldn't make it a happy one, but for people like Karen smoothness and speed were her watchwords.

At first Karen tried not to think, but that was hopeless. It blotted out precisely nothing. She tried then to think about Susan. She was worried about her, but lying there worrying achieved nothing. So she thought instead about the case, that is to say her bits of the case. The dead bodies and their manners of death. The clinical knife wounds and the exploded mess caused by the gun. She thought about Dominic Russell lying on the loft floor and the painting of Judas and the two mothers, and the neat slashes in the canvas, two parallel cuts on one diagonal and two on the other. So precise! What the hell was that all about?

'Do you want a rinse, Karen?'

Opening her clenched eyes, she realized Geraldine was talking to her. She leant to her side, took a sip from the plastic cup, and swilled the minty green solution around her mouth, before spurting it out into the white whirlpool bowl.

'Nearly finished, darling. Just lie back while I do a final check.'

She lay back. That was it. She hadn't thought of that. The cuts were neat and clinical, just as the stab wounds to Maria's heart and neck had been. They weren't the emotional slashes of a man who had decided to blow his brains out, surely? It had to be murder. She must tell Susan, give her a ring. It might help. Only Susan didn't want hunches or guesses from her. She wanted evidence, something definitive. And that was something she couldn't currently provide.

'All finished!' As soon as Geraldine had uttered these words of release, Karen sat up like a jack-in-the-box, anxious to escape the confines of the chair. Geraldine stifled a giggle. 'Steady up, I've just got to lower the seat.'

Karen waited obediently, then clambered out and wiped her mouth with the tissue that Geraldine offered. She turned round to look for a bin, but as she did something happened behind her eyes and a surge of dizziness struck her. She staggered and gave a tiny yelp. Geraldine Payne, alerted, grabbed her with her left arm before she could fall.

'Steady!' Her other arm wrapped round her patient, and she pulled her towards herself. They stood there for barely two or three seconds, locked together. Geraldine could feel Karen's breasts, soft against her own. She smelt the beguiling scent of her freshly shampooed hair, and memories resurfaced. Then, reluctantly, she released her.

'Are you all right?' she said hastily. 'Look, you'd better come and sit down for a few minutes. Lucy can make you a cup of tea. I know it's been an ordeal for you. But Susan will never forgive me if I let anything happen to you in my surgery.'

Karen Pointer nodded, her head still reeling. 'Sorry if I was rude earlier.'

'Forget it,' the dentist replied brusquely, leading her by the arm. 'Let's get you sat down. Then I've got more patients to see.'

'Dr Tull.' Holden paused, wanting to be sure she had got Alan Tull's attention. 'We're trying to trace what Maria did on that last day, just in case it gives us any clues. I know you were at work, but I wonder if you know what she had planned for that day. Work appointments, or a visit to the hairdresser, maybe?'

'Gosh, there's a question. To be honest, I don't know. Not for certain. She might have been going to see Dominic. They'd been as thick as thieves since she returned from Venice. I noticed that. Not that I told Maria I'd noticed. I didn't like it. It was all to do with stuff she'd sourced for him in Venice, I expect, but I didn't like it because Dominic wasn't exactly the straightest pencil in the pack, if you know what I mean.'

'Did Maria keep a diary?' However interesting Tull's comments were, Holden wanted to keep on her chosen track.

'Oh, yes, a little blue one.'

'Do you know where it is?'

Tull frowned. 'Wasn't it in her bag? You know that nice bag from Venice that you haven't yet returned to me.' It was sharpest comment that Holden had heard him say.

'You will get the bag back, in due course, sir. But the diary wasn't in it when we found it. Maybe it's lying around the house somewhere.'

'I suppose it could be,' Tull replied, though he sounded doubtful.

'Your wife used a computer, did she?'

'Yes, I bought her a laptop last Christmas.'

'We need to look at it, if you don't mind.'

'Look at it? What on earth for?'

'In fact, we need to look around generally.'

'Ah!' Dr Alan Tull hadn't become a very respected and successful GP by being a complete fool. 'So that's why you've come in force. Don't you need a search warrant?'

Holden nodded, and looked sideways at Fox.

Fox held his hand out. 'I've got one here, actually, sir.'

Tull's face hardened, and the softly spoken politeness drained from his voice. 'Well, damn you!'

'This is so embarrassing. I must be your worst patient.'

'I wish you were.'

Karen Pointer was sitting on an upright dining chair in a little room off the main waiting room. It was equipped with a kettle, a tray with four mugs on it, a small fridge that hummed away in the corner, and a sink. There were cupboards on the wall facing her, made of stripped pine with frosted glass doors that obscured their contents. Below them were pine shelves, piled with magazines to the left and formidable dental tomes to the right.

'We've got plenty of patients a lot worse than you,' Lucy added, conscious that that her comment needed some explanation. 'Late, rude, and always moaning about the cost. And stuck-up gits to boot. Only don't quote me on that.' She grinned and poured boiling water into one of the mugs.

'Milk?'

'Please.'

She added milk, two sugars and stirred. 'There, that should do the trick.'

'Lucy!' Geraldine Payne's voice rang out. 'If you don't mind, I need some assistance.'

'Or even if I do mind!' Lucy winked at Karen. 'That's Mrs Pearson. She's always a two-person job. Take your time. I'll pop back as soon as I can.'

Karen sipped at her tea and shut her eyes, leaning as far back as the upright back of her chair would allow. How stupid she was. How bloody, bloody stupid she was!

Back in Bainton Road, Lawson and Wilson had left the living room to go in search of laptops and diaries and whatever else that might be of interest. And DI Holden had decided it was time to change tack. 'On Saturday morning, Sarah Russell came to see you. Can you tell me what that was about?'

'Poor Sarah.' The words of sympathy slipped smoothly out of Alan Tull's mouth. 'And poor Dominic. I met him as an undergraduate, you know. Keble men we were. No women in those days. Still, that's of no interest to you.' He cleared his throat. 'Sarah came to see how I was. At least that was what I thought. But I should have known better. Sarah isn't exactly the tell-me-all-about-it-and-cry-on-my-shoulder type. Not that that's a fault. No criticism intended. She was concerned about me in her own brusque way. But what she really came to find out was whether I wanted to pull out of the J.B. Priestley play. You probably know it: *An Inspector Calls*. Such a good play. A touch old-fashioned, maybe, and the inspector is a male, I'm afraid, but it always goes down well!'

He chuckled, pleased at his own observation, but Holden did not respond in kind. 'So she arrived when?'

'Ah, times again. You police, you're worse than my receptionist!' He shook his head. 'I would guess she arrived about nine-thirty and left maybe an hour later, maybe a bit more than an hour. Sorry, that's the best I can do.'

She opened her eyes and looked around. She must have dropped off for a moment. She looked down at her mug, cradled in her hands and took a sip. It was still pretty hot. Not even forty winks. When she had finished she would go. Maybe by the time she had walked home she would feel better.

She looked around the room again, and her eyes alighted on the magazines, this time staying there. She put her mug down, and knelt down on the floor. There must be something to read, something to distract herself until she could face going home. The magazines were, of course, old, rejects from the reception room. Peter Andre stared out at her from the front cover of the top one. Karen made a face, and looked at the one underneath. Different name on the magazine, similar picture. There was easy reading and there was trash. She moved halfway down the pile, to Lewis Hamilton, delayed briefly, and then moved to the very bottom. She yanked it out – an Arts magazine. Nine months old – but then art doesn't go out of date much. Or does it? It must be one of Geraldine's. Or do dentists have a budget under the heading 'Reading material for the distraction and entertainment of customers'? She eased herself back on to the chair, took a sip of tea, and began to leaf through her find. An article on the origins of Art Deco seemed promising, but the first paragraph was of such deadening dullness that she abandoned it, glancing only at the pictures before flicking onwards. Gilbert and George were next, but even at the best of times she couldn't work up enthusiasm for them, and she moved quickly on. And then she saw an article that stopped her dead. It was entitled 'Zeus the Serial Seducer'. She read the text slowly, for it was in a sense topical. It traced the Greek god's sexual adventures through mythology and art. Some of it she felt she knew and some of the paintings illustrated were definitely familiar. She had seen Rembrandt's *The Abduction of Europa* in Los Angeles a couple of years ago, but even in her befuddled state the theme struck her with fresh force. The painting whose photo had been on Jack Smith's mobile and that the police had found at Dominic Russell's wasn't illustrated in the magazine, of course. It was far too insignificant, but its theme was the same: seduction or rape, whatever you might prefer to call it. Now what the hell was that all about?

'How are you feeling?' She looked up guiltily, like a child caught raiding the sweet jar. Geraldine Payne was standing at the doorway, with Lucy Tull at her shoulder. She wondered if they had been there long, for she had been quite oblivious of their presence until Geraldine spoke.

'Not too bad.' She shut the magazine and put it down, picking up the half-drunk tea instead. It was cold. She hated cold tea, but she drank it down nonetheless.

'Don't tell me you found something worth reading?'

'It passed the time.'

'You looked engrossed.'

'You've been very kind. I'd better go.' She stood up, but as she stepped forward she wavered, as light-headedness struck her again.

'Hey!' Geraldine and Lucy both grabbed at her. 'Steady!'

Karen felt ridiculously foolish. 'Sorry!'

'Don't be,' Geraldine said sharply, taking charge. 'Lucy is going to call a taxi, and she will go with you and see you back to your flat.'

'There's no need,' Karen replied, but there was no conviction and no strength in her words.

'There's every need,' came the firm reply. 'There's absolutely every need.'

*

181

The Tulls were a three-computer household. Not that Lawson and Wilson found three of them that afternoon. Joseph's laptop, like Joseph, was absent, though a plugged-in power cable suggested that wherever he had taken it, he wasn't planning on spending the whole day working on it. Lucy's tower PC was on the desk in her bedroom. It was an old one, at least three years, which in computing terms was verging on the unusable, Wilson reckoned. He tried to log on, but it was password protected, so he powered it off, unplugged the tower from its multifarious connecting cables, and tucked it under his arm. 'You never know what might be on even a museum piece like this,' he admitted, as they trudged down the stairs in search of the study. Here they found, as Dr Tull had said they would, a much newer laptop. 'I hardly ever use it myself,' he had insisted. 'It was Maria's really. I get quite enough of the damn things at surgery. Mind you, Lucy's pretty much taken it over now. She's been moaning for months about how slow hers was, but I wasn't going to replace it. She's been earning good money, so I didn't see why she couldn't buy one herself. But now she won't have to.'

The laptop was not password protected, and Wilson gave a whoop of excitement as soon as he realized. 'I'll see what I can find.'

A flash of irritation lanced through Lawson. How was it that Wilson had assumed the role of IT expert? She wasn't exactly a computer dimbo herself, but it wasn't worth arguing about. At least, not now.

'Yeah, and I'll see what I can find too!' she threw over her shoulder as she headed out of the study. It wasn't just an idle parting shot. If she was a murderer with an even half-functioning brain, and she had got sensitive, incriminating photographs, she wouldn't leave them sitting on a computer. She'd copy them off on to a pen drive and hide it somewhere safe. Lucy or Joseph – whose room to search first? Well, on the basis of who was most likely to have killed Maria, she'd have to go for Lucy, the stepdaughter. The stepdaughter. It was a term that in these days, when reconstituted families are commonplace, had rather dropped out of fashion. But the concept of the evil stepmother was one that had been implanted in Lawson at an early age when her father had read her fairy stories at bedtime. The story of Hansel and Gretel had always been, for her, the fairy story that had most fascinated and disturbed her as a child. It was the stepmother, not the witch, that was the most disturbing character for her, a manipulative, ill-defined character who schemed to separate a father from his beloved children. She was the figure of nightmares.

So, it may have been entirely because of the Brothers Grimm that Detective Constable Lawson turned left at the top of the stairs and entered Lucy's room. There she began to make a methodical search of the room: first the desk, then the chest of drawers, and finally the cupboards. Nothing. She looked around the room again. Where else? There was a glass-fronted corner cupboard with a few china ornaments. She opened that, carefully examining each of these, but there was no pen drive hidden behind or under or in any of them. If there was one, it must have been hidden with great care, maybe taped to the underside of one of the pieces of furniture, or, of course, she might carry it with her in her handbag, or hide it at work.

She sighed, turned and made her way out of the room and up the other end of the short corridor to Joseph's room. If Lucy gave the impression of being organized and careful, then Joseph did the opposite. Maybe, if he had something to hide, he was the sort of guy to stick it in the bottom of his sock drawer and think it was safe and undetectable. So, she made her way straight to the chest of drawers next to his bed. The top drawer was indeed his sock drawer, but the expression sock drawer implies a degree of order – socks matched up two by two in neat piles, or rolled together in balls – which was entirely absent from Joseph's drawer. A sock scrimmage, Lawson thought would be a better description, but at least she could move her hand around all four corners of the drawer without feeling she was making a mess. But there was no pen drive. The next drawer was pants, and the third and last was shorts. She pulled them out. Underneath were a couple of magazines of the sort young men prefer to keep hidden from their parents. On the cover of the uppermost one was a woman with remarkably large breasts pouting at the camera. Lawson didn't bother to even look at the second, because as she removed them from the drawer she saw that they had been hiding something of much greater potential: a brown envelope. It was plain, and unmarked, and it was sealed, though not tightly. Lawson carefully eased it open, and gave a grin of delight. 'Yes!' she exclaimed to the room triumphantly. 'Yes!'

She knew she ought to report this to Holden ASAP, but she was aware that she hadn't finished searching the room. She moved fast now, going through Joseph's desk drawers and wardrobe, but as with Lucy's room she drew a blank. Still, given what she had found, this was no big deal. She trotted quickly down the stairs, and breezed into the study.

'How's it going, Constable?'

Wilson's frustration, as the tone his reply made clear, was reaching a crescendo. 'Nothing,' he snapped. 'Absolutely, bloody nothing!'

'Have you checked the desk for pen drives?' She spoke calmly. 'There aren't any in Joseph's or Lucy's rooms.'

'Yes I bloody have!' His face was flushed. 'Anyway, how come you're so damn cheerful?'

Lawson was tempted to take him on, but she had found something and he hadn't, and besides, there was more than one way to challenge him. 'If I was wanting to hide a sensitive file on a PC, do you know what I would do?' She paused, but only briefly. Wilson said nothing, but she was going to tell him anyway. 'I'd rename the file something really meaningless, and I'd change its extension, and I'd hide it amongst the system files. Wouldn't you?'

Wilson looked up at her for the first time since she had entered the room. What she had said made sense, but he had no intention of saying so. 'What's that?' he asked, pointing at the envelope that Lawson was carrying.

'It may not be relevant to the case,' she smiled. 'But I think I'd better show it to the DI first, don't you think? Anyway, keep at it.'

She turned and left the room, pausing in the hall in the front of a long gilt-framed mirror. She inspected herself, ran a hand through her hair, and puckered her face. Not bad, she mouthed silently. At which point, there was the noise of a key being thrust into the front door, and in came a tousled Joseph Tull. 'What the hell are you doing here?' he demanded.

'It's nice to see you too,' Lawson replied breezily.

The taxi trip took less than five minutes, with at least two minutes wasted, first waiting to pull out across the stream of oncoming traffic in Beaumont Street, and then queuing to turn right at the lights opposite Worcester College. The rest of the run was straightforward, apart from the speed bumps and a pause while another taxi executed a U-turn in the middle of Walton Street. Once at their destination, Karen paid the driver, and then led the way uncertainly to the lift. 'I normally walk,' she insisted. 'But look, I really will be all right. If you want to go home or back to work—'

'Geraldine will skin me alive if I don't make sure you are okay. And besides, I need a pee.'

After a prolonged wait for the lift – how on earth could it be busy at this time of day, Karen wondered – and a swift ascent, Karen unlocked the flat and entered it, with Lucy in close attendance. While Lucy disappeared off to the loo, Karen moved zombie-like to the small rectangular space that represented her kitchen area. She filled the kettle, and turned it on. She ought to offer Lucy a cup of tea. But even though the kettle soon boiled, she got no further in the process. It was as if her brain was stuck in neutral and no amount of revving would get her body to move. Meanwhile Lucy, her bladder emptied, materialized in the archway that separated kitchen and living room, her head held at a slight angle. Karen wished, ungratefully, that she would go away, because she just wanted to lie down. But Lucy was showing no sign of moving.

'How are things going with you and DI Holden?'

Karen looked at her, and for some reason felt uneasy. It wasn't as if she and Lucy hadn't been in the same room before. Obviously they had been in the same reception area several times, but this was different. 'I'd rather not discuss it.'

'Why not?'

She felt suddenly irritated beyond all reason. She didn't expect to be given the third degree in her own flat, and certainly not by her dentist's sidekick. 'Because it's none of your business!' The words snaked across the short distance between them like the crack of a whip, doing their best to keep Lucy at a distance.

'I was just trying to be friendly.' She spoke in a tone of injured innocence. 'Most people like to talk about their boyfriends. Why should it be any different with dykes?' Karen flinched, but fought the temptation to react. Instead, she turned back towards the abandoned kettle, in the hope this might cause her inquisitor to withdraw.

'OK,' Lucy said suddenly, 'let's change the subject if it's too sensitive for you. Where's Susan got to in the case?'

Karen jerked round. 'I can't talk about that.'

'I won't tell. It's just between you and me.'

'It would be completely unprofessional.' Karen spoke firmly.

'I need to know.' Lucy's voice was low, but intense. Karen shivered. Why the hell wouldn't Lucy just go? She needed to lie down, and she needed to talk to Susan, or at least to make contact with her. But Lucy was unrelenting. 'I need to know who stuck a stiletto into my father's wife. Was it Dominic Russell? Did he kill her and Jack Smith, and then himself. Is that what happened? I need to know. Tell me, and then I'll go.'

Karen didn't answer. She couldn't have, not even if she had wanted to, because fear had taken hold of her throat with a strangler's grip and it was squeezing hard.

'We found this in your chest of drawers, Joseph.'

Joseph Tull was sitting in the same armchair as he had been a week previously, when questioned over his whereabouts at the time of his mother's death. As before, DI Holden was doing the questioning – with DS Fox and DC Lawson attending, and Dr Alan Tull looking anxiously on – but the casual nonchalance which Joseph had displayed at that earlier meeting had disappeared.

The reason for this lay on the glass-topped coffee table that lay between interviewer and interviewee – a pile of £20 notes that Holden had just tipped out of a large brown envelope. The gasp that came from Alan Tull indicated the surprise it was to him that his son should have such a sum of money hidden away, but it was Joseph's reaction that Holden was interested in. She thought she saw a brief flash of panic pass across his features, like a small cloud blown swiftly across the face of the full moon, but maybe that was merely in her imagination.

'So?' he replied, aggressively.

'So, where did you get it?'

'That's my business.'

It was the sort of sullen response that was designed to irritate. Holden's mouth tightened, and the vein down the left side of her head began to throb. She leant forward and spat her words like a burst from a sub-machine gun. 'It's my business too, until I decide it isn't! So don't mess me about, Joseph. Where did you get the money from?'

'You haven't been selling drugs, Joseph?' Alan Tull broke in. 'You promised me you wouldn't.'

'No, Dad, I haven't!'

'So where did you get the money?' Holden insisted. She would like to be doing this without Alan Tull in the room, but he had resisted that suggestion, and the key thing was to get some answers out of Joseph now.

'I was given it.'

'By whom?'

'A family friend.'

Holden stood up suddenly, and walked away from the sofa towards the door that led through to the hall. She leant with her back against it, but said nothing. Alan Tull was watching her, alarm in his eyes, while Joseph sat unmoving, resisting the impulse to look round at her, determined to win this battle of wills.

Eventually Holden spoke, quietly but firmly. 'So you were blackmailing this family friend?'

'No!' Joseph twisted round as he said this. 'I asked her and she gave it to me of her own free will.'

Fox laughed raucously, as if Joseph had just told a crude joke. 'That's what they all say, sonny!'

Joseph twisted round, suddenly furious. 'My name's not sonny!' he snarled, as if that was the worst thing that anyone could possibly have said to him.

Holden strode back across the carpet and sat down opposite Joseph Tull again. She wanted to regain control, and she wanted some straight answers, and she wasn't sure any more winding up from her sergeant would help. She'd stick with the softly, softly approach, at least for now.

'Look, Joseph,' she said, 'you do have to explain to me exactly how you obtained this money. If you prefer to do it without your father present, or indeed with a solicitor present down at the police station, then that is your choice. Otherwise, I'd like you to tell me who gave you the money, and how and why that was.'

'OK,' he replied. His lifted his left hand and pushed his long sweep of blond hair back off his face.

'So, first of all, who gave you the money?'

'Sarah Russell.'

'And she gave all £700 of it in one go, did she?'

'No, she gave me £400 initially, and another £300 later on.'

'And this was payment for some sort of service that you rendered?'

He laughed. 'What are you implying? That she was paying me for sex?' And he laughed again. 'You must be bloody joking!'

'I wasn't implying anything, but it's a lot of money.'

He smiled, 'I'd call it guilt money.'

'Guilt money?' Holden smiled back. She was making progress. 'Perhaps you can explain exactly what you mean?'

'It's not what you think it is. You see, the fact is I wanted to prove a point. I was out one night, with Hugo Horsefield. He got thrown out of Cornforth, and he was moaning that he just been kicked out of this bar job after only a week because this other guy thought he was a stuck-up git. So I told him he needed to get smarter. And he said what did a tosspot like me know about being smarter. And I said that sometimes you just need to get some leverage on people, and he told me I was talking a load of horse shit, and what did I know about earning money. Anyway, there was a bit more of that sort of thing, and in the end I said that I bet I could raise more money in a month than he could, no sweat.'

He paused, and looked around as if to assess how what he was saying was being received.

Holden was watching him, her eyes unblinking. She leant forward even more. 'That's all very interesting, Joseph, but what about Sarah Russell?'

'I didn't really know how I was going raise money, but then I was on the way to a class one day, and I saw Sarah Russell in the street with Geraldine Payne, and they seemed to be having – how shall I put it – rather an intimate conversation, and I suddenly thought, what the hell, that's how I'll beat Hugo. So the next day I went to Sarah's office at Cornforth, and I told her I had a serious financial problem, and of course she wasn't the slightest bit interested, so I asked her how Geraldine was, and that got her on the defensive, and I mentioned how they had seemed to be very friendly the day before in St John's Street. Anyway, that changed her attitude.'

'So she gave you the money?'

'Yes. She gave me £400 the next day.'

'So Sergeant Fox was right. You blackmailed her.'

'I wouldn't describe it as blackmail.'

'What the hell would you it describe as?' Fox jumped in noisily. Joseph Tull was, in his book, an overprivileged, spoilt piece of shit, and he had no time for any of his pissing about. 'You threatened her and demanded money. Would you prefer to call it extortion?'

'What did I threaten her with?'

189

'To tell her husband that she was carrying on an affair with Geraldine Payne.'

'I did wonder out loud what he might think if he found out, but I told Sarah that her secret was safe with me. Then I said I had to go as I was late for a class. The next day, she summoned me to her office and gave me £400. She said it was just to say thank you. Those were her words. Just to say thank you.'

'And what about the other £300?'

'She gave me that a week later.'

'And that was entirely out of the kindness of her heart again!' Fox gave another of his harsh laughs.

Joseph Tull turned away from Fox and back towards Holden. 'Look, if you want to call it blackmail, I don't care. I'll give the money back to Sarah if you want. It's just that I have the theory that everyone has a weak point. Find that weak point, apply a bit of pressure, and then see what they do. That's all I was doing. To be honest, I thought she was a tougher cookie than that. Hell, I don't have any compromising photographs of the two of them snogging or anything. I don't know for sure if they were having an affair. But she handed over the money readily enough. So, Inspector, the question you and your sergeant should be asking yourselves is why. Why did she not want her relationship with Geraldine Payne to become known to her husband? And does it have something to do with the death of my mother and the death of Sarah's husband? Because one thing I do know is that I didn't kill either of them, but somebody bloody did!'

'Excuse me, Guv!' All their heads turned. Wilson was at the door, and excitement was writ large across his face. 'Sorry to interrupt, but I've found something on the laptop. Two things in fact.'

Karen Pointer shut the lavatory door behind her, turned the lock, and then leant with her back to the door as she tried to gather her thoughts. Her breath was coming in deep, harsh gulps, and she tried to fight it. Steady, she told herself, keep calm. Slow down! She was used to getting up close and personal to dead bodies, but not to murderers – assuming she was right. Lucy had used the word stiletto. 'I need to know who stuck a stiletto into my father's wife.' The police had never used it in their news releases and interviews. They had made a conscious decision not to do so. They had merely referred to Maria Tull and Jack Smith being stabbed with a knife. But Lucy had said stiletto. Which meant either that someone had been talking out of turn or that Lucy was the killer. She had to tell Susan, but suppose Lucy was listening at the door? She pulled her mobile out of her pocket, found Susan's number and called it. As she did so, she moved over to the toilet and placed her free hand on its handle. Damn! There was no ringing at the other end, merely the brief silence that signifies that the mobile you are trying to contact is turned off. The silence slipped instantly into the pre-recorded message. God help me! The words rose noiselessly and unsummoned into her head. The last thing she would have called herself was religious, but the words came nevertheless, surfacing from childhood perhaps, or from some deeper level of unconscious knowledge. God help me!

She pressed the toilet handle, and whispered into her phone. 'For God's sake come, Susan. I think it's Lucy Tull, and she's in my flat.'

'Are you OK?' called Lucy from close outside.

'I'm fine!' she called back. She ran the taps, and washed her hands, to make the charade complete. For a moment she considered staying in the toilet, the door locked, but that would be to give the game away. Lucy hadn't twigged, surely, that she had made a mistake. All she had to do was behave as normal. She dried her hands, unlocked the door, and practised a smile. It would all be over soon.

They were standing around Wilson, who was hunched over the laptop.

'They were hidden away in the system files,' Wilson was saying. 'They had been completely renamed, so they took a bit of tracking down.' Lawson felt smug and irritated at the same time. Her hunch had been right. But it didn't look like Wilson was going to admit that now. Later, though, she'd have words. 'Here's the picture of Jack Smith. And here's the one of the classical rape painting.'

'No sign of the Judas painting, then?'

'No. Not so far. But I can't be certain it isn't hidden around here somewhere.'

'Dr Tull, does anyone else have access to this laptop except for your family?'

'Not as far as I know. But I hardly ever use it.'

'And I've got my own laptop,' Joseph added quickly.

'Which leaves us with Lucy.'

'What are you saying?' There was alarm in Alan Tull's voice.

'Where is Lucy?'

'You've got it all wrong,' Alan Tull was saying, apparently oblivious to the question. 'Lucy wouldn't do anything like that.'

Joseph looked at his watch. 'She should be at work still,' he said unemotionally.

'What's the address?'

'Beaumont Street.'

'That's not so far.'

Two minutes later Holden and Fox were driving back along Bainton Road towards the Woodstock Road. Or they would have been had a delivery lorry not stopped in the middle of the road to disgorge a sofa and pair of armchairs. Lawson and Wilson had been left behind with strict instructions to detain Lucy Tull if she arrived home. Fox got out to hurry the delivery men up, but Holden was unconcerned. A minute or two shouldn't matter. She pulled her mobile out of her jacket pocket, and realized with disgust that it was still powered off. She had forgotten. Her blooming mother. She pressed the red button and waited for it to kick into life. A text message soon flashed up. She viewed it. It was telling her she had a voice message. She keyed '121' and waited. It was from Karen. She recognized her voice, but her words were faint and indistinct, and besides, Fox had just got back into the car and had started talking. 'Shut up, Sergeant!' she snapped, and pressed '1' to listen to the message again.

'Christ!' she swore, and with such intensity that Fox jerked his head round even though he had now reached the Woodstock Road and was trying to negotiate a safe moment to turn out on to it.

'She's with Karen!' There was panic in her voice. 'She's at Karen's flat.'

Fox was staring at her, trying to take this information in. Holden could see his blankness, but could feel too the tide of absolute panic rising through her body. She willed herself to speak more slowly, but the fear was all but overwhelming.

'Lucy Tull is at Dr Pointer's flat. For God's sake, get there. Don't bloody hang about.'

'Where does she live?'

'Jericho Court. Over Aristotle Lane. If you turn into Polstead Road, and then take a right and left at the end.'

Fox was already out on the Woodstock Road, and heading south fast. This might not be his part of Oxford, but he knew where Polstead Road was, a road of huge houses so far removed from his own ex-council semi that it was way beyond a joke. Shit. Five hundred metres had passed ridiculously quickly and he found himself braking hard and sharply. He flashed his headlights and hooted too, but even so it took several seconds for the oncoming, almost stationary traffic to make a gap into which he could turn. That's the problem with plain-clothes coppers and plain-clothes cars. Other road users treat you with the anger they reserve for the BMW drivers of this world. A toxic mixture of anger and contempt.

Some forty seconds and several terrified pedestrians later they were approaching Jericho Court and Holden was screaming at Fox to stop. She pushed her door open and, before he had cut the engine, she was out on the pavement and sprinting towards an eight-storey block of flats that rose impersonally before them.

Holden did not wait for the lift. She took the stairs two steps at a time, driving herself upwards as if her very existence depended on it. She was a slim woman, but she never jogged, never went to the gym, and rarely swam except when on holiday, so by the time she had reached the second floor her muscles were starting to scream their complaints against this improbable and unreasonable imposition. As she rose higher, the pain spread to her lungs, and her head, and soon her whole being was demanding that she relent. But dread drove her on, forcing her legs to stretch and climb, stretch and climb till she was beyond pain and she stood finally on the seventh floor at the door to Karen's. She paused only then, to catch her breath and to screw herself up for whatever she might find beyond the door. Then she put her key into the door, twisted it, and pushed straight into the flat.

'Karen!' she shouted. All her training and all her common sense should have led Holden to utter this word in the manner of someone returning home after a day at work – 'Hi there, I'm home!' But she didn't. She shouted, in a shout gripped and moulded and empowered by the deepest fear. She looked around the living area and saw no one. 'Karen!' she called again, as hope and desperation battled with each other. And then she felt a breeze on her face, and saw the long net curtains flapping in that same current of air. The French window on to the balcony was open.

Her movement, previously frantic, was now slow motion. Through the curtains, she could see the shadow of a person. The figure did not move. Like a shop's marionette, it stood there, as if looking out across the canal that lay below, or maybe looking in through the curtains, watching. It was impossible to tell which. Thoughts, fears, assessments ran through her mind, but these were processes that took fractions of seconds, and almost immediately she resumed her forward progress. She was conscious she had no weapon in her hand. If it was Lucy on the balcony with a knife, she would need something, but looking for one did not occur to her. Her only thought was to get to the motionless figure out there, see who it was, and then react. It was as simple as that. Nothing else was possible. But please God, let it be Karen!

Detective Sergeant Fox should have been at his Inspector's back. He had followed in her footsteps across the manicured lawn that fronted the flats. But as he reached the entrance, he almost collided with a man who was himself sprinting round the corner from the back of the flats. He was wearing uniform green trousers and polo shirt, and as soon as he saw Fox he started shouting. 'Have you got a mobile? I need to ring "999"!'

It took Fox a few seconds to extract more information from the man, who was gibbering with shock, and then he was running again, hurtled his big frame round the corner of the flats, down the side and then round the next corner. And then, despite, all his years of experience, he stopped dead and for two or even three seconds stood unmoving.

The woman's body – for a woman it clearly was – was spreadeagled across the black railings which fronted the edge of the canal. The body had landed centrally, so that the spikes had pierced the width of the body just above the waist. Her legs were splayed, facing him, and her head and arms hung slack over the other side, above the dark, slow-running waters of the canal, so that he could not see the face. Fox shook himself, and moved forward again until he reached the railings. It seemed impossible that the woman could have survived the fall, but he stretched for and grabbed hold of her left hand, feeling for a pulse. She was, undeniably, dead, and he released her wrist. It was still warm. Finally, he pulled himself up on the railing, so he could see her face. It was, oddly, undamaged and even serene. It was the face of Dr Karen Pointer.

Fox turned and looked up. He, of course, had never visited Karen Pointer's flat, but he could see only one person above him, on the balcony below the topmost one. He couldn't see who it was. He assumed it was Lucy Tull, but, whoever it was or wasn't, he knew for certain that his boss was in danger. He started to run again, back round the flats. But on breasting the second corner he had to take sudden evasive action to avoid a grey-haired woman coming the other way. 'Is she all right?' the woman said, apparently unconcerned that a man of considerable bulk had very nearly flattened her. But Fox wasn't interested in either answering her or stopping. At the bottom of the stairwell, he hit the lift button in case it was waiting there. He would run up the stairs if he had to, but he knew the limits of his own mobility. Miraculously the door opened instantly, and he pushed himself inside it. Eight floors. He hit the button for the seventh. As the lift moved steadily upwards, he tried to work out on which side the canal would be, and so where the entrance to Karen's flat was likely to be, because he was pretty sure there would be at least two flats per floor, and he didn't want to waste time trying to enter the wrong one. The door opened at seven, and he rushed out, turning left. The door in front of him, with a '7b' on it, was ajar. At least he wasn't going to have to force it. He took a gulp, like a diver about to plunge off the high board, and thrust his way through the entrance.

'Hello, Inspector.' The figure on the balcony moved forward, pushing the flapping curtains to the side with her left hand.

'Where is she?' Holden spoke quietly, firmly, as her training kicked in over her emotions. 'What have you done to her?'

'There's been a terrible accident,' came the reply.

These words and the unutterable knowledge that they conveyed hit Holden like a tidal wave, deluging her so completely that she felt she must be swept into oblivion. Then the wave retreated, sucking and pulling every present, past and future hope out of her so completely that oblivion would have seemed bliss. But Susan Holden was a woman whose instincts had from her earliest years been honed towards fight not flight, a woman who lived in the reality of life, and not the fantasy of wish fulfilment. She was a survivor, and it was this instinct that cut in now, as Lucy Tull advanced slowly towards her, her left hand hanging loose at her side and her right hand held menacingly behind her back.

'Stand still!' Holden demanded. 'Hands out to the front!'

Lucy Tull stopped, and brought her hidden hand into view. In it, she held a knife. It was a kitchen knife, with a wide blade, the sort of heavy chopping knife you dice meat or vegetables with, that Karen had diced her meat and vegetables with. 'Such a terrible accident,' she said blankly. 'She just fell.'

Holden spoke slowly. 'Put the knife down!'

'You don't believe me, do you?' Her voice was now high and shrill, and she lifted her right hand so that the knife was pointing directly at Holden. 'You're trying to trick me!' Her voice had now changed to a hiss, and the pupils of her eyes had shrunk to such a degree that they were almost invisible. She stepped forward again, swaying slightly like a boxer weighing up a dangerous opponent, and her face was an emotionless mask. But it wasn't her face that Holden was watching. Holden moved the weight of her body forward, feinting towards Lucy's left, and then, as her opponent's knife hand slewed across to counter the move, she hurled herself forward, grabbing for Lucy's right wrist as she did so. Her hand closed tightly round its target, but as it did so a lightning flash of agony cut into her lower arm. Then her left hand joined the right, and together they gripped and twisted so violently that Lucy Tull screamed and the knife fell to the floor. Holden now pushed hard with her shoulder into Lucy's unbalanced body, and sent her sprawling across the floor.

Briefly she paused, scrabbling for the knife, and then hurling it way behind her, well out of reach of her assailant. But Lucy was back on her feet and retreating, back through the swirling curtains and out on to the balcony. For a moment, Holden paused, wondering where the hell Fox was and why he wasn't there backing her up, but she had no intention of waiting. She had got Karen's killer cornered, and she was going to nail her if that was the last thing she did.

'God, didn't she scream as she fell!' Lucy's voice, high and loud and mocking, sliced through the curtain. Adrenaline flooded through Holden's veins, fuelling her rage, and like a thing demented she burst through the flimsy barrier of curtain that separated her from her quarry, for her quarry was what Lucy Tull had now become. She crashed into her, and together they staggered and lurched against the balcony railing. Down below them someone screamed, but Holden was aware only of herself and Lucy Tull. She twisted round, trying to get a lock on her opponent, and for a moment she did, but then an elbow crashed with stunning force into the side of her head, and her grip slackened, and Lucy broke free. Holden fell to the ground, but instantly thrust herself up, conscious that if Lucy escaped back through the windows and into the flat, then she herself would be in serious danger – if not from the knife she had tried to throw away, then from the other four knives that she knew lived in Karen's butcher's block. Again she threw herself at Lucy, catching her by the door. This time she was more successful, grabbing and twisting Lucy's right arm, and forcing her round and down so that Lucy's chest was pressed against the top of the balcony railing, while she leant with all her own weight on top of her, willing her into submission.

'It's over, Lucy,' she said loudly. And then even more loudly she shouted the words again, as if merely by words she could compel her struggling opponent to surrender. 'It's over!'

But it wasn't over. For perhaps two or three seconds, the pair of them remained there, like a tableau frozen in time, for all the world like two spectators looking over a balcony to get a better view, or two friends locked in a romantic embrace as they shouted down to friends below. And that was when Holden finally saw Karen Pointer, her body spreadeagled across the black railings. There was an explosion of red across her white blouse, and her arms and legs were stretched out in gruesome symmetry. Holden shuddered and emitted a wail of agony.

Then Lucy Tull spoke, as if in response, her voice less shrill than before, but full of excited glee. 'And when she hit the railings, wow! She didn't half squeal! Just like a pig!'

Later, as she rolled every moment of those frantic events over and over in her head, Susan came to the conclusion that Lucy must have invented this, and had said it to throw her off her guard or maybe to provoke her into an uncontrolled reaction. She did hope so, for any other thought was too much to bear. But in those impossible moments, the only way she could hold on to reality was to ask the key question 'Why?' she bawled, bending her head low over Lucy's right ear. 'Why did you do it?'

'Why?' Lucy had giggled, as if in embarrassment, like a girl hearing a rude joke for the first time in her life. Then she stopped giggling. 'Why don't you ask Marjorie?' she replied. Holden momentarily released some of the pressure she was exerting as she took this in, and Lucy, sensing it, made a final effort to break free. But to no avail.

'Guv!' It was a man's voice behind her. 'I'm here. Hang on.' Susan Holden knew it was Fox's voice, and she cursed inwardly. She had heard and felt and suffered enough, and she wanted no help, and no interference. Not now. With an enormous grunt she tightened her grip on her struggling victim, and heaved. She felt the weight of Lucy's body begin to lift, and she heard a sharp crack as Lucy's wrist fractured under the pressure, but she pushed all the harder, until quite suddenly all resistance evaporated, and Lucy Tull hurtled over the balcony's edge and out into oblivion.

CHAPTER 11

The following Friday, at approximately 10.45 a.m. Susan Holden pulled into the car park in front of the Raglan Hospital, brought her vehicle to a halt in the furthest empty bay, and switched off her engine. She did not get out. For some ten minutes, she sat there, unmoving, with eyes tightly closed and arms folded across her body, as if immersed in meditation. But meditation requires an emptying of the mind, something she could not have begun to do in her present circumstances. Inside her head there were thoughts, images and emotions which whirled wildly around in such a maelstrom that she felt that sooner or later her brain must explode.

Eventually she uncrossed her arms, and put her right hand on the door handle. She knew she had to do it – to open the door and climb out and walk into the hospital and confront Marjorie Drabble – but the act of so doing seemed beyond her will and strength. But it was the least she could do for Karen, she told herself – to find out the truth, to find out what had driven Lucy Tull to kill. She cared not for Maria Tull and Jack Smith and Dominic Russell. Only professional pride would have driven her to root out the reason behind Lucy's killing of them. But professional pride had ceased to matter now, and not just because she had been suspended while the circumstances of Lucy Tull's death were fully investigated. Everything had ceased to matter except the reason for Karen's death. If only she had worked it out sooner, she could have saved her. Her left hand was thumping the dashboard, once, twice, and again. If only, if only, if only! She raised her head, and found herself looking into the eyes of a short, bald-headed man in a suit. He was staring at her, and he looked disconcertingly like her dead father. A surge of nausea swept up through her stomach, so that she felt she would vomit then and there. She pulled viciously at the door handle on which her right hand was still resting, desperate to escape the nightmare that was engulfing her. It swung open and banged hard against the silver BMW parked next to her, and the man scurried off towards the main door of the hospital, afraid of confrontation, maybe to report her. She didn't care. Holden gulped in the fresh air, as she fought to regain control of her body, and she noted with surprise – and relief – that the man moved, despite his shape, with remarkable nimbleness, and in that respect he was quite unlike her father. She sucked in another deep breath of air. He was no ghost. It was no nightmare.

As she entered the reception area of the Raglan Hospital, she felt a curious sense of déjà vu. There was the same sense of entering a rather smart hotel, elegant but restrained, where people move purposefully but quietly, and conversations are held in hushed tones. The receptionist, whom she thought was different from her last visit, looked up and peered over her glasses, as if daring her to proceed without first checking in personally with her. Holden moved dutifully towards her.

'Can I help you?' The receptionist spoke briskly, but with a cut-glass accent that suggested that even the receptionists in the Raglan Hospital were recruited from the choicest inhabitants of North Oxford.

'I've come to see Marjorie Drabble.'

'Are you a relative?' There was a tone of puzzled disbelief in her question, as if the woman standing in front of her did not match her idea of what a relative of Mrs Marjorie Drabble would look like.

'A friend,' she lied. 'I'm Susan Holden.'

The woman frowned. 'I see!' Two words that can mean so much, depending on how they are spoken. 'Well, sit down. I'll put a call through.' And she turned dismissively away.

Holden walked over to the seating area and sank into a large cream-coloured leather armchair so soft that for a moment it threatened to swallow her. There was a coffee maker on the table across the room, and the flask was half full, but the effort of getting up felt enormous, so she shut her eyes and tried to make do with the aroma.

'Excuse me!'

Holden jumped. Ms Reception was standing over her, and was prodding her lightly on the upper arm. 'Mrs Drabble will see you now.'

Holden stood up quickly, or as quickly as the depth of the chair would allow.

'Have you been before? Do you know where her room is?'

'Yes.' She reached down and picked up her shoulder bag. She wondered if she'd been asleep for ten seconds or ten minutes. Not that it mattered, but the receptionist remained standing there, as if reluctant to allow this rather dubious visitor to move unchaperoned around her hospital. 'Thank you,' Holden said firmly, 'I'll find my own way, I'm sure.'

'Oh!' came the disapproving reply. 'Well, it's room 203.' And with that the woman turned abruptly round, withdrawing towards her reception desk, where she would, Holden had no doubt, lie in wait for the next unwary arrival.

Holden made her way to room 203 with rather less difficulty than she had expected. The door was shut, so she tapped softly on it and let herself in. Marjorie Drabble was lying in her bed, but was propped up on three or four plumped pillows, apparently asleep. Holden closed the door quietly behind her and walked over towards her.

'Sit down where I can see you,' Marjorie Drabble said, gesturing with her hand. If her eyes were open, they were only just so.

Holden sat down. 'Can I get you anything?' It seemed a better thing to say than to ask how she was.

Finally Marjorie Drabble's eyes opened fully. 'I understood you were off the case?'

Holden nodded. Her suspension wasn't exactly a secret, not since Don Alexander had revealed it to his *Oxford Mail* readers the previous day. 'This isn't an official visit,' she said quickly. 'I was just hoping that we could have a chat. Off the record.'

'What if I say "No"?'

'Then I will have to leave you in peace.'

She gave a single laugh, followed by a cough. 'I get enough peace, thanks. Pass me some water, will you, and then you can ask your damned questions.'

Holden got up, poured some water into the glass on the side table, and offered it to her. She grasped it in two hands, and helped herself, taking several gulps, before she passed it back to the hovering Holden.

'No notes, no hidden tape recorder, no nothing. Promise me!'

'I promise.'

'And may God condemn you to eternal damnation if you break your promise!' The ferocity of the ill woman took Holden quite by surprise, and for a few moments she busied herself with replacing the glass, and picking up a greetings card that had fallen on the floor.

'Well, get on with it then!'

Holden sat down, and composed herself. She had listed several questions in her head, but inevitably they were no longer there when she wanted to draw on them. She cleared her throat. 'When I asked Lucy why she had committed these murders, she told me to ask you.'

'Did she now?' Drabble looked at her quizzically. 'When did she say that?'

'Just before she died.'

'Did you push her?' The question hit her like a punch in the solar plexus.

'What do you mean?' Of course, Holden knew what she meant, but evasion came easily to her. 'We had a struggle. She had already killed Dr Pointer. She had stabbed her and then she had pushed her over the balcony on to the railings below.'

'Stabbed her?' There was real surprise in her voice. 'That wasn't in the paper.'

'No, it wasn't.' Holden couldn't see any point in withholding this information. It would be in the public domain soon enough. 'But that's what she did. She stabbed her, and then she pushed her over the edge.'

Drabble was staring hard at her. She grunted. 'So, it was revenge was it?'

'Revenge?' Holden was floundering. 'I'm not quite with you.'

'Liar!' She laughed. 'You killed Lucy out of revenge. Yes or no?'

'No!' she replied sharply. Perhaps too sharply. 'We had a struggle on a balcony seven floors up. You know that. I guess I was stronger, and she ended up falling.'

'You mean you pushed her.'

Holden was non-plussed by this turn of events. She had come to try to tie up the loose ends about Lucy's motives for murder, and here she was being, in effect, accused of murder by a terminally ill old woman. She tried to defend herself. 'When you're fighting like that with someone, there's a lot of pushing and shoving.'

'You were lovers, right, you and Dr Karen Pointer.'

Again, Holden was startled. That had certainly not been broadcast in the *Oxford Mail* by Don Alexander. Not yet.

'There's no point in denying it,' Drabble said firmly. 'I can see it by your face. And besides, Lucy told me. It's amazing what she learnt in that dentist's surgery. She heard Geraldine Payne and Karen talking about Karen and you.'

Holden again made no response. What was there to do except admit it, or deny it, and she couldn't deny it. She wouldn't do that.

'So when Lucy killed your Karen, you saw red, and you killed her. Deliberately. Not that anyone can prove it was deliberate, but I think we both know it was.' She had been leaning forward slightly as she made her argument, but now she lay back, and again shut her eyes. Holden was relieved to get this break. Her mouth was dry, and she wished now she had helped herself to coffee in the reception area. There was no second cup on Marjorie Drabble's side table, so she couldn't even pour herself some water. She ran her tongue round her lips, and tried to think how to regain control of the situation.

'OK, then!' Drabble's eyes were open, and there was both triumph and amusement on her face. 'It's your turn.'

Holden looked back at her. She had thought a lot about this since Karen's death. In fact, when she had not been grieving or weeping, her only coherent thoughts had been about this. She began. 'The question that I keep hitting my head against is why now? I can understand that Lucy hated her stepmother, but why did she kill her just ten days ago, and not ten weeks ago or ten months ago.'

'I'd have thought that would have been obvious. She had just discovered Maria had been having an affair with the plumber.'

'Yes, I suppose so,' Holden admitted uncertainly, 'and that would explain why she killed Jack Smith soon afterwards, but—'

'But what? That all seems very straightforward to me.'

'I can think of at least two buts.' Holden paused, but her eyes were fully alert, watching the frail old woman in front of her, whose brain and spirit were anything but frail. 'Why don't you ask Marjorie?' That had been what Lucy Tull had said. Which meant, surely, that Marjorie Drabble knew more than she was letting on. 'But number one: can it really have been the first time that Maria had had an affair?'

'Possibly not. But maybe it was the first time Lucy found out.'

Holden rubbed her nose with her right forefinger. It wasn't so much what Drabble had said – she herself had thought along the same lines – but the readiness of her answers, as if she had been expecting this interview and had prepared for it accordingly.

'Yes,' she admitted, 'I expect you're right.' But she was hoping that she herself was right too, that by enlisting Marjorie Drabble's help in all of this, she might also be lulling her into saying something more than she intended. 'But that doesn't explain why she killed Dominic Russell, does it?' She waited then, curious to see if the response this time would be as quick. And, of course, she wondered what exactly Marjorie would say in response.

The answer to that was, initially, nothing. 'All this talking is making me thirsty,' she said. 'Perhaps you can order us a pot of tea? Just dial zero. In the meantime, I'd like a couple of minutes' break.'

Holden did as she was told, and sat down again until there came a tap at the door, and a smartly uniformed middle-aged woman entered balancing a tray with a tea pot, milk jug and a pair of cups and saucers, all in the same blue-rimmed white china. Holden poured them each a cup. 'White, no sugar, please,' Drabble said, opening her eyes, and shuffling herself into a more upright position. She took a sip as Holden moved back to her seat. 'So, where were we?'

'Dominic Russell,' Holden responded. She wasn't convinced that Drabble had forgotten, but maybe with the combination of pain and drugs she had. 'I was saying that I couldn't see why Lucy would have killed Dominic Russell.'

'So do you have any theories?'

Holden shrugged. Drabble was suddenly being very cagey. She had been full of immediate responses concerning the deaths of Maria Tull and Jack Smith, but now she seemed to be deliberately avoiding giving any answers. 'Maybe he had had an affair with Maria,' Holden mused, 'but somehow that doesn't ring true to me.'

'Why not?' Again, she was much more ready to ask questions than answer them.

'My impression was that Dominic was more interested in younger women than women of Maria's age.'

'Oh?' Another uncommitted response.

Holden said nothing. Maybe silence would push Drabble into opening up. Or making a mistake. For whatever else, Holden was convinced she was holding back on something. 'Why don't you ask Marjorie?' The words rattled insistently in her head. So she sipped her tea and waited.

Drabble too sipped at her tea, until she had finished it, and she held it there loosely in her hands. And then, quite suddenly, she spoke. 'What about the painting? I understand they found one next to Dominic's body, and it had been vandalized.'

Holden smiled politely. 'Yes, quite right.' She finished her cup of tea, and discarded it on the windowsill to her right, before turning back to face Drabble. 'But, you know, the painting was not that valuable. A few thousands of pounds, but not hugely valuable, except possibly if you're a Christian who strongly disapproved of the idea of Judas's mother being comforted by Jesus' mother. Would Lucy have had had views on that, do you think?'

'I don't know. But I doubt it. She didn't talk about religion or going to church, as far as I can recall.'

'So what exactly did she talk about when she was with you?' Holden said quickly. It was time to apply some pressure.

'Gosh! Let me see.' Again there was the impression of a woman playing for a bit of time. 'Well, she was very considerate of my health. I suppose she was worried I might change my mind and sue her father. My son Graham was very keen that I should—'

But Holden had had enough of pussyfooting. 'You knew her mother. Her real mother, that is. Christine, wasn't it? You told me last time Lucy liked to ask questions about her.'

'Did I. Yes, well I suppose we did talk about her. Lucy wanted to know what she was like.'

'Like the dresses and styles she wore and the music she listened to?' Holden continued to press, speaking quickly and firmly. Even her questions sounded like statements. 'Isn't that what you told me last time? I'm fairly sure it was.'

Marjorie Drabble, who had been sitting up ever since she had received her tea, now lay back into her pile of pillows and gave an exaggerated sigh. 'I'm feeling a bit weary.'

Holden made a noise that was halfway between a grunt and a laugh. But she wasn't ready to concede any ground. 'You only have to ring the bell, and the nurse will come running, and I'll be forced to leave. Not that that it is any skin off my nose. Lucy is dead anyway, and we know she's the murderer. It's just dotting the i's and crossing the t's. That's what I want to do, for my own satisfaction. I can't bring back Karen from the dead. And she died because she found out about Lucy somehow, and Lucy realized.'

She stopped, to gather breath, though she wasn't quite sure what else she wanted to say.

'She died because you didn't catch Lucy first!' But the stark truth of what she had said struck Holden with a ferocity of such intensity that she felt an almost physical pain in her stomach. Christ, how could she say that? How could she lay the blame on her?

How? Because, at some level, it was true. Holden was crying now. She felt the tears running down hot over her cheeks, stinging the pores of her skin, but she made no attempt to wipe them away. Her whole body reverberated with huge wracking sobs, and for the first time since Karen died, she abandoned herself completely to grief. And in this abandonment, she found – eventually – comfort.

'I'm sorry.' The apology didn't register at first. It was a small voice, barely audible above the storm. 'That's wasn't nice of me,' it persisted. Holden raised her head, and discovered Marjorie Drabble looking at her. And there seemed to be genuine concern in her eyes.

Holden wiped her face, and nodded. 'I don't know what came over me.'

'In fact, I'm not a very nice person, you know,' Drabble said, continuing her own train of thought, and speaking more loudly, as if determined to be heard.

Despite her own emotional pain, Holden was alert to the change of emphasis in Drabble. She wondered how to respond, for the woman seemed to need a response. 'My mother,' Holden said, taking refuge from her own uncertainties, 'would say we are all sinners.'

'How comforting!' Drabble's reply was sarcastic, but softly modulated. 'But not for me.'

'Would you like to tell me why you feel you're not a very nice person?'

Drabble laughed, and it was a genuine laugh of pleasure. 'Oh, Susan! I hope you don't mind me calling you Susan? But in the circumstances, I'd like to. You really don't give up, do you? Well, yes I would like to tell you. I need to tell someone, and you're the one I'd like it to be. No sanctimonious confession to a priest for me.' She laughed again, but her face had turned serious, deadly serious. 'I'll tell you, and you only. And it goes no further than us two! All right?!'

'You have my word.'

'Well, that's good enough by me. I just hope you don't hate me by the end, because if it wasn't for me your Karen would still very likely be alive.'

Holden felt tears welling up again, and she swallowed hard as she tried to regain control of her emotions. 'I think I know that already,' she said. 'It's the detail I don't know.'

'Would you mind just straightening me up, first? I've got a bit uncomfortable.'

It took a couple of minutes for Holden to complete the task of plumping pillows, pulling tighter the sheets to remove folds, and hoisting the admittedly rather lightweight old woman into a more upright position. The cancer had taken its toll. Holden gave her a glass of water, and poured herself the lukewarm remains of tea from the pot. Then she went back to her chair, sipped at her cup and waited for Marjorie Drabble to begin.

'What stupid, stupid things we do with our lives!' She was looking past Holden, and out of the window, her eyes apparently focused on some distant point where everything made sense.

'Lucy first came to me on the Thursday, the Thursday before Maria's death. She came, as I told you before, to plead for her father. My son Graham was all for throwing the book at Alan for failing to diagnose my cancer, but I never really wanted to, and when she started to cry, I couldn't deny her. Why should I want to? Her mother Christine and I had been such good friends. And I guess it's no surprise that it was Christine who we talked about most, because Lucy really wanted to know all about her – the mother she never really knew. So I told her how Christine loved Laura Ashley dresses, and Indian skirts, and joss sticks and Chinese takeaways, and Edna O'Brien's novels and all that sort of thing. You name it and we talked about it!' Drabble stopped, and a smile crossed her face as she remembered her friend of long ago.

'And did you discuss Christine's death?' The question popped out of Holden's mouth almost new born, for it had only been conceived in the recesses of her mind as she listened to Drabble, and yet it seemed suddenly so obvious when the key link between the women was Christine Tull.

'Yes, we did.' She nodded slowly as she said this, but otherwise went silent.

Holden waited. Outside the door, footsteps approached, but then passed on further down the corridor. 'And?' she finally prompted.

'I told her the truth. Just as I will now tell you the truth. But I don't want to be interrupted, so just let me tell it the way I want to, and at the end – maybe – I'll answer any questions you have. Right?'

'Right,' Holden agreed. After all, what else could she say?

'You know some of the details, I'm sure. There must be a police report on it somewhere, and it's no secret. It's just not something people talk about any more. In fact, they never did. Christine died driving home from Leamington Spa. She lost control of the car, and ran into a tree, and died instantly. When they ran tests, they found she was way over the alcohol limit, so it looked like it was her own stupid fault. The only problem for that theory was that it seemed out of character. Christine was a one or two glasses of wine at the most type, and of course she left behind Lucy, who was barely one year old, so it was just not something people much cared to talk about, at least not anywhere near Dr Tull. But that isn't the whole story.' She stopped then, though whether to get her breath or whether to get some sort of feedback, Holden wasn't sure, and anyway it didn't actually matter.

'Are you OK?' Holden asked. 'Would you like some water?'

'You see,' Drabble continued, ignoring the question, 'she was in Leamington Spa at a publishing event. She was a books editor, and they were doing a launch for a new series of arts books, and one of the contributors was Dominic Russell. So he was there too, and one thing led to another, and he seduced her. He always fancied himself, did Dominic, not to mention anyone young and pretty in a short skirt, and poor Christine was completely taken in.'

Holden's mind was in overdrive as she took in and assessed this new information. Could she fully trust Marjorie Drabble? She had thought that in these circumstances she could, but she wasn't entirely sure. 'How do you know?' she interrupted.

'Christine told me, of course. How else? We were the best of friends, and she rang me in a complete state about 9.30 that evening. She was so upset she was almost incoherent. She told me how Dominic had invited her round to his room before supper to discuss some ideas he had for future books, and the next thing was he was plying her with drink and . . . well, she didn't have a chance. She was almost hysterical when she told me. I tried to calm her down, and I thought at the time that I had managed it, but no. She was meant to stay in Leamington that night, and I assumed she had, but apparently she checked out at about 10.15, telling the receptionist she had to go home because her daughter was ill. And, of course, she never made it.'

'So, when you told Lucy all this, how did she react?'

'How do you think she reacted? She was almost apoplectic with rage.'

'I see.' But in reality Holden saw as through a glass darkly, and even as she thought about what Drabble had said, a string of questions were accelerating round her head like hyperactive children at a four-year-old's party, running wild and refusing to be controlled. For example, when exactly did this conversation take place? And when Drabble told Lucy all this, were Maria and Jack already dead? And did she know that Lucy had killed them? And if so, why did she tell Lucy about it? Because she wanted Dominic dead? And if so why? And if so, did she encourage Lucy to kill Maria and Jack too? What the hell was Drabble's motive in all of this?

Holden stood up, and turned to look out the window, though her brain was so overloaded that it barely registered what the eyes saw. After several seconds, she turned back and looked down at the sick old woman in the bed, trying to divine what was going on inside her head. *Mens sana in corpore sano*. It was a Latin verse that her father had taken delight in claiming in his lighter moments. So was the opposite true too? Sick minds in sick bodies. How sick in the head was Marjorie Drabble?

'Did you want Lucy to kill Dominic?'

'Does it matter?'

For someone who only a short while previously had appeared keen to make a confession, this was a curious answer. Was she playing some more complicated game? And of course it mattered. It was integral to her own desire for resolution. She felt the tide of anger, rising through her body, invading her head, and she fought to hold it back. 'Did you encourage Lucy to kill Maria?'

'Why should I?' The reply was instant.

'Yes, or no? I thought we were being truthful towards each other.'

'You haven't been entirely truthful, yourself,' came the response. 'You haven't told me the truth, the whole truth, and nothing but the truth about Lucy's death, have you?'

'Lucy is better off dead than alive. Period.'

Drabble laughed, a laugh of genuine amusement. 'You're dodging the question, Inspector, but never mind. I know what the true answer is, even if you can't admit it. But as for your question, no I didn't encourage her to kill Maria. But she told me about it afterwards. Actually, I guessed she had done it, because she came to me the next night, and burst into tears when I said how sorry I was, but I knew she had no love for her stepmother, so I knew it wasn't grief that was eating away at her. So I asked her outright, and she admitted it immediately, and she talked and talked and I listened, and at the end I assured her that her secret was safe with me.'

'So what about Jack?'

'I guess I'm not guilt free there. I asked her what she intended to do about Jack, and she said she didn't know, and I told her she should do what she wanted to do. A couple of days later she returned, and told me she had killed him too.'

'You think he deserved that?'

Again she laughed, but it was a harsher sound. 'Actions have consequences. That's something my grandmother used to say, and that's something I believe.'

Holden pursed her lips. Marjorie Drabble was a hard one to read. She sat down again on the chair, and leant forward. 'So,' she said, 'if that is the case, what was the action that led to Dominic Russell's death? His seduction of Christine?'

Another laugh rang out, and echoed round the room so loudly that Holden wondered if the nurse wouldn't come running to see what on earth had caused such unseemly behaviour. But no one came, and eventually the laughing petered out, and Drabble's face grew stern. 'Isn't that enough?' she demanded.

'So you told Lucy because you knew that she had killed Maria and Jack, and so you also knew there would be nothing to stop her killing Dominic too. You killed Dominic by proxy, in fact. Is that right?'

Drabble folded her arms, and looked straight into Holden's face. 'I did say I wasn't a very nice person.'

'That isn't an answer to my question.'

'I know.' She smiled what was almost a smile of sympathy. 'You answer my question about Lucy's death, and I'll answer yours.'

Holden hesitated, but only briefly. She too wanted to confess to someone. Needed too, even. A memory from childhood, painfully vivid, came to her: she was standing on the high diving board at the swimming pool, waiting to jump, and a line of children, mostly older than her, stood behind, urging her to get on with it or get out of the way. And she had been so scared, and yet she was determined to do it, because her mother was in the viewing gallery, watching. So eventually she had breathed in, pinched her nose, and had jumped. And much to her surprise, she had survived.

She took in a deep breath. 'I pushed Lucy over the balcony because she murdered the first person I have ever truly loved.'

There, she had said it, and she shut her eyes. But the feeling of relief that she craved did not follow. Instead, she felt her throat tighten, and even with her eyes closed tears began to well up, and then her whole body started to shake again. And all she could feel was an intense, head-splitting feeling of hatred for the woman who had shattered her happiness. She had absolutely no regrets.

'Thank you for telling me,' Drabble said. Her own eyes were red, and she dabbed at them with the corner of a sheet as she waited until she had got Holden's attention. 'I got Lucy to kill Dominic because I was incapable of doing it myself.' Drabble said this in a determined, raised voice. 'For years and years and years I had wanted him to die. Well, not just die. I used to fantasize that he would get cancer and then die a very long and very agonizing death, and that after death he would discover that God did exist and that God was a vengeful God who would condemn him to everlasting torment. You see, the bottom line was that I didn't have the guts to do my own dirty work. But when this golden opportunity turned up in the form of Lucy Tull, well!' She paused, and rubbed the back of her hand across her forehead, on which beads of sweat had now begun to form. 'You see, Susan, Christine wasn't the only person to fall prey to Dominic's charms. Six months before that, I had had an affair with him. Not a one-night encounter like poor Christine, but nearly three months of furtive meetings and often, I am ashamed to say, rather exciting sex. The only problem was that in my naivety I got pregnant. When I told Dominic, he dropped me like the proverbial hot potato, and I was left not knowing whose child I was carrying – Dominic's or my husband's. I never did try to find out. What was the point? At least the two possible fathers were the same skin colour and the same hair colour, and both even then showed a tendency to carry too much weight. In fact, the more I thought about it, the more I realized how alike they were, except in temperament.'

'So that child was Graham?'

'Yes. Of course he has no idea, and must never know. You do understand that?'

'I do.' What else could she say? She had promised to maintain secrecy. And she had meant it. And besides, some things were best kept secret.

'And I suppose Graham is the other reason why I did nothing. Even if I had killed Dominic myself, the chances are I would have been discovered, and then what? People like you start digging and asking questions, and before you know it Graham is left with the awful knowledge that he may be a bastard. I may not have been a perfect mother, but I am better than that.'

Both women now fell into silence. There was, suddenly, nothing left to say. Nothing left at all. Holden eventually stood up, stretched, and then stepped closer, bending down over the bed. 'I'd better be off, Marjorie,' she said quietly.

Drabble looked up at her. Her face was wiped clean of emotion. Only exhaustion was visible. 'Thank you for coming, Susan,' she whispered. 'I've enjoyed our chat.'

Holden bent lower, and kissed the woman on the forehead.

'Goodbye, Marjorie.'

Holden turned and moved towards the door. Drabble watched her go. She saw her open the door, and watched it swing noiselessly shut behind her, and only then did she lift a hand in silent farewell.

It was barely 5.30 in the evening, but it felt later. Susan Holden made her way towards the front door. It had been one of those grim autumnal days which underline the fact that winter isn't so much round the corner, as already up your front path and hammering rudely on the door. Holden wondered, without enthusiasm, who else might be hammering on her door right now. The last few days had impressed on her something that she had known, but ignored for some time – that she didn't actually have many friends. Most of her time had been spent at work, or doing things with work colleagues, or humouring her mother, or trying to forget all of those things. So the chances were that it would be a door-to-door sales person, one of those wretched people who try to sell you dishcloths you don't need, or who offer you a 'free inspection' of your exterior brickwork, or a student trying to sign you up to some no doubt terribly good cause. Alternatively, it could be her mother, come to check up on her. That was as far as her imagination took her.

She undid the security chain on her door and pulled the door wide. She didn't need a ruddy security chain, didn't need to peer through a thin crack to check on the identity of her visitor before allowing them in. She wasn't decrepit. Whoever it was, let them come in. She was ready for them.

'Hello, Guv!'

'Fox!' She wasn't ready for him.

He stood there, his hands in his coat pockets, and a slightly forced smile of greeting on his face, as if posing reluctantly for a photograph. His face and hair were glistening, and Holden realized that behind him it was raining the thin, miserable rain that had threatened all day but never quite materialized.

'I was just passing, Guv, and I thought—'

'For God's sake, come in. And I'm not your Guv at present, as you well know.'

He eased himself past her, and then started to fight his way out of his coat. He had never been inside her house before. He had called there on a number of occasions, but only to pick her up or drop her off. There were pegs in the corridor and he was conscious that his coat needed hanging up rather than dumping in a damp pile somewhere. 'Actually, I'm on the way to the Phoenix, but I'm running a bit early, so I thought I'd call in and see how you were.' As lies goes, it was barely adequate.

'What would you like to drink? Tea or alcohol.'

'I'd go for a small whisky, if that's OK.'

'Ice, water?'

'No thanks.'

'Let's go and sit in the kitchen. It's nicer there.'

The whisky bottle was, Fox noted, three-quarters empty and was standing defiantly in front of the kettle. He sat down at the table, and watched in silence as she found two tumblers and poured out two generous portions.

'It's not the same without you,' he said suddenly, as she set his glass in front of him.

She sat down opposite, and smiled back. It was good to have a visitor. Any visitor. Even Fox. 'I hope that doesn't mean it's better with me out the way?'

'It's bloody marvellous,' he said in a deadpan voice.

'Glad to hear it!' And she laughed, though rather unconvincingly. Then silence fell, an uncertain and – as far as Fox was concerned – an uneasy silence. He knew he had to say something, but he couldn't bring himself to tell her just yet.'

'We thought you'd like to know about Sarah Russell and Geraldine Payne.'

Holden looked up, relieved. She was wondering why the hell he had really come. To check that she hadn't fallen apart? But this was comfortable territory – the nuts and bolts of the case.

'You know', he continued. 'About why it was that Sarah succumbed to blackmail by Joseph Tull.' He paused, as he wondered how precisely to phrase his words.

'I'm listening,' Holden said, the familiar impatience back in her voice.

'Well, we interviewed them both. Geraldine and Sarah, that is.' He paused.

'And?'

'It turns out they weren't having an affair. Geraldine admitted to being a lesbian, not that that was news, of course. But Sarah Russell insisted she wasn't. It was just that she'd had it up to her ears with her husband. She wanted a divorce, but she hadn't told him because she was trying to make other living arrangements first, and Geraldine was her confidante.'

Holden frowned, her mind fully focused. 'I hadn't realized that Geraldine and Sarah were great friends.'

'It was more complicated than that. Remember, Jack Smith found the Judas painting in Geraldine's house.'

'Of course.'

'Well, they both admitted that they thought that Dominic Russell was helping Maria sell it on, so with Maria dead, Sarah became Geraldine's best bet to recover it for herself. But Geraldine was also Sarah's support. Sarah had been wanting to leave Dominic and get a divorce. No surprise there perhaps, but Sarah also reckoned Dominic was cheating her. She was an equal partner in the business, but profits had been dropping, and then she discovered that Maria had set up a big deal for Dominic when she was last in Venice, but he had denied it, saying there was only one painting involved. So she was pretty damn sure that he was doing other business but putting it through a different company.'

'You have been busy. Well done!' She spoke like a teacher congratulating a five-year-old, but she meant it, though frankly it wasn't that earth shattering. It was rather prosaic, in fact. Money and petty jealousies. When push came to shove, that's often what it did boil down to. Grubby little motives. She took another sip of whisky. 'Sounds like you don't need me.'

Fox looked across at her. Self-pity wasn't something he was used to seeing in his boss. Perhaps, as Lawson had wondered out loud back at the station in her know-it-all way, perhaps Holden was cracking up.

'Don't be bloody ridiculous, Guv. We all want you back. And both Lawson and Wilson sent their best wishes. They're very concerned for you.'

'That's kind of them,' Holden replied. And she meant it. She missed them. She missed not being in the office – the routine, the camaraderie, the banter – and she missed her team. They were important to her, and yet here she was under suspension, not knowing when she would be allowed back. Or if. She cleared her throat noisily, as she felt her eyes begin to moisten. 'And how are Lawson and Wilson?'

Fox didn't answer immediately. He was looking intently into his glass, as if within its contents he might find the elusive answer to all things temporal and eternal. Or, at least, something intelligent and helpful to say. Lawson's and Wilson's concern, and his own too, was not merely about her suspension, but it was also about the death of Karen Pointer. It seemed that he had been just about the last person in the station to know about Holden and Pointer's relationship, and he knew he ought to say something, but he could think only of the obvious things like he was really sorry or how they were all thinking of her back at the station, but these sounded bloody feeble when he rehearsed them in his head. Perhaps sympathy always feels forced and inadequate to the person expressing it. But whatever, that wasn't why he had come.

'They're fine,' he said finally. Although it wasn't entirely true.

Holden took a sip at her whisky. 'Anyway, I'll be back before you know it.'

'Of course you will, Guv.' But neither of them was convinced. 'I want you to know that I'm on your side, Guv.' He had meant to work his way gently into this conversation, but he found that sort of thing difficult. The crucial thing was to get it said, to get it out there on the table. 'Lucy Tull's death was an accident,' he insisted, and he brought his left hand down heavily on the table to emphasize his point. 'Hell, it could just as easily have been you falling over that balcony, couldn't it? In fact, it was a case of either you or her, and thank God it was her.'

Holden looked down at her glass, and took another, deeper sip, taking refuge in it from the jumble of her thoughts, and in particular the one thought that wouldn't go away – that it might have been better if it had been her. That way, she too could have embraced oblivion or whatever it was that awaited people after death. At least she and Karen would have been there together.

'There's something else you need to know, Guv.' There, he had said it. Started the ball rolling. That was the hardest bit. That's what he told himself, though he didn't believe it. Soon he would get to the end of telling her, and then he could leave.

Holden was looking at him. Her face was etched with pain and tiredness and grief, but overlaying it all was a look of resignation of such awfulness that Fox suddenly felt terribly afraid for her.

'Well, tell me then!' she said in a voice that was barely above a whisper, 'Don't keep me in suspense.'

'It's to do with Karen Pointer,' he said. 'We thought you should know. Her inquest is next week, but in view of everything we felt you should know first. Before it becomes public knowledge.'

He picked up his glass, and took another slug of whisky, in the hope that it might help. 'Someone filmed her death,' he said quietly.

'What?' Fox had seen plenty of people in shock, and had had to pass on the worst kind of news to people, but rarely had he seen blood disappear from a person's face with quite such dramatic speed. 'What are you talking about?'

Fox swallowed. He would tell it how it was, stick to the basic facts, and no more. Then he would go. 'There's a block of flats adjacent to Karen's block. It overlooks the canal like hers. It looks pretty much like her block, actually. A woman was out on her balcony. It's near enough the same height as Karen's, so she had a good view of what happened. And when she realized something was going on, she used her mobile phone to film it. She got a ten second video clip. Not of the precise moment of death, I should say, but of the struggle just before it.'

'So, has she sold it to the media? Is it going to appear on the six o'clock news?'

'No, we're holding it as evidence. But I guess we're lucky she didn't just post it on YouTube.'

'Christ!'

'Well, we are fortunate at the moment, but in the future who knows.'

'So it shows them struggling on the balcony, does it?'

Fox hesitated, and when he did reply it was only a signal word. 'Mostly.'

'Mostly!' Holden's response exploded across the gap between them with such force that Fox flinched backwards. 'What the hell do you mean by "mostly"?'

Fox leant confidentially forward. Oddly, the burst of temper encouraged him. It was more like the woman he knew. Tough, direct, no bloody nonsense. 'The neighbour heard a lot of shouting initially. She was on her balcony, and was just finishing her fag, when she heard all this noise. Really wild, scary shouting she said it was. And the next moment a woman came out on the balcony. That was Lucy. And then moments later another woman – Karen –

came out, and she was doing most of the shouting, it seemed.'

'What do you expect?' Holden was on her feet now, and her voice was raised, almost shouting in sympathy. 'Karen was probably petrified. She was trying to scare Lucy. She knew she was the killer.'

Fox held up his hand, and held it there as he waited for Holden to calm down. He hadn't finished yet. 'Karen had a knife in her hand,' he said simply.

'What? Karen?'

'Yes, Karen.'

'Are you sure?'

'It's on the film. There's no doubt at all. Karen had a knife in her hand when she came on to the balcony. And then she attacked Lucy with it.' He paused again, but this time there was no question or interruption from Holden. 'She actually caught Lucy with it, a gash across the lower left forearm, but after that the knife was dropped or got knocked out of her hand, and anyway when the film cut out after ten seconds, the two of them were struggling hand to hand, and Karen was being pressed back against the wall. According to the witness, she fell to her death only seconds later. The witness then rang 999, before heading for the lift, to try and come down and help. She's a bit arthritic so running down the stairs wasn't an option. It was her I nearly knocked over when I ran to come and help you.'

'It was self-protection.' Holden was still standing up, and she was lecturing Fox loudly, her right hand in the air, emphasizing her point of view. 'Don't you see, Karen knew that Lucy was the killer. She had worked it out. She left me a message on my mobile. She must have been scared witless. So she took the knife out of her butcher's block to defend herself. Don't you see?'

'Of course I do.' Fox tried to sound calm and logical, but underneath he had gone to pieces. 'But it's not my view that counts.'

Holden strode across to the side door that led to the garden. She banged her forehead against it with such force that Fox stood up in alarm.

Then she swung round and pointed an accusing finger at him. 'What other view is there?'

'A lawyer could make a case to say that Karen was the aggressor. That she lost her temper or her mind, took one of her own knives, and tried to stab Lucy, who had just kindly helped her home from the dentist.'

'When I saw Lucy, she had the knife in her hand. And there was blood on her. I could see it. She had stabbed Karen and pushed her over the edge of the balcony. Just as she stabbed her stepmother and Jack Smith.' Holden's voice had risen to a frenzy, and her previously white face was now suffused with red. 'And what does ten seconds of film prove? Maybe Lucy got the knife first, in the flat, then Karen disarmed her, and then Lucy retreated to the balcony, while Karen picked up the knife for her own protection, and followed her out.'

'Maybe,' agreed Fox, but there was no conviction in the way he spoke.

'Karen wasn't like that.' Like a tempest that has blown itself out, Holden's voice had collapsed, and these words were barely audible to Fox. He wanted to leave right then, but he knew he couldn't. It wouldn't be right. Besides, he needed to cover everything now, and to leave nothing unsaid.

'I'm on your side, Guv. I agree with you. Karen was terrified that Lucy would kill her, so she got hold of a knife and went for her. But the only thing is it doesn't look like that on the film. And then there's the forensic evidence.'

'What do you mean?'

'All the blood on the knife was Lucy's blood. There were no knife wounds on Karen. She was alive and uninjured at the time she fell. Of course, there are two sets of fingerprints on the knife handle – Karen's and Lucy's.' He paused, conscious of the blow which he was about to administer. 'But analysis suggests that Lucy Tull held the knife only after there was blood on it. And that Karen held it beforehand.'

'God!' Holden was still standing near the garden door, and now she dropped her head forward into her hands, and began to rock forwards and backwards in distress.

Fox, who had himself risen from his chair, now moved a step towards her, fearful that she might suddenly collapse. He ought to do something comforting, like put an arm round her, but hugging his DI – that really was no-go territory as far as he was concerned. Best just to get everything said. 'And then there's the fact that you pushed Lucy over the balcony only a few seconds later. Not to mention the fact that you and Karen were lovers. You know what a good barrister will say, Guv, don't you? That once you'd disarmed Lucy, being a police officer with training you should have been able to get her down on the floor and disable her safely. Only you didn't.'

He paused, and Holden stopping rocking. She straightened up, and looked at her sergeant. What did he really think about her? Was he just being nice? Mind you, he was dead right about the barrister. She was sure about that.

'Luckily,' he was saying, 'nobody filmed you and Lucy fighting. But at least I was there to see what happened. I saw how when push came to shove, it was just one of those things. She lost her balance just as you disarmed her, and then she fell to her death.' He paused. He knew, and she knew, it hadn't been quite like that. But he knew too where his loyalties lay. 'I'm quite clear about that. Absolutely clear! I'd stake my professional reputation on it.'

Holden let out a howl of pain. 'I don't care,' she wailed. 'I don't care what people think and what people say. I let her down. I let Karen down. If I'd been smarter, I'd have saved her. It's all my fault.'

'It's our fault, all of our faults!' Fox insisted.

But Susan Holden was not listening. For she was pacing around the kitchen now, her left hand on her forehead, while her right hand slapped increasingly harder and harder on the back of her neck. Fox watched, paralysed, unable to intervene in her pain. She stopped eventually, in front of the side window a metre to the right of the door. It was an old sash window, and it gave a view of nothing. Or as good as. Not that Fox could be sure, because since the clocks had changed, 5.45 meant not light or dusk, but darkness. Fox doubted if even in the full light of day it could offer any view other than the fence or the neighbour's side wall. The glass was uneven, old – not necessarily as old as the house, but old enough. Easy for a burglar to smash. He could see no sign of security bolts on the frame. That did surprise him. She knew the score, after all. She knew how vulnerable that window must be. He must point that out. Later.

'Eoooh!' A thin wail of agony, more intense even than the earlier one, was emitting from Susan Holden's lips. Fox was wrenched back to the present moment. He tensed. He had to do something. But what?

However, Holden had fallen silent again. She turned her head round, looking back at her sergeant, and smiled. Then everything happened in slow motion, as if the world had turned to treacle. Her smile faded to a slit, and she turned her face away. Fox lifted his hand in comfort or supplication or greeting. But she was already adjusting her balance, transferring forward her body weight, and throwing her whole being into the window. Fox saw her upturned face crash into the glass. For milliseconds it appeared to resist and hold firm, but then it disintegrated into a shower of fragments, as Detective Inspector Holden (temporarily suspended on full pay) hoped desperately (but vainly) for death.